Borders
UNDER
Arms

Based On a True Story

Some names have been changed for privacy

by

Ludmila Loisy

As told to
Alan Caillou

 www.trafford.com

North America & international
toll-free: 1 888 232 4444 (USA & Canada)
phone: 250 383 6864 ♦ fax: 812 355 4082

In Memory of
Martin

Dedicated to Don,
With love like that of the Earth to the Sun

PROLOGUE

Czechoslovakia, that part of the old Austro-Hungarian Empire that is known as Bohemia, lies in Central Europe across that continent's most historically important trade routes. Its land area is some forty-nine thousand square miles, roughly the size of New York State, and about half that of England. Made of hills, mountains and plains, its population has been fairly steady in recent times at about twelve million souls.

On October 28, 1918, in the aftermath of World War One, the country was proclaimed the Republic of Czechoslovakia by Thomas Masaryk, a Czech exile living in England. He worked vigorously for the independence of his homeland together with Edward Benes, a Czech diplomat and journalist. Benes worked locally to free his country from the yoke of the Austro-Hungarian Empire. As an independent state it prospered mightily for twenty years.

On September 30, 1938, Britain's Prime Minister Neville Chamberlain, fearing an outbreak of war between Germany and France, into which England would inevitably be drawn, signed an agreement with Adolf Hitler for the cession to Germany of Czechoslovakia's Province of Sudetenland, where the population was largely German. Two days later, Hitler occupied this territory.

The Sudetenland was forested mountain country in the west of Czechoslovakia-on Germany's border. It was very strongly fortified indeed, with concrete fortresses and heavy armor in great abundance. The whole province was regarded as a solid defense line against any German attack. With its loss, the mainland of Czechoslovakia, and its abundance of Skoda arms factories was defenseless now and a natural prey for Hitler's militaristic ambitions. "Peace in our time," he had promised. "This is positively my last territorial demand."

Six months later—on March 15, 1939—Hitler invaded Czechoslovakia against almost no resistance and held it for nearly six years until, in 1944, Russia attacked from the west—welcomed now by the Czechs—and seized power, reaching Prague in May 1945 and driving the Nazis out. Eduard Benes became President of the Republic. Three years later the native communist element in the country had increased its strength formidably, causing Benes to resign, and the Russians made Klement Gottwald the new Prime Minister. Gottwald was the most rabid of communists, under whom a violent Stalinist suppression of all opposition began. It was to last for eighteen years, until such opposition by the citizenry had become so strong that Russia found it necessary to reinvade the country with a much stronger force than that which had accomplished the first assault in 1948.

Once again, resistance was minimal, limited to stone throwing and such emotional responses as emptying garbage from upper story windows onto passing Russian armor.

And this time, beginning at eleven p.m. on August 20, 1968, the invading force was powerful indeed. More that two hundred thousand troops of the Warsaw Pact crossed the border in the first twenty-four hours—from Russia, East Germany, Poland, Hungary, and Bulgaria—and a further two hundred thousand were airlifted with their armor into Czechoslovakia's two principal cities, Prague and Bratislava, only twenty-four hours later.

Their object, it was stated by the Soviet Presidium, was to end the liberalization that was spreading explosively among the Czech people. The Warsaw Pact operation was ordered into the fray by Russia's Brezhnev and Kosygin as an attempt to persuade America, France, and Britain that this was merely a Pact operation which entailed no threat whatsoever to the security of these countries, which all displayed a certain uneasiness, though no action was taken to save Czechoslovakia from the ghastly morass into which it would now sink.

From now on, the most rigid Leninism was forced on these historically gentle and now isolated people, cut off from the rest of the world, save the Soviet satellites, as they were, to a degree of coldly calculated despotism that even today has not been fully realized.

This repression was to last for more than twenty years, resulting, as time went by, in increasingly explosive rioting by the more liberal populace, accompanied by strikes and mass protests which, in turn, meant a disastrous downward trend in the economy.

Foreign trade with this once wealthy country ceased entirely, bringing it to the verge of poverty.

Eventually, the hapless Soviets were to find that censorship and applied terror on a scale never before experienced still would not overcome the resistance of the Czech people. On the contrary, it weakened Soviets so badly that they simply threw in the towel, and at the end of 1989 Vaclav Havel, a dramatist, poet, and down-to-earth realist of high intellectuality and integrity, was elected premier by the victors of this internecine warfare; and the upward climb for the country's reason and prosperity began, increasing quickly until the present day, where it has once again found its proper place in the modern world.

Eliska Ludmila Kucera was not to know of this recovery until long after she had found her freedom in America; her escape with her family took place in the summer of 1983, at the time of the country's worst possible enslavement.

CHAPTER ONE

Eliska suddenly woke up in the middle of the night, every nerve in her body almost ready to explode. She could feel the pulse under her skin, and her body was wet with perspiration. It was that wretched nightmare again, the same visitation that had plagued her so terrifyingly for five nights in a row now, scaring the nighttime wits out of her.

She reached for the bedside lamp in the darkness, threw the switch, and swore aloud when nothing happened; they'd cut her power again, damn their eyes. There was a candle there in its little holder, and she lit it with one of those matches that would strike anywhere. In its faint glow, she slipped out of the rumpled bed and moved around the room, touching each piece of furniture, even the wallpaper she liked so much, as though to assure herself that she really was here at home, in the apartment where she belonged. In the dream, she had been racing along the bank of a river-could it have been the Vltava, somewhere closer to Prague? If so, what the devil was she doing up there, calling for the only man who could help her now, screaming hysterically, she remembered, "Zdenek! Zdenek! Where are you when I need you so badly?"

Well, it made some sort of crazy sense, which was where he was now, for some Agricultural Conference or other, a whole week of trying to make those idiots use their common sense and close down the factories that were savagely polluting the river, the land, and the environment in general. But they were Government owned of course, and she knew, as he himself must have known, that this was not only a lost cause, but one that might well get him into serious trouble.

Serious trouble? These new days, in Czechoslovakia, ever since the 1968 Warsaw Pact takeover and the resultant enforcement of the strictest

Leninism, it never meant a fine, or a reprimand, or a short suspension if you chose to argue with the Commissar. It got to be regarded as what they called "evil capitalistic ideas," and unless you were very glib and could talk your way out of it, you finished up in prison. Here, today, an already dubious social philosophy had gone mad.

Zdenek was a very tough young man of imposing intelligence and even more remarkable audacity, and in her more romantic moments she thought that one day, just maybe, she ought to marry him. That is, of course, the dreaded Secret Police didn't get their cruel hands on him first.

This was always a possibility, and even he shuddered at the thought of it. "Prison," the good Zdenek had told her once, "is not a nice place to be. Often they have to make space for more jailbirds, and they do it the easy way. The burial grounds are beginning to overflow." The awful horrors of the prisons in this new society were well known.

But in her dream, there was a road running alongside the river, and a big, black, well-polished car of the kind the Secret Police used, was driving slowly along it. She knew the car well. It turned onto the grasslands between them, speeding bumpily towards her. She raced for the water and leaped into it. It was the sound of the rifle shot that mercifully awoke her. But once, in the nightmare, she had caught a glimpse of the driver, and she knew him well too—a fat, bald-headed man with a chubby baby-face that seemed always ready for a smile. The eyes belied much smiling; they were small, and shifty, of the kind that moved from right to left, to center and back to right, with no movement of the head at all, a habit that, at their first real-life encounter, Eliska had found terribly disconcerting. His voice was a disaster, a deep, husky croak that she had always thought was generally a symptom of well advanced syphilis.

The first time she had met this creature was more than a year ago, when she had wanted to take a short holiday in Split, Yugoslavia's beautiful beach resort, and she needed a passport, a matter in which the Secret Police were always interested. It seemed that Czech citizens crossing the borders for those "short holidays" very often opted never to return; and who, except the Commissars, could blame them?

The Commissars did indeed blame them; these "temporary expatriates" were known to spend much of their time and effort in lamenting the tragedy that had overtaken their homeland, spreading their angry propaganda wherever they could. Sure, the Yugoslavs were communist too, but it was a philosophy they mostly took with no more than a grain of salt.

Now, she looked at her watch; just after a quarter to five, and it was still dark. The kids were still sleeping, two children by a terrifying earlier marriage, now mercifully ended. "That divorce," her friends would say, "was the best thing you ever did in your life." She would nod, "When I found out what he was doing, I felt that I would end up killing him. Divorce was an easier way out. Thank God I got custody of the children." Even today, it was painful for her to think about it.

Today was a day of the utmost importance, a day for lying as convincingly as perhaps she had ever lied before.

No, she thought, that wasn't quite true; if you wanted to survive in this jungle, you had to spend half your day lying. And to whom would she be lying today? Would it be to that baldheaded, fat little bastard again, what was his wretched name, Mirek? Yes, monstrous, mortifying Mirek . . . But no; this was not a matter for the Secret Police.

She went to the kitchen and used the gas stove to make herself some toast and a very strong espresso, and took them with her into the bathroom. She looked at herself in the mirror, looked at her eyes, unusual pale gray, perceptive and very lovely. Would they give her away when she was lying? She made a mental note—keep the eyes bright, even happy, no sign of worry there at all.

Good, not the slightest problem, just a matter of self-control, something she was good at. She nibbled at her breakfast while she made herself presentable, choosing at last the jade green dress that went so well with her long and silky blond hair. Her immediate boss in the Governmental Electric and Telephone Service was a pleasant and friendly young man named Peter Tuka, holder of a Masters in Economics, and a Party Candidate as his job required. No one of much importance, but why not look nice for him too? Actually, she was quite fond of him.

She checked her watch when she was ready, nearly seven o'clock and the trolley she normally took to work would be leaving soon if it was on time. Last night her eldest son, Martin, had said cheerfully, "Gonna sleep late tomorrow, Mom, don't wake me, I'll make my own breakfast." So she left a note for him on the kitchen door: "Suggested menu for the day, Martin darling—scrambled eggs and bacon. Make sure that Michal eats his porridge."

This morning she decided to walk, the air was fresh and cool, and the region's almost constant rain had let up for a while. But the walk took her longer than she had expected, and she was a little late.

11

Peter was smiling at her as he handed her a coffee. "It's almost cold, I'm afraid."

Eliska nodded. "I know I'm late, and I'm sorry. I preferred to walk today to get some exercise."

"No problem. As usual, there's nothing to be done today that can't well wait till tomorrow."

"Yes, that's true enough, isn't it? The whole country's falling apart, wouldn't you say?"

Peter was still smiling, a smile of true amusement. "No, I wouldn't say that, and you shouldn't either." But then he was frowning suddenly. "Comrade Franek called, he wants to see you at ten o'clock. It's something about your apartment, I hope it's not bad news."

Eliska thrust the incipient shivering away quite forcibly, "My apartment? My God, I hope so too!"

It was no more than bantering, but he said, "Your God? What God is that?"

"Mine, Peter. Not yours, I know that."

"And do you hold it against me?"

"Of course not! You surely must know how fond of you I am, not so?"

He reached out to touch her. "And I of you. And right now, it may be that you will need my support. A good word from your boss, a good Party Member, counts for a great deal these days. Be assured, you can indeed count on it."

She put her hand on his, and felt its warmth. "Thank you, Peter."

"May I say something very personal?"

"Of course!"

"The feeling I have towards you . . . If it weren't for my, well, my ambition, I suppose . . . I'd allow myself to fall in love with you."

It amused her a trifle, "Ambition and romance? How can the one possibly conflict with the other?"

"These days, I'm afraid it does."

"These days?"

"These days. Ten years ago, it was quite different. But then . . ."

Somewhat to her surprise, he laughed out loud. "Ten years ago, I was twelve years old. And you? Also a child, I suspect."

His good humor was contagious, "Ha! Flattery will get you nowhere at all. And I have no problems with my age; ten years ago I was twenty-eight. Give or take a couple of years, old enough to be your mother!"

"Then it's a hopeless case on both counts, isn't it?"

"It is? Tell me where the ambition raises its ugly head."

He sighed. "Yes, ugly head is right, but we're back to 'these days'. The Party regulates not only whom we marry, but also whom we take as our mistresses, you must know that."

She nodded, "I've heard it said."

"And I'm dead set on taking over the whole of this department. Director Peter Tuka sounds very nice to my ears." He was talking very fast now, and very seriously, "It may sound ugly, yes, but I've come a long way considering my age, I'm by far the youngest superintendent in the whole company, and that's because Comrade Franek knows damn well that I'm not only the best-educated superintended he has, I'm also the most reliable, the most trustworthy, and best Party man too."

Eliska said a trifle coldly, "And the Party doesn't approve of romance, I've heard that said, too. It horrifies me."

"Only when it's with the wrong people."

In the little silence, he saw that he had shocked her, and he made a gesture of utter helplessness, then said, "The wrong people in their opinion, not in mine, and to tell the truth, this attitude of theirs horrifies me too. In my more sensible moments, dear Eliska, I thank God for people like you."

"The God you don't believe in?"

A young man of impulsive moods, his state of mind had changed completely, and he was smiling again, "I can't think," he said, "of anyone else in the whole of our country I would say this to . . . But once in a while, I have this crazy feeling that maybe there is a God out there somewhere, biding his time. Just maybe. Like waiting for reason and logic and human decency to find their way back here again. And if anyone but you were to hear me say that . . . Well, it seems that hard labor in prison these days is mostly digging graves. I don't think I'd be very good at it."

"It's hateful never being able to say what you think. Yes, it is best we keep the romance, I'd say, just in our very secret thoughts."

"Let's do that. So go and see if you can find something to waste your time on till ten o'clock. And remember what I said. If you need help with Franek—just scream."

"It's carved in granite," Eliska said. "On my heart."

He laughed, gratefully. She went about her business, shuffling papers, form after form after form, permits for this, refusals of that, almost all of it useless and boring in the extreme, the kind of distraction that could put you to sleep if you didn't watch out.

But not all of it. Among all that useless documentation she was just wasting time on was an order from Comrade Franek that intrigued her personally. It was a command to shut off the electric power in her own apartment. Alone, this kind of instruction was not enough to satisfy the bureaucrats. Party regulations required that it be counter-signed by the head of her department. And there was the signature, carelessly scrawled, "Peter Tuka, Superintendent."

Ten o'clock was getting close at last and Eliska walked slowly down the long bare corridor to what was without a doubt the finest office in the whole of the town, from which Comrade Franek ruled more than just this company.

He was a powerful man, she knew, a Party Chairman who, some said, was in line for the country's vice-presidency. It almost automatically made him a man to be respected, or perhaps even feared, though she had heard nothing about him that might worry her. He was well-known as a competent womanizer, currently having an affair with his secretary who held him completely under her thumb; and for Eliska, this made him somehow less fearsome. This was to be her first meeting with him in the whole year she had been working here.

She knocked on the door and opened it when she heard the word "enter", and saw the famous secretary, youngish, but with an air of authority that seemed to be her own, looking at her sharply and then checking her watch. "Rather too well developed," Eliska was thinking, "but nice-looking, and certainly very well-dressed, and I wonder who her hair dresser is? And is that gorgeous auburn color her own? No, it can't be".

"Right on time, exactly," the secretary said. "Good. That door there. Knock first, three times, and then go straight in."

Eliska nodded, and did as she was told. She found the Chairman's office overwhelming. It was enormous, and there were splendid paintings on its walls, some that she half-recognized from visits to the Narodni Gallery in Prague's superb Sternberg Palace, still open for the benefit of the tourists, although many of the more 'decadent' French paintings had been removed. The ornate furniture, much to her surprise, could have come from Prague Castle itself. Some of it, indeed, had.

Comrade Franek himself was also a surprise. He was tall, and slender, with piercing eyes under very bushy eyebrows, and most elegantly dressed. And, Heaven be praised!, he was smiling. "I believe you wanted to see me sir," Eliska said, and Franek's reaction was instant. "Sir?" he asked. "Please don't call me that! I haven't been a sir for more that ten years! A simple 'Comrade' is preferable."

"Of course, Comrade. It was simply a matter of my respect for authority."

"My, yes, that's very commendable. Do please sit down, I always feel uncomfortable when a lady stands in my presence. Especially one so lovely. And your name is Eliska, is it not?"

"Yes, sir. Comrade."

"Watch it, young lady . . ."

"Of course, Comrade, a slip of the tongue."

"It's the tongue that so often betrays us, is it not?"

"My apologies, Comrade. It will not happen again."

Franek sighed. "I hope not. You are already, I am afraid, in very serious trouble."

So here it was. "I am? I honestly cannot think why, Comrade."

And then, "It says here that a year ago you applied for a permit to move into an apartment because, in your own words, you had nowhere to live. Is that true?"

"Yes, that is true."

"And you were given a document to sign, is that also true?"

"Yes, it is indeed."

"Kindly be so good as to describe this document to me."

"It was an application," Eliska said, "to report to a seminar in the Marx-Lenin Workshops. A five-year seminar, I believe."

"And did you sign it?"

"Yes, Comrade, I saw that it was the kind of document that, properly signed, could only mean very rewarding study in matters that have always been close to my heart. I mean . . . Five years of delving into the minds of Comrades Lenin and Marx. A delight, Comrade! Euphoria! The greatest possible satisfaction!"

Franek sighed, wearily: "The question I would like answered was, did you sign it?"

Was he looking into her eyes? She said, emphatically, "Yes, Comrade, of course I signed it."

"And then returned it for activation?"

"There is a possibility that it somehow got lost, and was never returned."

Franek said, "May we replace the word 'possibility' with 'fact'?"

15

What could she do? She said, "Regretfully, Comrade Franek, it is fact. Yes."

"But you were given, none the less, a permit for a year's occupation of that apartment?"

It startled her, "A year? I thought it was to be permanent!"

"Permanent? These days, dear lady, that is a word that has been stricken from our vocabulary. And your year is up today. You have to evacuate your tenement by tomorrow."

The shock was sudden and overpowering, a bolt from the blue that she could never have anticipated. For a brief moment, she was quite speechless, and then, "But . . . tomorrow! But why? Please, Comrade, please tell me why!"

"Very simply, "Franek said, "Because the day after tomorrow some of our own people will be taking it over."

"But that doesn't even give me time to move my belongings! Apart from anything else!"

Franek leaned back and put his feet up on his beautiful eighteenth century desk, "Belongings? What belongings have you in mind?"

Eliska said desperately, "My furniture, my washing machine, my oven, my refrigerator, all my personal effects . . ."

"As of tomorrow," Franek went on, "all these effects, as you call them, will be Government property. And kindly do not even consider sneaking these things out of the place tonight. Our people will need them too."

"But Comrade, please, to find somewhere else to live . . . It's not possible, what can I do? Please, I beg of you, help me."

"My mandate, dear lady, is not to help you, even if I could. It is to see that the Party's regulations are strictly obeyed."

"But . . . But where can I go?"

"That is your own personal business, is it not? A matter in which I would not be so bold as to interfere."

"It's a calamity, Comrade, It's a calamity! And there must surely be some way of avoiding it! By—I don't know—maybe a way of re-interpreting the regulations! Comrade, this is a benevolent Government we have, there must be the means by which it can help good, and simple citizens like myself!"

For a while, Franek looked up at the ceiling and rubbed his chin as though he was considering matters of great importance. He took his feet off the desk and stood up, and paced around, and then nodded as though he'd come to a momentous decision.

He sat a t his desk again, and looked at Eliska sternly. "There are some things, I suppose, that I might be able to do, stretching a few points. Would you . . ." He broke off and looked through his papers again, and held up two of them at last. "This," he said, "is the order for your evacuation. Given the right circumstances, I could, at very considerable risk to myself, cancel it with the stroke of my pen. It may surprise you, but even I, these days, have very critical superiors. And this one . . ." he showed it to her. "This is an application to join the Government seminar at once, a course of study which has been designed to improve the thinking of our citizenry. I can make it for one year instead of the usual five. Sign it, and you can stay in that apartment for another year. So . . . Will you, here and now, in my presence, sign it?"

"Willingly, Comrade, and with gratitude!"

He pushed the paper across the desk to her and watched, and when she handed it back to him he inspected the signature and nodded, and then took another paper and signed it himself and gave it back to her with a broad smile. "This," he said, "is your authority to stay where you now reside for another year. Keep it with you at all times. And I hope that pleases you. Because . . ." He was frowning now. "Because I have an awful feeling as though my neck were under the blade of a guillotine, just because of a simple, humanitarian gesture. Well, that's just a foolish fancy, I suppose."

Eliska wanted to scream. She was thinking, "Enough, you simple-minded idiot!" But she said politely, "A fancy indeed, Comrade. The importance of your position is itself a defense against all ills."

"Yes I'm sure that's true. Good. Then that is all, you may go now."

Eliska folded the paper and put it in her purse, and rose to her feet.

"Allow me," she said, "to thank you once again. Good day, Comrade."

"Good day."

He was already scrawling his signature on other forms, and she was thinking, "Papers, papers, papers, no end to the papers to be signed . . ."

When she reached the door and was about to open it, he said, in the friendliest possible manner, "Oh, Eliska?"

She turned back.

"One more thing," he said. "Would you like to have a small private dinner with me?"

There it was, but she found she could smile, too. "I would consider that a privilege, Comrade."

"Splendid. So let us meet at one of the bars first, shall we? The Vejvodu? At six o'clock this evening? And then go on to my place for dinner. I have a truly excellent cook."

"The Vejvodu at six," Eliska said, smiling. "I look forward to it."

"And let me show you something."

It was one of those damned papers again. He held it up and said, "The order to move you out of your apartment. Signed by no less than three very important officials. And yet . . ."

With something of a flourish, he took a rubber stamp and thumped it down on the document, and held it up again so that she could see the slightly smudged word: REVOKED. "You see how simple it is?"

Her mind was tumbling over. "Yes, what a bore you really are, Comrade," she was thinking, "an upstart, a lout, and a clown as well." But she knew that she had to let him know, one way or another, and she smiled broadly, to show him there was a joke coming up. "Have no fear, Comrade," she said, "as I already suggested, I know what a privilege it is. And I will be there, of a certainty."

He held her look for a moment, not quite sure of himself, and then, "Good. Six o'clock, then, at the Vejvodu."

She turned to go, but he was still not finished with her.

"Eliska?"

She turned back.

"Be informed," he said, "that I truly enjoy meeting with a woman who knows the value of carefully chosen words, knows how to use them like rapiers. I always find the connection to be . . . exciting."

She nodded slowly, then turned again, and this time, she made it.

As she closed the door behind her, she found that the secretary was looking at her quite strangely, almost asking for something, and she knew what she had to do now. Could she get away with it? She was sure she could.

She smiled, a smile of true happiness, and said blithely, "What a sweet man Comrade Franek is! He's given me another year's permit for my apartment, isn't that good of him? At considerable personal risk, he said. And it's not as if we were friends, I mean, I've never met him before!"

As she spoke, so cheerfully and freely, like an idiot on the loose, she was conscious of a slow hardening of the secretary's face, something first in a narrowing of her eyes, followed by an almost imperceptible change in the shape of the jaw. Pugilistic was the word that came to mind; or was it all her imagination? She thought not. It was that time, then, when push becomes shove, and she said, not losing her carefree demeanor, "He also

18

invited me to dinner at his house, I can't wait to see it, it must be marvelous! With cocktails first at the Vejvodu, isn't that great?"

For a long time, the secretary did not answer, and when she did, what she had to say was not quite what Eliska had been expecting. The voice was quiet, calm, and very controlled. "I have never before had the dubious pleasure of meeting you," the secretary said, "but I do know who you are, of course. Comrade Tuka is something of a casual friend, and he has mentioned your name on occasion, Eliska. He thinks very highly of you, which means that you are not, as one might have expected from those comments, an idiot, or a whore, or both."

"Correct so far," Eliska murmured.

"Kindly do not interrupt me. Does it mean, instead, that you have been trying to make a fool of me? For what purpose, I cannot for the life of me imagine! What is it that persuades you to talk like that?"

"The only persuasion I have that is relevant at the moment," Eliska said, "is my belief that women should stick together. We have to help each other when we can."

For a very long time indeed, the secretary did not answer, but just sat there, staring out into space, unblinking, as Eliska waited in silence.

She said, at last, a little heavily, "You could have told me the problem at once, you know, directly."

"Had I known you then as well a s I think I know you now," Eliska said carefully, "I would have done just that."

"I think you know rather too much about me, but it is, after all, what everyone in town seems to know."

"Your business, not mine."

"Very well . . . ." The secretary took a long, deep breath, "If I were you, I would not waste my time going to the Vejvodu tonight. I can assure you, Comrade Franek will not be there."

A little silence again, and then, from Eliska, "Will I see you again from time to time?

"It is possible."

"I would very much like to."

The secretary said, "Good day, then. Or perhaps I should say, have a good day." And as Eliska left, there was a feeling on both sides of a comfortable relief, of something important actually accomplished.

She found Peter waiting anxiously for her in their office. "How was it?" he asked, and she laughed. "A minor problem there, but it got solved, by his secretary. I like her. And I don't even know her name."

19

"Pavla," he said. "Pavla Zeyer. And the apartment?"

"Another year, at least." She showed him the permit. "And it helped a lot that you told her about me."

He grinned, "Just boasting of my good fortune in knowing you. So why don't you hang around and do nothing again for the next few hours?"

It was to be a long, slow day, but five o'clock came at last and she took the usual trolley back home, to within two blocks of where she lived. And she saw, to her surprise and her pleasure, an ancient green Volkswagen parked discreetly round a sheltered corner; Lenka's car.

This was the closest friend she had, one of the closest ever, a friendship that had to be discreet because there were some—like the dreaded Secret Police—who suspected that Lenka just might be connected with the city's very active underground. So where was she? Out of sight somewhere, no doubt, waiting and watching, a common enough occupation for this little group of anti-government activists. A bomb here, a fire there—blame the underground.

In a very few moments, Eliska was home. She left the apartment door slightly ajar while she went to the kitchen to make coffee and prepare a hefty meat sandwich. Dear Lenka, slim as a sylph, with a wonderfully graceful figure, had the appetite of a horse and was constantly hungry.

"If you were a dog," Eliska had once cheerfully told her, "I'd run you down to the vet for worming."

She heard the front door open and close quietly. She laid a little piece of parsley on the sandwich—cold roast lamb with a tomato slice and a little garlic—and took it to the living room. And to her dismay, she saw that her friend was on the verge of crying. She put her plate down and hugged her. "What is it, Lenka? Tell me."

Lenka wiped away the incipient tears. "Thank God for my friends! He knows I have enough enemies."

"So tell me."

"You still have some of that rum? I really need it."

"Sure. It does tend to cure all vexations, doesn't it?"

She took the bottle and glasses from the cupboard, and poured. "Come and sit down and tell me what the problem is. You know I'm good at helping out."

They sat together on the sofa and Lenka sipped and asked, "You know who Jitka is? Doctor Jitka Halek?"

Eliska nodded. "I've met her a couple of times. I can't say I like her very much. She's underground too, isn't she? I can't hold that against her, of course. And I've heard that she's a lousy doctor."

"No, she's not, but her specialty is, well, not very useful to most of us. She's an expert on poisons. She's not in the cell I belong to, and as I expect you must know, one cell is not supposed to have much to do with any of the others, which is good security. But her group specializes in bombing while mine is mostly intelligence."

"And . . . ?"

"She's blown her cover. They've arrested her."

"Oh my God!"

"And God alone knows what they'll do to her. And that's not all. Zdenek might be in trouble here."

"Zdenek?" There was a terrible fear clutching at Eliska's heart.

"Only might, we can't be sure," Lenka said. "We're waiting for more intelligence to come in."

She gulped the rest of her rum, refilled her glass, and took a long, deep breath. "You know, of course, what Zdenek is doing in Prague?"

Eliska nodded, "The Agricultural Conference. He has a report to show them. To discuss with them."

"Did you get a chance to read the report?"

Eliska nodded again and felt that she was vibrating with tension. "Yes, it's about pollution, what everyone's so concerned about, with very good reason, I'd say."

"You know where he got it?"

"No."

"Doctor Jitka damn Halek gave it to him, didn't have the guts to get it up there herself."

"Hell's bells. Even so . . ."

"Even so, my ass! You know what selenium is?"

"No."

"Neither did I till Jitka told me about it. The glass factories use huge quantities of it; it helps to make glass clear. Apparently, it neutralizes its natural green color. It's a very insidious poison, and that's the stuff polluting the river. The horses eating the grass in the area, which absorbs it, are losing their manes and tails, growing abnormal hooves, and then dying. There's been an outbreak in humans of lung, kidney, or liver deterioration. There've been a few deaths and half a dozen bodies were quietly disposed. Selenium poisoning. And its origin? The Government factories up stream. You see what I'm driving at?"

"My God . . ."

"There's nothing at all being done to clean up those factories. They say it's too expensive. It figures."

Eliska's heartbeat was almost painful. "And what about Zdenek?"

"One of our people is at the conference," Lenka said quietly. "He's a very senior Party Member, but he's very senior in the underground too, in my own cell. He's been detailed to shut Zdenek up before he even mentions those factories, or selenium, or anything equally stupid. Whether he can do that or not, who can even hazard a guess? You and I both know that Zdenek is not the kind of man who likes to run from any kind of danger; he would rather attack it head-on. And he's dead set on reading that report and yelling his fool head off because the Government doesn't give a damn about pollution, not even when it kills. Ha! And why should they? They kill people who challenge them, don't they? So what are a few more dead bodies lying around?"

"We have to do something about it," Eliska said furiously, "and we have to do it now, today, at once."

"Too late," Lenka said, as she looked at her watch. "The conference was scheduled to end at five this afternoon, and it's now nearly half-past seven. A few drinks all' round before they finally call it a day. Zdenek may already be on his way home. Will he come straight here?"

"Yes, of course he will."

"Then we have to do something. I'm more accustomed to than you are, which is simply, just wait and see. He'll be here soon, I have that feeling."

"Unless . . ." Eliska said, trying hard not to let her voice shake, and Lenka nodded.

"Yes," she said clearly. "Unless. We wait and see."

It was something to which Eliska was not much accustomed to. She drank a little of her rum and rose to her feet. "Looks like the children aren't home," she said. "I'd better go and see."

"You're not still worried about Martin, are you?"

"No!" Eliska told her emphatically, "not a moment of anxiety ever. All done, all over, finished with, absolutely."

"Couple of damn good kids you have there."

"I know it."

She went to her eldest son's room, and came back a moment later with a slip of paper, which she read aloud with evident pleasure. "Gone to a movie, a Russian flick about how they won World War Two unaided. Michal's up the road playing with the Stransky's kids, they are okay. See you tonight. Mom, we both love you so much you're never going to believe it."

Lenka, too, was pleased, "As I said—a couple of damn good kids."

"Never a truer word has ever been spoken."

"But are you still keeping an eye open for latent trouble? With Martin?"

For a long time, Eliska did not want to answer, but Lenka was very dear to her. So she said at last, "I hate myself for it, but perhaps I am, even if it's almost subconscious? He was getting so very, very close to what his father wanted him to be that perhaps, just perhaps, there is something deep in his psyche, unknown to him, that might one day burst out and overwhelm his better instincts. Instincts that at the present can only be called admirable. But demit, he's only seventeen years old, Lenka! He's a teenager! And you and I, a different generation, live in a world that is foreign to them as theirs is to us!"

She drank a little of her rum, and said, "I am as close to Martin's heart, the greatest son in the world, as I hope he is to mine. So what the hell am I talking about, can you tell me that?" But then the phone rang, and she picked it up at once, "Hello?"

And it was Zdenek, at last, "Hello? Hello? Eliska, is that you? Yes, well, thank god, it's taken me nearly an hour to get through to you. Hello? Hello, can you hear me? I'm in Tabor, Eliska! Isn't it time they fixed these damn phone lines? Time that Peter Tuka of yours got off his ass and worked on them. Can you hear me?"

Exasperated, Eliska shouted, "Zdenek, speak up! I can't hear you!"

And the voice came back, "No, what would I be doing there? I'm in Tabor, halfway home. I should be there . . . what?"

"At least," Eliska shouted, "tell me where you're speaking from! Are you still in Prague? Zdenek, I have to know! Are you still in Prague?"

And he answered her, "Hey, I got that! No, I'm in Tabor."

Eliska was in desperation.

"You're where? Where did you say?" Was he hearing her at last?

"I'm in Tabor, You know, Hussite Tabor, with all those underground tunnels. Tabor! If this damn rain eases up, I'll be home in forty minutes or so."

"So are you okay, Zdenek? Are you okay?"

"No, I'm not okay. I've had it up to here! The whole damn thing's a mystery. I'll tell you about it. I think the Secret Police may be after me. Hello? Hello! Darling, can you hear me? Are you still on the line? Eliska, can you hear me? This phone is acting up like you won't believe!! I say again, for God's sake, get your Peter Tuka off his ass! Hello? Hello? Eliska, are you still there?"

And then a new voice came in, a carefully cultivated female voice, "We are sorry, but this connection must be terminated. Repeat, we are sorry, but this connection must be terminated." And the phone went dead.

And all they could do now, both of them, was—as Lenka had said—just wait and see.

A storm broke then with a burst of sudden thunder, and the rain came pelting down, the kind of rain that could turn the streets of their town into torrents. It was an added torment for them, as it would hold up the motorists interminably.

But at long last, there was a very welcome sound out there on the sodden street, a beep-beep-beep that signified the arrival of a car. The Skoda that had seen much more efficient times in its long life, but was still regarded as a very prized possession.

"Zdenek!" Lenka said, and Eliska nodded. "Yes, at last!" She found that it was necessary to wipe away the beginnings of unwanted moisture in her eyes, "Thank God!"

She was waiting at the opened front door when he arrived, soaked to the skin, his hair dripping wet, and when they embraced and kissed each other, the beautiful jade-green dress was getting saturated too. "On top of everything else," he mumbled, "I got a flat tire, in all that damned rain."

It was hard for her to break away, "So what happened up there, darling?"

He shook his head. "I don't know. It's a mystery."

But there was something Lenka wanted to know, urgently, and she asked, "Did they get your report?"

"They got it," he answered, "sort of. That's what the mystery's all about. Then, on the way home, one of those damned big black cars was following me, all the way. When I got that flat, it just parked behind me and waited. I drove off, and they came on following me, and when I parked the Skoda outside," he grimaced, "that's when they drove off. And I don't like it one little bit."

"Let's sit down and talk about it," Eliska said. "You want to get into some dry clothes first?"

He moved over to Lenka and kissed her on the cheek. "And I'm glad you're here with the only woman I ever loved. There's nothing to beat the comfort of intimacy."

"Dry clothes," Lenka said, and he shook his head.

"That can wait. What I have to tell you can't. So let's do just that, sit down and talk about it, shall we? See if we can find an answer of some sort to what seems to me to be a very nasty problem."

Eliska found another liquor glass and filled them all. They found chairs and sat down, and the two of them waited impatiently for Zdenek to tell them his story.

CHAPTER TWO

It was obvious from the start that Zdenek was trying very hard to hide the furious anger that was consuming him, forcing on himself calm that he felt was necessary. "Not only a mystery," he said, "but an insult to me personally as well. I was all set to read them a report about the horrendous incidence of selenium poisoning on the riverbanks. In my temporary stupidity, I thought that perhaps they might persuade the Government to clean it up." He grunted, shook his head, and looked to Eliska. "That's the paper I got from Jitka Halek, an angry and detailed outcry about the awful pollution everywhere. I told you about it. I think you even read it, no?"

Eliska nodded, "And I suggested to you that it might be pure dynamite, you remember?"

"Yes, I do. Maybe I should have paid more attention to what you said."

"That is absolutely true."

"Well, there was a thirty-minute break in the meeting for what they call 'Thinking Time'. It's when they break out the vodka and the rum. They even had some Russian brandy, not too bad, actually. That's when this guy sidled up to me, very unobtrusively. I had no idea who he was and asked if I would please give him the paper I was going to read. How did he even know I had it? As I said, a mystery! I told him, 'No, I don't want to do that.' But he said, very earnestly I thought, that it would be far better if he were to read it himself. As an added persuasion, he said he had a certain authority here, and showed me his card, which said: Party Chairman Comrade Ivan Sramek. I'd never even heard of him, and . . ."

He broke off abruptly, hearing Lenka catch her breath, and turned to her. "You know who he is?"

"Later," Lenka said. "go on."

"Well," Zdenek went on, "there really wasn't anyone standing very close to us, but I had the impression that he was sort of shielding me from the others, and it puzzled me a little. He was speaking very quietly, but he lowered his voice even more, and said, 'Please give it to me. Believe me when I tell you that I am saving your skin and Jitka Halek's too.' There was something going on here that was quite beyond my comprehension, and I figured I'd better do as he said. It's no use trying to argue with a chairman, so I gave it to him. He slipped it into his breast pocket and looked around, and then—more mystery—he said, so quietly I could hardly hear him, 'From now on, say nothing, keep quiet whatever you do. The danger is not only to you, it's also to Jitka. And for her, the danger is deadly.' And then he was gone, just moving off and pouring himself a drink."

He sighed, got up from his wet chair and began pacing back and forth. He went on, "That's when I saw this woman on the other side of the room staring at him, then looking at me, and then back to him again. It was somehow . . . . quite sinister."

He gestured helplessly, "Am I overly suspicious? Perhaps, but then again, perhaps not."

"The life we have to live these days," Eliska said, "if something arouses your suspicion . . ." she left it hanging.

Lenka nodded, "You walked away from it. Zdenek, it's a lesson we all had to learn some years ago."

"I'm sure you're right," Zdenek said, "and that's what I did. I went over to the bar table where Sramek was and helped myself to a drink too, a strong one. I thought I might really need it, and I said, almost whispering and not looking at him, 'The woman in the dark blue dress'. And not looking at me either, he said quietly, 'I know. I can cover.' And then, beaming a huge smile, he went over to a small group nearby, raised his glass to them, and joined them."

But then the phone rang, and Eliska snatched it up at once. "Hello?" In a short moment she was smiling, and then on the borders of laughter. "Playing what? Cops and Robbers? And that's a game? Their thinking is a long way from ours, isn't it? Yes, of course he can. Sure, you too."

She replaced the handset and said to the others, "Mrs. Stransky, calling from the Post Office. Michal is playing Cops and Robbers with her kids, all five of them! And, please, may he stay the night again? They're a very nice family."

"Too many damn kids," Zdenek said. "And where's Martin? Why isn't he here?"

"He's watching a movie about the Russians on the Eastern Front. He loves that sort of stuff."

"Yes, of course. He would."

Eliska turned away. "So where were we?" she asked.

"The thinking and drinking time at the conference was nearly over," Zdenek went on, "and when we sat down at last, they all talked and talked and talked, more boring rubbish than I've heard in years, enough to drive a sensitive man crazy. But the time came at last for Comrade Sramek's big moment, and I still can't believe what he did! He read the paper, yes, but changed its content completely, adding stuff off the top of his head here and there to make it seem absolutely different, turning it into—he was searching desperately for the words—into a paean, a song of praise for the damned authorities! Can you imagine what that did to me? My mission at that conference was to give them all hell, and here was Comrade damn Sramek destroying all my best hopes completely!" Zdenek's natural good humor was returning, and he was even beginning to smile now. He said, "An end, for Heaven's sake, to my selfishness, because that is what this has been about! I apologize, But some good did come from it. Jitka Halek, it seems, was arrested this afternoon and has been hauled off . . ."

"That's true," Lenka said, interrupting him. "The secret Police picked her up late this afternoon."

He stared at her, "the S.P.? Or the regular police? We have to be sure about that."

"The Secret Police, I'm sure. They even had her cell number, Lodge 5. They knew the whereabouts of the wine cellar they regularly meet in, and the time of their scheduled meeting."

"Oh, my God! You know what that means?"

Lenka could not have been more certain. "I know exactly what it means! It means that their cell has been infiltrated."

"Without any doubt," Zdenek said, "that's what must have happened."

"Perhaps," Eliska suggested, "the whole of the underground movement as well?"

Both Zdenek and Lenka answered her at once, "No, that's not likely . . ." and Zdenek let her continue, "We would have known within an hour of Jitka's arrest."

"But is it not probable," Eliska asked, "that they have decided to bide their time? To wait a day or two? A week or two? A month or two? Or even longer until they make a decision to descend on you in force? Isn't that a possibility, at least?"

For a moment, no one answered her, so she hit it harder. "The cops of the Special Police Department," she said, "are, as we all know them, debased, uncultured, and hellish sub-humans; that's all they can ever hope to be. But they are like guard-dogs, well trained by experts in human weaknesses; it's never the dogs in charge, it's the trainers. Those are the headache people. These are the ones you should throw your talents at. Infiltrate their headquarters, for God's sake!"

Lenka was filling up the rum glasses all round, sipping her own. But it was Zdenek who broke the little moment of silent thought. "It is possible, yes." He said heavily. "I suppose that's true. But there are more urgent matters on the table now. About Jitka. Yes, she was hauled off to prison this afternoon. But hear what Comrade Sramek had to say about that. When he'd finished reading he said: 'Comrade Doctor Jitka Halek—whom we all know to be a good, hard-working Party member—composed this report, and this morning she showed it to the proper authority, who promptly, and in gratitude, set about the heavy and expensive task of cleaning up the pollution.'"

Zdenek sat down again, and he was more worried now. "You see the problem here, don't you?"

Eliska raised her eyebrows. "Problem?" she asked. "No. I'd say that when a man in his position says Jitka is a Party member, someone there is going to wonder why she was arrested. It can easily lead to her release."

Lenka shook her head. "No. It's certain that someone is going to check with what Sramek called the 'proper authority,' and they'll find out at once that he was lying. Bad news all around."

"Unless," Eliska said, "a way can be found to get her out of prison and hidden away before someone does that. Not easy."

"Or even necessary," Zdenek said. "One of the men there, who said he was from Security, gave us all the news of Jitka's arrest, and I couldn't believe the show Sramek put on! He quite literally screamed at this man: 'Well, get her out at once, you hear me? At once! Comrade Doctor Halek is a good, hard-working Party member, and I want her out now or heads are going to roll! And yours will be among them!' This fellow scurried off to the nearest telephone and ordered her instant release. And that isn't all, either. Sramek looked at the woman in the dark blue dress, smiled at her,

29

and continued cheerfully. 'This report you have all listened to so attentively was given to me by Comrade Zdenek Zizka. I think it is fair to say that we all owe him a very deep debt of gratitude.' Heaven help us, everybody started applauding, and they crowded round and clapped me on the back, and shook my hand. I went up there to risk my neck giving them hell, and they made me a hero."

He turned to Lenka, "I have the impression that you know about Comrade Sramek," he said. "tell me who he is."

"Ivan Sramek," she said, "no one in this room, including myself, is supposed to know who he is. But I do, and we're all friends here, aren't we?"

"Loose talk?" Eliska asked, worrying about it. "That's supposed to be dangerous. I think it almost is."

Lenka grunted, eloquently, "I say again, all friends. And Comrade Sramek, one of Prague's most formidable of our enemies, happens to be also the toughest of our friends. He's in the underground, with us. He's head of Lodge Seven, Infiltration, and he's wonderfully good at it."

Both Zdenek and Eliska were visibly angry, and Zdenek said clearly, "Very careless talk, Lenka darling. You must know our rules about that, no?"

She was shocked, "Of course I do. I helped draft them," she said. "But we're friends here, no?"

And he asked her, "Then are you suggesting that our rules make that exemption?"

"No," she answered, "of course I'm not!"

He pushed her harder. "Do you dispute our belief that the cause is stronger than friendship?" Her face was white as a sheet, and Eliska was watching closely.

"No, I don't," Lenka said, desperately defending herself against what she knew to be a very serious offense. "I just think that in our normal lives, outside of our hidden activities, we have far too much Leninist discipline thrown at us! It makes me vulnerable, yes, to—what shall I call it—permissiveness?" She took a long, deep breath.

"I'm sorry. I know I must watch it. I will."

"Then we're friends again," Zdenek said. "And if I was too hard on you . . . well, you did ask for it, you know. But I'm sorry too, anyway. Put it down to the rebel in me." He grimaced. "I had a very rough day up there, and I'm glad our good friend from Lodge Seven got Jitka freed."

"Lodge Seven?" Lenka knew it was meant for her, as Zdenek had said, 'friends again.' She laughed a little, and Zdenek grinned back at her, his old self once again.

"I lost my own battle," he said, "but Jitka ... well, I never liked her very much, but that doesn't mean I could put up with the image of her in one of our nice new prisons! And we have to give some thought to where we can hide her. Isn't she too well known here in Ceske Budejovice to hide out somewhere on a semi-permanent basis?"

Eliska looked at Lenka. "We're a pretty big town these days," she said. "What's our population? About sixty, seventy thousand?"

"Last count I heard," Lenka said, "it was ninety-five."

"Well then ... it doesn't have to be in the center of the town, but how about finding her a place in one of the outskirts?"

Lenka nodded. "I think that's a good idea, but our people are probably working on it already."

"No." Zdenek said emphatically. "We must send her to Tabor. Under the circumstances, Tabor is the only sensible place. Nowhere else would be right."

There was a moment of silence and Lenka was frowning, wondering what was on Zdenek's mind. But Eliska nodded, "Yes, the Husites." As Lenka stared at her, she went on. "Both historically and—perhaps more important—symbolically, it has to be Tabor. Yes, nowhere else."

Her reference was correct. Here, in the Fifteenth Century, the Husites were a powerful body of Reformists, outraged by the rapacity and immorality of the clergy and of the landowners who supported them. They aroused the furious anger of the peasants by the tens of thousands, so that the movement became not only theological, but democratic as well, stronger and stronger as the years went by, with war after war, most won, some lost. They were courageous, stubborn, warlike, and of great importance in the development of Bohemia's culture and civilization. The city of Tabor, with all its underground tunnels, became their fortress.

And among all their leaders, none was more famous (though some said infamous) than the Bohemian General John Zizka, who was well recorded as being one of Zdenek's ancestors.

Before he joined the Husites, this lion-hearted soldier had already been blinded in one eye in the service of King Vaclav the Fourth, (who was to become unforgettable in later history as Good King Wenceslav) and in a later war against Wenceslav's brother, King Sigismond of Germany, and Hungary, he lost the other. Nonetheless, completely blind, he continued to lead his armies in the Husites' future wars until, in late 1424, he died horribly, in agony and great indignity, of the bubonic plague, known in those far-off days as the Black Death. Without him, the Husites struggled on, no longer so successfully until, in a major battle twelve years later against their constant enemies, they were virtually annihilated.

Now Zdenek Zizka said quietly, "Tabor is my spiritual home. Never forget that I am part and parcel of my ancestry. And I am proud of the family name."

In a little while, Martin came home and was polite and charming to everyone, and even quite amusing, telling them that the Russian pictures should have been billed as a comedy. But, sensing perhaps an air of gravity in the room, he soon excused himself, found his favorite book on chess problems, and went to his room to study it. He was struggling to create one of these problems himself, founded on the turn-of-century theories of Jan Dubrusky, Bohemia's most famous chess master, and finding it almost (but not quite) beyond his capabilities.

The violence of the rain had worn itself out, and Eliska went to the window to look out on the sodden street and at the darkening sky. And then, there was a slight buzzing sound from the kitchen, and she said to no one in particular, "Well! Thank God for small mercies!"

"Meaning what?" Zdenek asked amiably.

And she told him, "That was the fridge turning itself on. The power has been off all day, but now . . . maybe someone is feeling sorry for me."

"So what's on your mind about dinner? I'm starving half to death."

"Goulash soup?" Eliska asked. "Fried cheese? Fruit dumplings for desert?"

"All of the above," Zdenek said. "Just give me time to get into some dry clothes." He turned to Lenka. "You'll stay, won't you?"

But she shook her head, "Much as I'd like to, there are people I have to see, people who have to be hidden away for the foreseeable future. We do have someone in charge of that sort of thing."

Zdenek asked, "And can your Intelligence people check with my cell? They must know where we are."

"Sure, I'll find out."

"And let me know?"

"Of course. I should know something within a couple of hours or so. I'll call you."

"Is it too late to talk to them about Tabor?"

"Don't worry about it, Zdenek," she said. "I know what has to be done."
She was looking at Eliska now, and smiling, she said gently, "And it's time I
asked you that question again. Is your answer still going to be no?"

Eliska nodded. "I'm afraid so. The same old reason."

"There are a whole lot of people in the underground," Lenka said, "who
have children. It doesn't seem to be a problem for them."

"Then tell me something I've often wondered about. Those people with
families, do their children know what their parents are up to?"

Lenka thought about it for a moment, and then, "That's not a question
I can answer with any certainty. But an educated guess would be no. For
the kids to be kept in the dark is something we like to encourage, but a lot
depends, of course, on their ages."

"It must be very hard to hide from them, surely?"

"Yes, I'd have to agree to that."

"And if you were to change your mind and join us," Zdenek said,
"which, God forbid, I would insist that neither Martin nor Michal had the
slightest suspicion."

"Michal!" Eliska said scornfully. "He's a baby, for God's sake!"

"Yes" Zdenek said, "that he is. And we all know how talkative seven-
year-olds can be! But you must surely also know how much I respect your
decision here. I think you are right with your firm and constant refusal. You
have every right in the world to think of the children first."

Eliska reached out to touch his arm. "And that, dear Lenka," she said,
not unkindly, "seems to be your answer. Just like the last time, and the
next as well."

"Then so be it," Lenka said, "and I'm off now."

"And I'm off for a shower," Zdenek said, "and a change of clothes."
He kissed her chastely on the cheek before she left, and when he was
through with his wardrobe at last, the ripe scent of the goulash was filling
the apartment. Michal had been safely brought home, had been fed and put
to bed, and Martin had excused himself again, telling them he'd stopped on
the way back from the cinema to grab a chlebicky, a sandwich of cheese,
salami, eggs, pickles and tomatoes.

For Zdenek, the meal could not have been more satisfying. The goulash
soup was delicious, the fried cheese done to perfection, and the dumplings
were a delight. Half starved, as he had said, he ate like a horse until not a
morsel of food was left.

Then, the phone call came from Lenka, very discreetly, "There's a small
group," she said carefully, "sponsored by the Government, off on a very

good tour of the agricultural areas, and guess where they'll be staying? The very place we were talking about this evening. Isn't that great?" And she hung up.

"That was Lenka," Eliska said, "I think she's taken your lecture on careless talk very much to heart. The refugees are on their way to Tabor."

"Good," Zdenek said. "That's the way it has to be." And very soon, it was time for bed.

But it had been a long and heavy day for him, and he was overtired; it meant that he could not sleep, except in short and unwelcome snatches, a nasty dream confounding him with its repetition. It was well after midnight when, carefully, so as not to wake Eliska, he eased himself out of the bed, found his slippers and a spare blanket to throw over his shoulders, and went outside onto the little veranda that overlooked the silent street.

The night air was cold but not insufferable as he drew the blanket tighter around his shoulders. The sky was unusually clear—the welcome aftermath of the storm—and the moon, almost full, was very bright. When the slight breeze made its presence known with the rustle of leaves, the overall effect was very satisfying, and the word that came to his mind was 'romantic'.

It could have been an answer to his unspoken thoughts; he turned at the sound of the door, and Eliska was there too, dressed, as he was, in a blanket. Kidding him, she said, "It's not enough that you got soaked to the skin this afternoon? My darling, you're going to catch your death of cold now."

"I think not." He was embracing her, caressing her warmly, knowing that life was being very, very good to him; the touch of her flesh was cold under his fingertips, "Can you ever believe how much I love you?"

"I think I know that. I love you so much, too."

"I had a dream . . ." He was running a hand now through that long, silky hair, "too real-seeming to be a nightmare, "he shuddered, "but in it, I had come home, and I was bringing you some wild flowers I had found somewhere, but the apartment was empty. I called you, time and time again, and I was wandering around looking for you, and all I found was a note pinned to the kitchen door that hadn't been there ten minutes earlier. It said—and I remember the exact words: 'Our love is over, Zdenek, finished and done with, and you will never see me again.' I had put the flowers on the table, but they were gone too."

She tightened her arms about him. "You must know, my darling, it could never, ever happen! There's very little that's wrong between us, and never anything so severe. Never anything we can't keep under control."

into one of his moods again, all humor quite gone from him. "So," she asked, "what was it you wanted to talk about?"

He sighed. "It's about running away," he said brusquely.

"What? You mean to Tabor? Darling, with the Zizka name, that's the first place they'd start looking for you."

"Thereby endangering all the others too," Zdenek said, interrupting her. "No, that's out of the question. I was thinking of leaving the country, you, and me, and the kids too, all of us."

"Oh, my God . . ."

"You don't like the idea?"

Eliska was ecstatic. "Darling, I love it! Sometimes, when I let my imagination goes crazy, I've even thought about it myself!"

"You do? But you never told me."

"Of course not, for a very good reason."

"Which is?"

"Very simply, it's not even remotely possible."

Zdenek threw up his arms, gesturing wildly, "We can't say that; we mustn't say that! Somehow, somewhere, there must be a way! It's just a question of finding it."

"And applying it."

"Yes", he said emphatically, "finding a way to do just that."

The thought of the difficulties sobered her, and she sighed, "Darling, for so many years now we've all been in straitjackets here, with a totalitarian system forced on us more and more rigidly with every passing week, so strong that we've quite lost any kind of control over our lives."

"That is absolutely true, even understated," Zdenek said, "and somehow" . . . he interrupted himself. "Can you remember what the word freedom means?"

"One of today's great sadness," Eliska said angrily, "is that not so many years ago, our Czechoslovakia was well known as one of the freest countries in the world!. Yes, I remember . . . and I've been a terrible silent witness to the changes that have been forced on us here because all they've done is . . . confuse me beyond belief."

It was true.

Even from childhood, she had suffered the distressing perplexities of what she thought of as double message. Her mother wanted to send her to church to find God, while her father would rail at them furiously shouting, "God does not exist!" and—jabbing a finger at them—would scream out his own belief: "The only universal power to believe and obey is the Communist Party, can't you understand that? Why do you think they've closed the Cathedral and all the churches? Haven't they thrown all those thieving priests out of business? Why, do you think? Answer me that."

Answer it? How could she? The clergy at the time were notoriously rapacious, and how could she tell him that the nomenclature of the Party—its upper echelons—wanted all of the priests' power and wealth for themselves; which they very soon acquired?

And then, the good-looking young man she married at the age of nineteen became, later on, not only a communist, but a communist of the worst possible kind, the kind that seeks to convert others by the flagrant imposition of terror: "If you ever want to see your wife again, sign on as a Party member. And do so now."

As the years went slowly by, in a life filled with lies, deceptions, and hatred, she realized, with slowly mounting horror, that he would almost certainly try forcing his monstrous philosophies on their own young son once the boy became old enough to think for himself. With her spirit, her inner nature, and her inherent dignity sorely wounded, she decided that divorce, provided she could get custody, was the only possible solution.

She found the strength to overcome all the governmental obstructions to this endeavor and to win her case. It had not been easy.

"Confusion?" Zdenek asked, and he was beginning to smile now. "Yes, that was always a problem in our earlier days together, wasn't it? Perhaps your only weakness."

"Is it so noticeable, then? Does my confusion confuse you too?"

"Once in a while. Only a little. And now—we have to think in terms of absolute clarity. So . . . if we were able to search world wide for freedom, just suppose, dream a little more, where do you think we would find the most of it?"

"In America, where else?"

Zdenek nodded, "I'm glad to hear you say that, because that is where we are going."

"What? Zdenek, you can't be serious!"

"Never more serious in all my long and rather dull life."

"So! We drive up to Prague, and hop on the next plane to New York, right? Except that the only planes leaving Prague these days are to the Warsaw Pact countries. And I have no wish to finish up in Poland, or Bulgaria, or East Germany, or even in Hungary. Even if we were able to get the necessary permits."

"Ah, yes, the permits, that's going to be the major difficulty. The protectsia alone is going to impoverish us."

"Protectsia?" She had to smile at his use of this good old-fashioned word, which once had meant friendly help of some sort, but nowadays included unfriendly help as well. It sounded less venal than 'bribery.' These days if you wanted a favor from some official, you had to be sure to have an envelope full of bank notes handy as you were often going to need it. Little protection could also allow you to move around much more freely.

"It's not only that," Zdenek went on. "It's the fact that we're not dealing with just one authority. I do have a valid passport, but does yours need renewing?"

"Yes, it does," Eliska said. "When I start on that brain-washing seminar, that Marx-Lenin nonsense, it might be much easier to get that taken care of. They must know that I've signed up for it."

"It just might help, yes. But it's the plethora of clearances we need. In your case, once you have the passport renewed, it has to be stamped by, let's see . . ." he started ticking off on his fingers. "First of all, the senior Party Chairman for the whole district, then the Chairman here, which if Franek . . . Ha! That's not going to be easy! Then your immediate boss, that's Peter Tuka, no problem there, maybe; then the Special Police must okay it. Any more?"

"For the children," Eliska said, "we need that rubber stamp from the class teacher and from the head of the school board. I hope those six authorities give us their blessing and, my God, any single one of them can say no, with or without reason, and the whole thing falls apart. Four of us, six clearances per head, twenty-four all told. Darling, we can all be in our graves before we're finished with them!"

"Which is why," Zdenek said calmly, "I say that we have a lot of clear-headed thinking to do. So let's start by thinking about the borders that confine us, keep us here in the country we used to love so much, okay?"

"Okay," Eliska said. "We have East Germany, and Poland, and Hungary . . ."

"All Russian satellites . . ."

"No good to us at all. But then there's Austria, and the controller of our destinies, Russia. Did I leave any out?"

"No, that's all of them. And the one I best like the sound of is Austria." He sighed, "The Czech/Austrian frontier is the most heavily-guarded border in the whole of Europe, no vehicles allowed to pass in either direction, sharp-shooters stationed every fifty paces. If it's suicide you want, try to

39

cross that border. But it's where we have to get to eventually if we want to hop on that plane to New York."

"So couldn't we somehow smuggle ourselves out, forget the permits, not go over the major crossings, but through the woods somewhere?"

"What woods? On our side of the border, every tree, every bush, every shrub that could hide a body has been cleared away; they even have tanks there. Believe me, it's very heavy-handed. Don't you read the daily rag? They like to publish the numbers and even the names of all those traitors who try to cross the line. Last time I looked at those numbers, it was eighteen in one week. And four of us together? Two adults, one semi-adult, and one child? No, forget it, sweetheart! We have to be legal all the way there. Someone stops us and we must be able to wave a permit in his face. There's no other way."

"And the more we discuss it, the more I realize that it just can't be done."

"So we have to keep on discussing it," Zdenek said, sipping his drink, "until we find the weaknesses in our own arguments."

Eliska said suddenly, "Yugoslavia! Maybe it's not so difficult after all! We went there two years ago, we could do it again! Another two-week vacation! Only this time, we don't come back!" She picked up her glass and held it high, "So here's to the Yugoslavs!"

He didn't answer the toast. Instead, he said somberly, "Unhappily, it seems that a whole lot of people have been getting permits to go there and choose not to return. The Party is turning applicants down now almost automatically. I agree, if we can get there, it's a giant step in the right direction. Those people might even help us to get to Austria. They're communist, sure, but they say that we here in Czechoslovakia are not."

"What? They're crazy!"

"No. They say we left communism behind and became, instead, Marxist/Leninist-not the same thing at all. And God knows, that's the truth. I've heard it said that they even feel sorry for us, and if that's true, it means that we can maybe expect them to look the other way when we cross over."

Eliska said, decisively, "Then the whole thing might be less difficult than we are assuming!"

"No," Zdenek said, "don't ever think like that. Overconfidence can destroy us. And remember, this is a one-shot operation. If we fail the first time around, there'll never be a second chance. We'd have to wait for history to take its natural course, for communism to self-destruct, as one day it most surely will. But when? In another twenty-five years? Do you realize that next month will be the fifteenth anniversary of that damnable invasion?"

"My God, that's true," Eliska exclaimed. "Fifteen years of corruption and hypocrisy and . . . and humbuggery."

"That's what it is. Though it took them ten years or more to force this wretched regime down our throats, to overcome that old-fashioned decency of ours. A little more pressure, year by year by year, until we found ourselves in the horrible condition we live in these days."

"Which will soon, it seems," Eliska said, "be behind us, and thank God for . . ."

She broke off and raised a finger to Zdenek for silence, and they waited for a moment. And then there was the sound again, the sound of a tiny footfall. She swung round and stepped to the half open door, and there was her young son, turning to beat a hasty retreat. "Michal!" she called, not unkindly, "come here."

A little sulkily, a little scared, the child turned back and moved to her. "What are you doing here?" Eliska asked. "Were you listening to what we were talking about? That's really not very nice, darling."

He shook his head vigorously, "No, Mama, No! I heard . . . I heard a noise. I wanted to see what it was."

"Well, it was nothing except-except us chatting together, nothing important, nothing exciting. So go back to bed and be a good boy, go back to sleep. It's a long time yet before you have to get up. Will you do this for me?"

"Yes, Mama."

"And how about a hug and a kiss first?"

But instead, the child turned and ran back to his room, saying no more. Eliska sighed and went back to Zdenek. "It's not easy to be a mother, these days."

"Yes, I know that."

"Do you also know that in the schools the teachers are encouraging the children to listen to everything their parents talk about and then spend a little time with over-friendly Secret Police questioning them?"

"I know that, too." Zdenek was frowning darkly. "But, I also remember when I was his age, I too sometime liked to sneak downstairs and listen secretly to my parents' conversation. I think most kids do that. Nothing political about it, just . . . well, more or less innocent childish curiosity."

41

"I wonder how much he heard." She said, quoting, "The horrible condition we live in these days will soon be behind us. You think he could understand that?"

"Maybe. Personally, I could never under-estimate the intellectual capacities of a seven-year old. If the S.P. ever question him, I think it would depend on how they phrase their questions. But it raises another point. Am I correct in my belief that Martin does not know about my work in the underground?"

It astonished her a little. "Of course not, darling. He has absolutely no idea at all!"

"I won't try to persuade you that I'm fond of him."

"Please, darling, please . . . ."

Zdenek went on, plowing ahead, "But I do realize that he's a very, very bright young man. And a little secretive, right?"

Eliska thought about it for a moment, and said at last, "Well, I don't know . . . secretive? Perhaps. Admittedly, he doesn't often volunteer much information about how he spends his days. Perhaps we don't ask him as much as we should. I wouldn't call that secretive, no. It's the same old matter of the famous generation gap. We've both seen him with his friends often enough as he talks to them non-stop. And intelligently, too."

"Thoughtfully, would you say?"

"Yes, I'd say that. What's on your mind?"

"When we start out truly planning this momentous journey, from the very first step we take, the story is that we are trying to arrange for a short vacation in Yugoslavia, week or two on the beach there, and then back home again. That, and nothing else, is what we are doing, right?"

"Well, of course," Eliska said. "But that, I think, is not what is on your mind and doesn't answer my question. What is it, darling?"

"It's Martin," Zdenek said clearly. "From step number one, whatever that might be, from the very beginning, Martin must never know, not even suspect, that we are leaving the country for good."

"Oh my God . . . do you really distrust him so much?"

"No." He shook his head, "It's not a matter of distrust at all. You have to realize that compared to us at least, Martin is perfectly content with his life here. So many good friends, plays high-class chess all the time with some of them. He likes his studies, and he's never really known what it was like in the old days. There's nothing for him to compare to these days." He threw up his arms, and gestured, "As far as Martin is concerned, this is what life is like, for everybody, everywhere, and he has learned to adjust to it. So why should he leave it all behind him?"

Eliska's hands were at her face, and then at her blanket's hood, her fingers sliding through her long hair and setting it back over her ears, anything to give herself a little time to think. She said at last, her voice very low, "You're right, of course. I see that and I hate it."

"Does that mean that you think we should leave him behind?"

"No! Absolutely not! I want that better life for all of us, for the whole family, even if Martin can't yet appreciate the value of it!"

"It's agreed then? We keep it a secret from him?"

"It's going to bring a whole lot of misery down on me."

"No, it won't", Zdenek said. "By the light of the coming day, you'll see how very necessary tight security is if we want to pull this thing off. It means that you and I know what we are planning, but no one else. Absolutely no one must have even a casual thought that there's any change in the life we are leading now." He picked up his glass and drank a little, and he said at last, "Another thing . . . we have to sharpen our minds to a very incisive kind of discretion. If the wrong people begin to suspect us . . ." he broke off, worrying, and Eliska waited, till he went on. "What do we really know about the Secret Police, about how sophisticated they might be? Why were they following me all the way here from Prague? Why? Why, why, why? It must mean that they already suspect me of something or other, not what we are talking about now."

"Your work with the underground," Eliska said, and he shook his head.

"No, I don't think so, the slightest suspicion there is all they need, and they would have already arrested me. It has to be something else." He grimaced. "Whatever. I don't think they're sophisticated enough for hidden cameras, but they can bug our telephone easily enough, maybe even scatter a few microphones around. It means, sweetheart, that we will not, from now on, talk about this in the apartment, only outside in the open air."

Eliska nodded. "I think that's a very good idea. We can go for strolls in the park."

"Take a boat on the river."

"Drive out of town and look at some forests."

"Or some mountains."

"Only . . . there's one thing we might consider," Eliska said, thinking hard, "Telephones and Electricity, that's my own office; if they wanted to tap our phone, Peter Tuka would have to okay it. That's the way the machine works."

"And would he therefore pass the word on to you, risking his job?"

"I don't know. Perhaps. He's certainly a very nice guy."

"Yes, that's true. But he's a Party member, too."

Eliska agreed, "But only because he's after that Directorship. He'd move heaven and earth, if he could, to get it-ambition at its very worst."

A thought came to her, and she laughed softly. "You remember how they cut our electric power off yesterday?"

"I remember the click when the fridge came on again."

"That order came from my office. Guess who signed it."

Zdenek stared at her, "Not Peter, surely?"

"In person," she said. "Of course, he just automatically counter-signs every one of the hundreds of documents they shove at him every day. I doubt if he ever reads many of them. That's the way the machine works, too."

"Well, let's just remember rule number one: the utmost in discretion all the way down the line."

"Will do."

He held her tightly, his arms around her, and kissed her. Over her shoulder, he looked at his watch. "Nearly three o'clock. Shall we go back to bed and catch up on some sleep? Or something?"

"Let's do that."

Embracing each other like the lovers they were, they went back into the room and quietly closed the door behind them.

Zdenek looked at the telephone there and said, growling, "Our enemy. Government property that can be used against us."

One of the first almost unbelievable steps the Marxists with the invasion's new authority had taken had been the instant seizure of every single telephone in the whole of the country, reissuing a number of them only to Government employees. Eliska was one of them who had to be available at any hour of the day or night. All calls to or from these phones were recorded on a police reel-to reel that automatically switched itself on and off, whenever one of them was used.

These days, scrutiny of the citizenry's communications with each other was considered to be of vital importance to the efficiency of the Party watchdogs.

These days, in the new Czechoslovakia, there was no longer any such thing as a private telephone. You want to call someone? Try the Post Office. If there's a long line waiting, a little protectsia might help.

CHAPTER THREE

It was three days later that the true extent of the danger they were always in was brought home to Eliska with sudden shock, after a morning session in the office that could have been rough, but turned out to have its humorous moments, too. She had arrived quite late because the usual trolley she had taken to work had been held up by a downed telephone pole, fallen overnight in the storm. The repair crew was already working on it, but it looked like a very long delay, and there was a matter of enormous importance to her in the office that needed her urgent attention: it was the paper-count. She was not supposed to know about this because it was always done on random days, understandably without pre-notification; but in one of his better moments, Peter had mentioned it to her. She knew exactly how to get out of the trouble she might well be in. It was just a matter of falsifying a few documents, but would she be there in time? She could only hope for the best.

She told the trolley driver, a big, uncouth sort of man with a scar on his left cheek that looked like an age-old knife wound, "Take a detour, I have to get to my office in a hurry."

He looked at her, grinning. "Lady, I get off the route they give me, you know the trouble I'm in? We wait, lady."

Eliska flashed her card at him "Telephone Service. Make a note of the number 72A. Tell them I gave you an order, because that's what it is. So get going."

His face took on its habitual somber look. "Sorry, Comrade. How was I to know, Comrade? I will do as you say, Comrade. You got it. Okay, we make a detour."

He backed up, to the accompaniment of the noisy horns all around, and worked his way through the gridlock quite skillfully.

She was still more than an hour late when she stormed into her office, and there was a look on Peter's face that could have been anger, or merely amusement. It confused her a little.

"Pole number ninety-three is down," she said tersely. "Last night's storm, it held us up."

Peter nodded, "I know, I have the report, and there's this nice young man to see you." He grinned, "I gave him your coffee, maybe soften him up a little."

She looked at the young man, and young he certainly was, scarcely out of his teens, but a cop. Not one of the Secret Police, but a Regular, and he seemed a little hesitant, even embarrassed, as he studied the paper he was holding, not very comfortable with it. He said at last, "Comrade Eliska Kucera, is that correct?"

"Of course it's correct," Eliska answered, judging his character, just a boy, and already on the offensive. "Otherwise, why would you be here?"

He was almost stammering now. "There seems to be . . . to be twelve sheets of copy paper missing. I've studied your report, and the addition is correct, so . . . twelve pages missing, Comrade. There are twelve sheets not accounted for." He picked up his file and took out a typed page and handed it to her for her inspection. She ignored it, but the youth went on. "Eighteen days ago, one thousand sheets of copy paper were delivered to you, and you signed for them. Is that correct, too?"

"Yes, it is." She saw that paper-storage drawer had been removed from its chest, the block of unused paper beside it.

"According to your reports here," the young officer said, "you have used three hundred and two sheets, which should leave six hundred and ninety-eight still to be used. I have checked and rechecked those two figures, Comrade, and they are correct. However, I have made the count, and I find that there is only nine hundred and eighty-eight sheets accounted for. This means that twelve of them are missing." He added hastily, "I checked that number well; I counted them three times."

Eliska looked at the block and saw the grubby fingerprints up on the top right-hand corner.

"Yes, "she said, "I see that you did."

"And I must ask you now, you yourself, to count them too, in front of me."

It startled her, "What? Are you out of your mind? You want me to count, what is it, nine hundred and eighty-eight sheets of copy paper just for the hell of it?"

He was beginning to stammer again. "It is reg . . . regulations, Ma'am—I mean, Comrade."

"Well," Eliska said, "I flatly refuse to do it, so why don't you consider it done? I have counted the sheets and, yes, twelve of them are missing. Now it's your turn to say something."

"Then I must ask you," the youngster said, "what did you do with those twelve missing sheets?"

"My printer jammed, and I lost those pages clearing it. I just crumpled them and threw them away."

"But . . . I have no report of malfunctioning printer, which is Governmental property . . ."

"I fixed it myself," Eliska said, "and all this for a few lousy sheets of copy paper!" The young man was shaking his head slowly, his eyes cast down. "They might have been used," he said, "for an illicit dispatch to the underground. We must control all forms of communication, we really must, or—they tell me—there will be a kind of chaos in our country. He raised his eyes and looked squarely at Eliska. "Is that, perhaps, what they were used for?"

"No," Eliska said clearly, and how easy it was for her to lie! "As I told you, they were thrown away."

Peter was quietly stuffing a few bank notes into an envelope, and he let it fall to the ground. He bent down and picked it up and held it out to the cop. "I think you dropped this," he said, in the friendliest possible manner. But the young policeman stared at him and shook his head. "No," he said, very clearly, "I do not accept. What I accept, what my report will state, is that Comrade Eliska Kucera has satisfactorily justified the matter of the missing pages." He looked now at Eliska. "Good day, Comrade. A good day to you." And then he was gone.

"Well, I'll be damned!" Peter Tuka said. "What the hell do you make of that?"

Eliska echoed his question, "What do I make of that? I'll tell you! I think we just found a rare human species. We've found a cop with a conscience. A young man who hasn't yet lost his soul. I think I rather like him, though I wonder how long he'll last."

"And what really happened to those missing sheets?"

"Off the record?"

47

"You know me better than that."

"Well, perhaps I did write a few notes to friends of mine. But if I'd been on time this morning . . . I was planning on making a few alterations in my report. It would have been simple."

Peter said slowly, "Eliska, you must know how fond of you I am. We—and that's the authoritative 'we'—know that you are not a member of the underground. But there are some people around who suspect that one or two of your friends are. Please, I beg you, be careful."

In a moment, Eliska reached out and touched his arm, "I've a lot to thank you for, Peter. A giant looking after me."

"Not a giant," Peter said cheerfully, "an ogre. It's lunchtime already. Go get something to eat. Just leave me alone for a while, so I can worry some about my own weaknesses."

"I think I'll eat out today," Eliska said. "The cafeteria's serving hot dogs."

It was pleasantly warm outside in the sun, and she had not gone more than a few paces when she stopped in astonished surprise. "Vaclav! Well, by all that's wonderful!"

Vaclav Cubirka, at the age of thirty-five, was one of the country's leading authorities on the rich early Czech literature, a highly-regarded specialist in the rhymed legends of the fourteenth century and the chivalrous verse that had become so popular a hundred years later. There was never any studious look about him; rather, he always gave the impression of a happy-go-lucky sort of adventurer. He was tall, slim, agile, and quite wonderfully good-looking.

They shook hands warmly, four hands gripped together, and Eliska said, "How long is it since we last met? I thought you'd disappeared off the face of the earth."

"Not quite," he said, smiling, "just a long lecture tour, all over the place. And how good it is to see you, to be home again."

"But what brings you here?" she asked. "Were you coming to the office?"

"I was wondering whether to or not. I thought that you might perhaps be very busy."

"Ha!"

"So can we have lunch together? There's a whole lot of things I have to tell you."

"Good news, I hope?"

"Yes—and no."

"Oh. When did you get back?"

"This morning. From a very long tour that seemed quite interminable."
They were crossing the road, heading for the café around the corner, and he went on, "To Bratislava, Brno, Kosice, Olomouc, half a dozen smaller towns. And some of them are really falling apart, not just the . . . the feeling that nothing is being maintained properly, but . . . well, the people these days, they can't seem to take an interest in anything, not even in their own history which, God knows, is fascinating enough."

Eliska nodded. "I think it's the same everywhere these days. We're in a kind of deep freeze, everything in abeyance, like waiting for better times we're afraid we'll never see."

"I think you're right," Vaclav said, "and at lunch, let's sit outside and keep our voices very low."

"Whispering to each other," Eliska said, not very pleased with the thought. "It's almost a national disease these days, isn't it?"

They came soon to the little café, and as he pulled out her chair for her, Vaclav said, "They feed you on these lecture tours, and I don't want to see another piece of fried chicken as long as I live. Shall we have hot dogs?"

"What a splendid idea," Eliska said, and they chatted for a while about nothing. But when the waitress had brought them their lunch and had gone back inside, Vaclav moved on to more serious matters, speaking very quietly. "What do you know about Jitka Halek? Have you heard any recent news of her?"

"A few days ago," Eliska said, "she was arrested, then presumably released."

"And a man named Ivan Sramek?"

"Very little about him."

"Explicitly, what exactly?"

"Zdenek had a paper to read at a Prague conference," Eliska said, "roundly condemning the Party—the pollution problem, selenium poisoning from the glass factories. But it seems that this man Sramek took it from him and read it to the conference himself, changing it's intent completely. He said Zdenek, or perhaps Jitka herself, had already shown it to what he called the 'appropriate authority.' I worried about that, because it was a lie that could so easily be checked."

"Ah, well, that accounts for everything."

Eliska raised her eyebrows, "Meaning what?"

For a few moments, Vaclav was silent, rubbing his chin; he'd had a bad shave this morning. He said at last, "Olomouc, a very interesting city, you know it?"

49

"I know of it, of course, though I've never been there."

"It's supposed to be a center of learning, which might well be true. There's a beautiful tower there, something like thirty stories high, built, believe it or not, in the thirteen hundreds. Anyway, I had a very good audience there; they asked a lot of sensible questions. One of them, a woman, wanted to know why it was that the Austro-Hungarian Emperor was crowned there, in that particular city, instead of in Vienna. Of course, it was because the Viennese were killing each other off then by the thousands, and doesn't everybody know that? It was a very stupid question, and I wondered if she had some ulterior motivation there. I asked if I might know her name, and she said, 'I am Sarka Cap, a medical student.' And at that moment, I suddenly knew who she really was."

He took a long, deep breath. "Olomouc," he said, "a city of what? A hundred thousand people or so? And the two of us there by the remotest of chances. It was Jitka Halek, with not only a new name, but a new look as well. It's so easy for the ladies, isn't it? A new hair-style, a new color, less make-up or maybe more, and you have an entirely new personage."

"Oh, my God. But there's more to this story, I think, no?"

"There is indeed. In a place called Pisek, there was a strange automobile accident yesterday morning. Is this man Sramek a friend of yours?"

Ahead of him by far, Eliska was already deeply disturbed, "No, I've heard of him, but I never met him. And what can be 'strange' about a car accident, for God's sake?"

"This one certainly was," Vaclav said. "He was driving south from Prague, presumably taking a roundabout route home to Ceske Budejovice. On the bridge there, he apparently ran into a heavy truck, head-on, and could well have been killed then and there. He was driving an Audi, a pretty solid sort of car, but it was almost demolished. And then . . ."

He broke off. The waitress was passing by, and he said to her,

"Could we have two coffees, please? Espresso, I think." She nodded and went on her way, and Vaclav continued, "But there were two witnesses, an old man and a very young girl, and they both said the same thing, that after the initial collision, when the truck had changed lanes and was on the wrong side of the road, it backed up and quite literally charged the Audi, ramming it into the wall of the bridge and knocking down one of the statues there, then just drove off, its job done. In other words, Sramek was blatantly murdered."

Eliska wondered why it was that she was not really shocked. Why should she accept this so readily? She hated it. "And Jitka?" she asked.

"After I'd finished with the lecture," Vaclav said, "I found her waiting for me. We talked. The moment she heard about it, she knew that she'd be the next on their list, and she very sensibly fled. She chose Olomouc because she has friends there, also in the underground. It's a very small group, apparently, only two cells, but quite active. The rest—you now know."

"She'll have to stay there, I suppose, more or less permanently?"

Vaclav nodded. "At least until our country returns to its once civilized state, as surely it must do sooner or later."

"If it does, I just hope we're all not too old to enjoy it. Or dead and buried without ever seeing it. How will she live now? Doesn't that sound like the most ridiculous question you've ever been asked?"

"No, not really. The simple act of living, I know it's not as easy as it used to be, but her friends are going to fix her up with a job, under her new name, in one of the local hospitals, all of which are grossly understaffed. She can easily answer any medical questions they want to throw at her."

"I still find it very, very sad," Eliska said. Irritably, she added, "To get out of this, this deep freeze they've put us in, there's nothing I want more in the whole world! What they loosely call freedom, an idea I find tugging at me harder and harder every day."

She fell silent suddenly. Was she talking too much? Well, it was only Vaclav.

And then, this thought, too, made her shudder. "Discretion!" Zdenek had said, very forcibly. And yet, she was at least half in love with this wonderful, studious man. For quite a while it had seemed to her almost a trial of arms between him and Zdenek. Zdenek had won out—in spite of certain negative elements to the contrary—only because his firmer strength of will, his greater persuasion, perhaps even his lesser intellectuality, had at last overcome Vaclav's easygoing gentleness.

"More confusion," she said aloud, and when he looked at her inquiringly, she half-smiled. "Nothing. Will you be staying here for a while now?"

"The day after tomorrow," Vaclav said, "I start three days of lectures in Badrdejov. That's a long way to go for fried chicken. But it's a nice enough little town, sort of tucked away, and quite pleasant. And I didn't ask you how you've been, did I? How very thoughtless of me. I must say, you look marvelous."

Eliska smiled, "That's probably not true, but it's nice to hear."

"And gorgeous, too, as ever."

"Now you're getting carried away."

"No, not a bit of it. Maybe it's those lovely eyes." He was amused now by his own thoughts. "Would it be indelicate of me to tell you that I sometimes dream of them?"

"Indelicate?" Eliska asked. "No, plain balderdash? Yes. But I love it." She looked at her watch. "And maybe it's time I went back to the office, to do absolutely nothing for the rest of the day."

"To do nothing? Doesn't that bore you?"

"Quite a bit. But my boss gives me lots of time off. Peter Tuka, you know him, don't you?"

"We've met. I think he disapproves of me. He suspects that I'm in the underground."

"You're not supposed to let him do that," Eliska said, "Shame on you!"

"When are you going to join us? You really must, one day."

"A suggestion that's made to me quite often," Eliska said, quite without any ill intent, "and my answer is always the same. The children."

"But that doesn't apply to Zdenek?"

"That is a battle I lost a long time ago. And can we change the subject?"

Vaclav spread his arms wide, "Of course. And I'm sorry if I offended you."

"You didn't."

"So give me a new subject . . ."

"The time off my boss gives me," Eliska said, thinking that a little advance news would be harmless. "Coming up soon, I have two weeks off, and we're all going to Yugoslavia for a vacation."

"You are?" Vaclav's surprise turned to worry. "But the permits, will you be able to get them?"

She was smiling broadly now, "It doesn't seem to be as difficult as expected. I went to Martin's school the day before yesterday and got them for Martin, at least.

"That's the Technical School, Prague?"

"Yes."

"Well, they're more liberal there than most, considering the pressure they're under. It might be harder for you and Zdenek."

"Perhaps not," Eliska said. "I've signed on for one of those Marx-Lenin seminars."

He was shocked, "Oh, no! You haven't!"

She said cheerfully, "Yes. I'm turning myself into a really good make-believe communist."

"Ah ... and it does seem to help. The watch again. Will I see you before you leave for Bardejov?"

"I'll try and arrange something," Vaclav said, and his smile broadened. "Risking Zdenek's wrath."

Eliska shook her head, "Vaclav! He honestly does not dislike you!"

"Would you call it, then, pity for the vanquished? That would be grossly out of character for him."

"No, no, no!"

"But I bear him no ill will at all. What is it they say? May the best man win? That's how it turned out to be."

They shook hands warmly again. Five minutes later, Eliska was back at her no-work office job. But there was a major surprise awaiting her. "Four o'clock this afternoon," Peter Tuka said, "the cops want to see you. It's about your passport; they want you to bring it with you. I hope that doesn't mean a problem for you."

Eliska sighed, "Just more bureaucracy. They told me at the Passport Office that they'd have to check with the police. But they also said there shouldn't be any problem." She grimaced, "Are you sure you can cope with all this work without me?"

But Peter was scowling, not amused. "It's not the Regular Police who are sending for you. It's the S.P.S."

Eliska felt the blood draining from her face. "But ... but what on earth would they want with me?"

"Who knows?" He was obviously very angry, or was it merely worries on his mind? "Comrade Franek tells me that you signed up for the seminar, is that true?"

"Yes, of course it is."

"Well, even with the Secret Police, that ought to count for something in your favor." He looked up at the clock. "Nearly two more hours. Why don't you go on home, pick up your passport, and then spend a little time figuring out what kind of lies you can tell them—lies that will best suit your purpose. Which is, at this moment, the need to get a couple of rubber stamps going, simple enough. You know where their offices are?"

"Who doesn't? If only as the kind of place you never want to get close to. A long detour around it."

He hesitated, worrying, and then, "You might think about telling them that Zdenek can't go with you, that he is tied up at his workplace, whatever.

53

Then they'll realize that you are planning on returning, not staying abroad to propagandize—that's their main fear. Of course, even if it gets over this problem for you, you're creating another one for later on. But, step by step, think about it."

"I'll do that." And she did, as she soon wandered around the apartment, idly tidying things up. How could that other problem ever be solved?" And she couldn't go without Zdenek anyway! So the whole idea was nothing but a lot of foolishness! But the passport—maybe there was something in it that could help? She hunted for it, found it in one of the kitchen drawers, and there was what she was looking for—a two-year old entry stamp followed by its exit equivalent ten days later. The entries were smudged and not very neat, but she could at least read them: Entry: June 24.1981. and Exit: July 3.1981. She decided that this would be her best approach. But when the time came, it was not to serve her well at all.

The trouble started as soon as she came within sight of the S.P. building, a fortress-like structure in cold gray stone. She hated the feeling of trepidation that came over her, almost dismissing her resolve in its entirety. Then there were the black-suited escorts who accompanied her down those long depressing corridors, a new guard at each one, handing her over like a common criminal to the next guard at every corner. She wondered why they didn't slip the cuffs on her.

Then, to the boss's office at last, with a young male secretary there, good-looking and effete enough to raise a certain amount of surprise. "Comrade Eliska Kucera," said the guard, and the young man nodded. He rose to his feet, a little too elegantly, and said to her, "The Comrade Captain will see you at once."

'Comrade Captain'? Eliska tried not to sigh, at least there was a slight aura of comedy here. It was not to last for very long. She was shown into a not-too-orderly room that was filled with pale blue cigar smoke, and she felt her hackles rising; the man seated there, dressed in a very well-cut black suit, a white shirt and a black tie, and smoking the fattest cigar she had ever seen, was the man whose name she knew to be Mirek Voitech. "Madame Eliska Kucera?" he asked. She forced a smile. "No, Comrade Captain. I am Madame Kucera no longer. I have recently signed up for Comrade Franek's Marx-Lenin seminar, and I am proud to call myself a communist now."

"A communist now? Kindly tell me what you were before."

Rapidly thinking now, Eliska drew herself up to her full height, and said clearly, "Before, I was weak. Now, I am strong."

54

"Very nicely put," Mirek said, "though perhaps a little irrelevant. What do you think of us? Of the Secret Police?"

Eliska allowed herself a short moment for thinking, and then, with a very thoughtful sort of frown," I think that you serve a very useful purpose indeed."

"Which is?"

She was ready, ready with the neutral answer, "I think that your mandate must be to correct disorderly thinking among those who have not yet aligned themselves to this new way of life."

"This new way of life being what, exactly?"

"Order," Eliska said promptly. "Order, where once there was only chaos!"

"And would I be correct if I were to suggest that you must take me for an absolute imbecile? For a fool?"

She was aghast, "Good heav . . . I mean, no, no, no!" She said, very earnestly. "A fool, Comrade Captain, could never have reached your high position, I know that!"

"Well," the Comrade Captain said, "let us thrust all that aside for future consideration. The matter of the moment, I believe, is about your passport?"

"Yes, that is true." She took it from her purse, opened at the right place, and handed it to him. She said, smiling and full of good-will, "You will see, Comrade, that two years ago, you yourself were good enough to give me the necessary permits to visit Yugoslavia. For ten days. We returned in ten days, all very legal and above-board."

"You did? And I myself gave you the permits?"

"Out of the goodness of your heart."

"And now, you want to go back there for another vacation?"

"That is why I am here, Comrade."

"Comrade Captain, if you don't mind . . ."

"That is why I am here, Comrade Captain."

"And you want to go to Yugoslavia?"

"I thought I made that clear, Comrade Captain."

"As vacation?"

"A vacation. For the whole family."

"The whole family being . . . ?"

"Myself, my two children—Martin and Michal—and my companion, Zdenek Zizka."

"Your companion?"

55

"My companion."

"You are not married?"

"In time, we will be. Not yet. I believe the Party does not disapprove of this kind of arrangement."

"But you are not a prostitute, I imagine, Madame Kucera?"

At this moment, the cry in her gut was to reach out and strangle him. But too much was at stake, and so, "No," she said coldly, "that is something I never have been, and never will be." And how very hard it was, at this moment, not to mention the sweet young man in the adjoining room! But it would have been murder in the worst possible degree. She said instead, "I must ask you again, Comrade Captain, to use that rubber stamp you have. Please? A pass to Yugoslavia is all I am asking for."

Mirek leaned back in his chair and put his black-booted feet on his desk. He asked, "Tell me why you want to take your vacation in Yugoslavia."

"The sun," Eliska said, "the blue skies, the peace and quiet."

"Three qualities," Mirek said, "that the Soviet Union has in abundance. Is that not good enough for you? Have you never heard of our famous resorts on the coast of the Caspian Sea?"

"Yes," Eliska said, "but we still want Yugoslavia. Where we were two years ago, a beach resort called Split."

"Our Baku is better," Mirek insisted. But Eliska went on. "My son Martin is an expert in the game of chess; he has even invented a chess problem of his own. In Split, there are three very young men, also computer experts, one of them only ten years old, who believe they have solved it. We honestly have to meet with these young men again."

"Chess?" Mirek asked. "You dare to dispute the Russian superiority in matters of chess?"

Now Eliska, pride-filled, made a bad mistake. "My son," she said, "will happily take on any of your experts. Let's all make some media headlines, will you all agree to that?" She was mocking him, digging her own grave.

But Mirek seemed not to be offended; he was, after all, in charge of this enquiry, and he asked, "Can we perhaps return to the matter in hand? Your own political philosophies, for example. Do you agree that the Communist Party should control not only your career, but your personal life as well?"

"Of course," Eliska said evenly.

Mirek went on, "If I were to give you the Yugoslav permit, do you think that you are ready to represent our communistic ideology abroad? Do you think you are strong enough to resist the evil capitalistic ideas with which they will try to confuse you?"

"Yes to both those questions," Eliska said, and he grunted.

"So tell me," he said, "give me one good reason why I should believe you."

Was this her chance to catch up some of the ground she had lost? She thought that it might be. "I will give you, Comrade Captain," she answered, "the best of all possible reasons. I am pleased—more than pleased—to inform you that through the good offices of Comrade Franek, who is in charge of the office I work in, I have signed up for the Marx-Lenin seminar, and will soon be a card-carrying member of the Party, a position I will always cherish very dearly."

"Over-statement," Mirek said, "does seem to be one of your weaknesses. Are you aware of that unfortunate fact? It is, however, a very common weakness among women, so I assume that you seldom give such a matter any serious thought."

How could she answer this kind of challenge? She wanted so much to say something like "the hell with you, Comrade God-damn Captain," but she elected instead for a hollow little laugh and a smile, and a comment that was not exactly the best thing she could have chosen, "They call us the weaker sex. It may well be that this appellation is entirely justified."

"Then just one more question," Mirek said. "The invasion by armies of the Warsaw Pact in 1968, to save the idea of socialism in this country. Tell me whether or not you approved of that."

This was a question that demanded a very, very careful answer. On that unforgettable night, eleven p.m. on August the twentieth, Polish, Hungarian, Bulgarian, and East Germen troops, led by the Soviets, had crossed the Czech border at nearly a score of points, and a few hours later, heavy artillery, tanks and other armor were landed in both Prague and Bratislava, the country's two most important cities and there had been almost no resistance from Czech Military Forces. What, after all, could they do against this army of nearly two hundred thousand troops? Eliska thought about it for a long moment, then put on a frown, and said slowly, "At that time, Comrade Captain, very many people here really believed in the old German ideas, which could very easily have taken us into absolute Fascism. But the Warsaw Pact armies crossed our borders to save our respected socialist philosophies. And in this, they succeeded. And I, personally, am very grateful that they did."

Mirek, puffing out great clouds of blue smoke, leaned back in his chair, his hands clasped at the back of his head and said, "My mood today is a very good one. I think I will grant your request. A visa for Yugoslavia, and even a few other countries you might want to visit as well, a kindness to you. Give me your passport."

Eliska could hardly believe what she had heard a kindness from the monster Mirek? She said excitedly, handing it to him, "I cannot begin to tell you how grateful I am . . ."

But he waved an airy hand, "Think nothing of it, dear lady."

He took a box of rubber stamps from a drawer in his desk and laid three of them out in neat and perfect order. Then came the thump, thump, thump with quite a flourish, pages being flipped as he slammed the stamp home. He gave her back the passport and waited.

Eliska, too, flipped the pages; page seven, a pass to Bulgaria, and she smiled. "That's one I'll never need," she said, "but thank you anyway." Page eight, the stamp for East Germany, and what kind of a joke was that? Page nine, the Soviet Union itself, and she was beginning to wonder what was going on here. Page ten, nothing. Pages eleven, twelve, thirteen, all the way to the final pages and still nothing more.

She stared at Mirek, and forced herself to speak, "For Yugoslavia?" she asked. "You promised me, Comrade."

She was already feeling the welling up of tears, and at his answer they nearly burst out. "Next year," Mirek said. "One year from now, exactly, we'll talk about Yugoslavia some more. Tell my secretary on your way out, and he will arrange it."

She stared at him, the unspoken words were tumbling over and over in the back of her mind You fat, bald-headed little bastard! Is this how you get your kicks? By destroying other peoples' dreams? And enjoying it? May you rot in hell, you repulsive wretch. Those damn tears were on their way, and she forced them back. She told him coldly, "I will not give you pleasure, Comrade Captain, of seeing me cry. But be assured that this is what I will be doing tonight."

"I'm glad," Mirek said. "Go now. You are dismissed."

She slipped the useless passport into her purse, turned on her heels and left the office, slamming the door behind her. A silent guard was there to escort her on the way out, but she did not go straight home as she had intended. Instead, she walked slowly, and in the most acute depression, over to the City Park that was nearby and made her way to a spot she knew of where there was a bench in a small, thickly wooded area.

She had been to this almost private place several times in the past and had found that it seemed somehow to cut off the rest of the world, to leave any single person there in the purest solitude. The bench was made of neglected and decaying oak, supported by nicely turned wrought iron legs. She knew that in the old days, so distant now,! it was a much-favored spot for young lovers.

She sat there in the silence, and laid her arm along the bench's back, put her head down on it, and began to sob her heart out, letting the tears stream out unheeded.

In a little while, she was suddenly conscious of a presence there, and she pulled herself together sharply. It was a young man, still in his teens she thought, who was sitting close by her and staring at her, a worried look on his boyish face. "You got trouble, lady?" he asked. "Something I can maybe do to help? You want to tell me what's wrong?"

Eliska shook her head reaching for an answer "No, though I thank you. It's just . . . my cat died, my . . . my pet."

"Ah," the boy said "Me, I like cats, too. I tell you what you do. You have a real good cry, and in a little while everything is okay. You do that?"

She smiled. "Yes, that's what I'll do. It's a good idea."

He got to his feet. "So I go now. You will be okay?"

She nodded, "I'll be okay" and he was gone.

Eliska rose, too, stretched her arms, and drew in great breaths of that wonderful clean air. She looked around at the green, sweet-scented shrubbery, and said aloud, "Yes, everything's okay." She reached down to the bench for her purse, but it was no longer there. It was gone. She looked around for the nice young man who liked cats, but he was gone too, and she knew that by now he'd be far, far away, perhaps still running among the tress and the bushes, till he could be sure that the prize was really his for keeps.

All she could do was sigh.

She walked home, thinking hard all the way, and waited for Zdenek to return from his work, to give him all the news of her long day. First things first, her meeting with Vaclav, and was he scowling a little? No, she decided that this was what he ought to be doing and was avoiding doing it.

"I thought he was on one of his tours," Zdenek said, quite amiably. She answered, "He came back today, with news of that fellow Sramek. He's been murdered."

"What? Oh, God!"

She told him how it had happened. "More worry for me about you, darling, as time goes on. You're closely tied up with this business of the pollution report. It means that you are in danger too, and it scares the wits out of me."

"Don't let it do that," Zdenek said, "I'm clean."

"Clean?"

"In a manner of speaking," he grunted, and went on, "That Lenka! She has to be the most obscure lady on the face of the earth! You remember I asked her to find out if anyone in my cell was in danger?"

"Sure. So?"

"She called me this afternoon and, obviously, she knows how carefully monitored telephone calls are. What she said was, word for word was: 'We've checked your car very carefully, Comrade, and it's quite safe to drive, no danger at all. We'll give you the bill next time you come around. Good day.' And the only words of note are no danger and the piece about the bill, which means the explanation. But I hate this business of Sramek, nonetheless. And Jitka Halek?"

"A new personage," Eliska said, "and a new life under another name. And that's not all the news!"

She told him how the nice young man who liked cats had stolen her purse with the passport in it, and he was furious. "Just when we need it urgently!" he said. "Crime's on the rise daily, and most of it is the kids! The passport, for God's sake! We're lost without it!"

"But," said Eliska, "this might be a blessing in disguise."

It puzzled him, but only for a moment, and he said, "Either we think alike—or I'm reading your mind . . ."

"Perhaps both. The Passport Office itself?"

Eliska nodded, "Exactly. They're not nearly as rigid in their thinking as most of the Government departments, agreed?"

"Absolutely I've decided that in the past."

"And I'm quite friendly with a few of them there," Eliska said. "So what we'll do is this. I'll report the theft directly to them instead of to the police and suggest to them that they might want to do that themselves."

"Okay so far."

"And since they'll be giving out a brand new passport, they won't automatically send it on to the police. I'll just ask them nicely for a Yugoslav visa while they're about it. They do have that authority. I'd say we have a fifty-fifty chance of getting it, maybe much better than that."

"Yes, I think so. Tomorrow morning, I'm taking my own round to their office, just to renew it. That shouldn't be a problem."

He went to pour himself a drink and gestured to Eliska, "One for you, too?" But she shook her head, "I'll wait until a little later. You go ahead."

"So what do we have?" he asked, pouring.

She answered, "What we have, really, is just a couple of disputables, and I would prefer a whole lot of certainties. I suppose tomorrow will tell."

Zdenek nodded, and said calmly, "Then as Lenka would say, we'll have to wait and see, won't we?"

Eliska nodded back at him vigorously, "Yes. That's what we'll do. We'll wait and see."

CHAPTER FOUR

The morrow turned out to be a highly successful day for Eliska at least the first part of it. The whole week was going to be a busy one, and very soon, she hoped, they would all be on their way to better lands, so she had a quiet word with her boss, "I'm terribly sorry about this, Peter, but I feel I have to ask you for quite a lot of time off for a while."

It did not surprise him as much as she had expected. "Ah," he said, "the trip to Yugoslavia, right?"

"In part, yes."

"But does this trip mean that you have decided not to return? To spend the rest of your lives in Yugoslavia, widely condemning that state that we here in Czech land have fallen into? Right again?"

"No, no, no," she said, "absolutely not!" She was laughing at his little jokes, but was he looking too deeply into her eyes? She pushed the lie a little harder, hating it, but knowing how vital it was. "And I shall expect to work twice as hard as soon as I'm through with the travel details. We have a deal?"

"We have a deal," he said, more gravely now, "and I'm only too glad to help."

She told him, as a good friend, the story of her stolen purse with the passport in it, and he said at once, "When you apply for a new one, I think I can help you. They know, in that office, how well and how quickly we take care of their telephone problems. I've had a personal thanks from them on occasion, so . . . mention my name when you apply. My endorsement might speed things up. Better still, I'll call them."

She was hating it even more now, but she forced a smile. "I've said it before, but that's no reason why I shouldn't say it again—you're always helping me along, Peter, one way or another. I can't tell you how grateful I am."

"It makes me very, very, happy. Have you exchanged your currency yet?"

She shook her head, "Top of the list of things I have to do. This afternoon or tomorrow morning."

"Are you looking for Yugoslav dinars or American dollars?"

"American dollars?" Eliska asked, trying her best to look shocked. "Peter. Heavens above. If I wanted dollars, I'd have to go to the black market for them, wouldn't I? Nothing could be further from my mind than that!"

She wondered if perhaps she was overdoing it, wondered, too, what Peter was up to, throwing the idea of dollars at her like that. She sighed; you could never tell with this man.

He said lightly, "Yes, indeed, but you know that the people at the bank will keep you waiting forever, don't you?"

"But they know me well there: we're on the best of terms."

He nodded, "It's highly probable that they take care of their friends, and to the devil with anyone else."

"I think you're right. At least, I hope you are." And she was to find that their guess was correct, though this money exchange problem could have been a formidable one. The system was somewhat like a lottery—take a few applications out of the hat, so to speak, every few days, and the rest can take their chances. But with Eliska, it was not so. The lady teller found her correct file and read the application carefully, paying no attention to anything else at all, including Eliska. She was in her fifties, perhaps, nicely dressed, with a rather long sort of face, but quite good-looking, if a trifle severe. She said at last, "Three adults and one child. And you write 'ten days or possibly two weeks.' Which is it to be? We have to know that."

Eliska suggested, smiling, "Well, to be safe, can we make it two weeks?"

The teller was not pleased. "Does that mean that you hope to return with four days' worth of dinars to sell on Ceske Budejovice's black market?"

"Ah, of course," Eliska said hastily, "I hadn't thought of that. No. I mean. Nothing is further from my mind! I consider myself very much a law-abiding citizen; I'm proud to call myself that. So can we settle for just ten days? I'd be most grateful."

The teller sighed. "You will not be staying, of course, in one of their luxury hotels? They do like to flaunt their capitalistic ideas. I presume you do not?"

"It's a beach house," Eliska said, "quite small. Two years ago they charged us thirty dinars a day."

"Hotel—three hundred dinars," the teller said, writing it down, "plus thirty dinars a day for each of the adults and two dinars for the child. That's for meals and other incidental expenses." She was scribbling it all on her pad. "I make that a total of six hundred. And I feel we're being quite generous."

"Yes, indeed," Eliska said politely, "and that's fine."

The teller found the currency exchange chart and scribbled some more. "So if I may have a check for twelve hundred and twenty korunas, you shall have your dinars."

She was happy to do so, and the whole of this essential part of the operation had taken less than half and hour. Her euphoria, she thought, could not have been at a higher level. And yet . . .

A hurried hour's walk took her to the passport office, where the young man on duty said affably, "Madame Kucera! Only a short while ago we had a call from our good friend, Peter Tuka. We know about the theft of your passport, and, believe me, the moment that abominable young thief tries to sell it, we'll nab him! However, that might take quite a long time, if not forever." He laughed a little, "I imagine I shouldn't say things like that. Our image here is supposed to be one of great efficiency. I only wish that were true."

Eliska laughed with him, rather liking this attractive young man. "So how long will it take for a replacement?"

He spread his arms wide, "Did I mention our efficiency? Allow me to prove it." He reached down under his counter and came up with the new passport. "There," he said, "already made up, and all we need now is your signature."

She could not believe it. She turned pages and saw the photograph there, at least ten years old, when that glorious hair was half its present length and the blouse she was wearing was a disaster.

"For heaven's sake, where on earth did you find that photograph?" she asked.

He looked a little saddened now. "The Secret Police," he said "require us to keep photographs of passport applicants back to the time of the first issue. Doesn't make much sense, does it?" But then he brightened. "However, you will see that we've given you that visa for Yugoslavia that Peter said you wanted."

"Oh, that's very good of you."

"We figured that traveling abroad is not very easy these days, and there's no reason we should try and make it more of a problem." He pushed a form across the counter. "Sign this, and you're all set to go."

Euphoria? The word, the feeling, was sticking in her mind, and she found it hard to accept so much good fortune. "Wait 'till I tell Zdenek," she was thinking as she hurried home. And much to her surprise, Zdenek was there when she arrived, making himself an over-sized chlebicky for lunch. "What on earth," she asked, "are you doing here this time of the day?"

He grinned broadly, "I do believe I could ask you the same question," he said. "I'm in charge of my department as you know, and since I had things to do, I simply handed my day's work over to my deputy, came home, picked up my passport, and took it 'round to the cops for that stamp of theirs so that it can be renewed."

"The cops?" The word itself was beginning to worry her, but he quickly reassured her.

"The Regular Police, not the S.P. They won't cause any difficulty.

I have to pick it up at four o'clock and take it 'round to the passport people for the visa, and then, by God, we're almost ready to go. I can't believe it's all been so simple."

Eliska could not accept it quite so readily. "I hope you're right," she said. "It's been a good day so far, an excellent day, I'd hate for it to be destroyed now."

"It won't be, trust me. And you?"

"My passport," she said, and she showed it to him, "with the visa already there. And I've resigned from the Telephone office. That Peter Tuka is really a very nice guy. It was he who arranged for them to stamp it for Yugoslavia."

"Good," Zdenek said. "That's going to work out very nicely for us." He was looking at her a little strangely. "But there's something else on your mind, isn't there?"

It did not surprise her that he always seemed to read her thoughts so easily, and she nodded. "Nothing important, really," she said, "but Peter . . ." She broke off, thinking, and went on at last, "I keep getting this idea that Peter is not only the head of my department in the office, trying hard all the time to get the Directorship. I think he's a great deal more important in the hierarchy than he pretends to be. Irrational thinking, I'm sure, but . . . that's how I feel."

"If you're right," Zdenek said, "don't knock it! It can only help us along the way."

"Uh-uh!" Eliska said, "why don't I come with you to the Passport Office? They know me well there now, and there's this young man . . . well, I think it might help if he knows that we're together, that you are part of me, and I'm part of you. What do you think?"

"I think that's a very good idea," Zdenek said correctly, "although I imagine that that's fairly common knowledge all over town and accepted everywhere. Why should it not be? I have to go to the police first. The two offices are only a few blocks apart, so why don't you come with me there, too, and save a long walk home in between."

"Another good idea," Eliska said. "I've had far too much walking to do today. I'm sure it's bad for my figure." And so it was decided.

They talked together about nothing in particular for a while, and then suddenly and unexpectedly, Lenka arrived. And to their astonishment, she had a finger to her lips indicated silence, please. She went straight to the phone, unscrewed the mouth-piece and took out a tiny chip no bigger than a little finger-nail and held it up to show them, a finger still to her mouth. She took it silently to the verandah and dropped it on the floor there and stomped on it angrily and repeatedly 'till it had the appearance somewhat, of a squashed cockroach. She returned and said, looking at Zdenek, "I realize that you don't like me to talk about my cell, but I think you know that its major mandate is Intelligence. This morning, we discovered that your phone had been tapped."

Staring at her, Eliska said, "Oh, my God!"

Lenka turned her look to her "Think back, Eliska dear. They did it at twenty after nine this morning. They were here for exactly four minutes. What have you been discussing since then?"

"Nothing of importance," Zdenek said emphatically. "Just small talk." And Eliska agreed with him. "But," she said, "for God's sake, I was in the office around that time, handing in my resignation! I can't believe this!"

"You want to know something else you can't believe? Guess who signed the order for the tap?"

Eliska stared at her. "No! No I don't believe that either!"

"Peter Tuka," Lenka said. "In person. He gave the order a few minutes after you'd left."

Zdenek was signaling to them now and he said, "It's a beautiful day, why don't we get some fresh air? That's what the veranda's for, isn't it?" and when they were all outside he went on, speaking very quietly now, "Damn it, we're breaking our own rules. We must get into the habit of talking only out here."

Eliska agreed, "Care and more care all the time, yes, and that ought to be easy for us by now." She turned back to Lenka, frowning, "But this is a Telephone Department operation, right? I mean, it doesn't involve the Secret Police?"

"As far as I can gather," Lenka said, "that is true the S.P. aren't concerned here."

"And am I correct in assuming that you have one of your agents in our office? You must have!"

"No comment," Lenka said, and Zdenek nodded his approval.

"But," he said to her, "have you ever tried to solve the enigma of Peter Tuka himself? He's something else again, and some of us have often wondered about him."

"So have some of us," Lenka said. "And, yes, we've tried, with no results at all. Everything indicates that he's exactly what he says he is, nothing more, nothing less."

"I shouldn't be asking you these things, I suppose," Zdenek said heavily, "but since they affect us so closely . . . could you be wrong there?"

"It's possible."

"Probable?"

"No, absolutely not. It's just a long-shot possibility, and quite remote."

"So let's be sensible about it," Zdenek said, "and not condemn a man who's known as a very nice guy just because we can't find any proof to the contrary. Both you ladies agree?"

"Agreed," Eliska said.

Lenka nodded. "But we'll still keep trying. And I'd better be on my way now. I've a lot to do this afternoon."

"Can't thank you enough," Zdenek said.

Eliska added, "Yes, and we'll take that as a very serious warning! We could have been so easily . . . well . . ." She was smiling broadly, "hoisted on our petard, so to speak. We should be moving off soon, too. We're getting our passports fixed for a ten-day vacation, the best way, which is to say, absolutely legal. Mine's done already, it's just Zdenek now."

"Which we are quite sure," Zdenek said, "will present no problem at all. The whole day's been a very lucky one for us."

"See you both again soon," Lenka said. "In the excitement I forgot what it was I came here for, I take it that my phone message was plain enough?"

"Of course. The second part of it?"

"Let's go out together," Lenka said, and they both understood her intent.

Out on the street, they went to where Zdenek had parked his Skoda, and Lenka said quietly, "The second part . . . the reason the Secret Police so often decide they want to follow you around, we've found out what it is and why it doesn't put you in any immediate danger. It's not an ordered surveillance at all; it's just that whenever they see your car, they like to see what you're up to and because it appears that someone once suggested that you had contacts in the underground. They absolutely don't know that you're part of it, one of its originators, in fact. They don't know that at all. They're just hoping that one day they'll find you with someone who actually is under surveillance, or going to some wine cellar where they know a meeting is going on. And then—bingo! They've got you. But I know we all know how superbly careful you are, so that's not likely to happen,"

He was frowning darkly, "But that makes no sense at all! If they suspect me in the slightest, they're going to arrest me! And believe me, yes, I'm pretty tough, I believe, but once they started on their Moderation Three with me, I'd be screaming with the best of them. And pretty soon I'd be talking. Shameful, isn't it? But personal ideas and personal realities are often very far apart from each other, aren't they? I have no illusions, Lenka. And deep inside me, I know that they'd break me." He found that Eliska's hand was on his arm, and he laid his over it and squeezed it gently.

"No," Lenka said, with a great deal of assurance. "They're afraid to arrest you on speculation; it has to be with what they call 'due cause.'"

"That," Zdenek said, "is-forgive me—the most ridiculous assumption I've ever heard! Since when are the S.P. being finicky about who they arrest?"

"It's your name," Lenka said, and he stared at her.

"My name?"

"Zizka." Lenka said, "There aren't many of you around, are there?"

"Except," Zdenek said with a touch of friendly sarcasm, "a few hundred thousand all over the country."

"Here, in Ceske Budejovice."

"Ah. Maybe a few hundred of them, at a guess. I don't really know any of them at all."

"They all enjoy, probably unknowingly, the same protection that you have."

"I wish I knew what you're talking about."

"You really ought to. You remember when they arrested a Zizka in Bratislava two years ago? Ivan Zizka, I think his name was. He got rollicking drunk in a bar, threw stuff around, and a whole lot of people, too."

"Ah, Ivan! Yes, I think he's my second cousin three or four times removed. I've never met him. I don't know him as a drinking man."

"Will you kindly listen," Lenka said wrathfully, "to some common sense?"

"Sorry. Go on . . ."

"They sent four cops to arrest him, and he beat the daylights out of all of them."

"A true Zizka," Zdenek said.

Lenka answered him, "And if you don't shut up, by God, I'll beat the daylights out of you, too, okay?"

"Sorry again."

"Darling," Eliska said to him, "have you been drinking?"

"No," Zdenek said. "Tonight, when this splendid day has come to its inevitable end."

But Lenka went on. "The cops there finally got an alarm out, and four squad cars rushed in—a total of sixteen more police officers—and at last they got him into jail." She was beginning to enjoy this. "But he was a Zizka, a descendant of the hallowed Hussites, and the bartenders don't have a union now, but the next day there wasn't a single bar open in town. The steelworkers called a strike, so did the Skoda factories. The farmers were blocking all the roads with their produce trucks. And more than thirty thousand demonstrators were raising hell in Town Square."

She was suddenly deadly serious. "Do you remember the days, so many years ago, of those strikes and demonstrations and the resulting chaos?"

"Yes, I do."

"It can happen again, Zdenek. It's the one thing the Secret Police are terrified of. Because it's the one instance that can start it all over again and throw the whole damn regime—which pays their exorbitant salaries—out of business. All that took place because they arrested Zizka without—ha! No, even with—due cause! It means that your danger is not imminent. Make a mistake, yes, it will be."

"Something," Zdenek said, "that I try to avoid at all times. Are you going home? Can we give you a lift?"

"Thank you, but no," Lenka said. "No way I'm going to let you know where I'm headed."

"Very proper," said Eliska. "But keep in touch, right? And thanks again for you-know-what."

She was gone. Zdenek started the car and it promptly stalled. He swore, lifted up the rear-end engine cover and checked the plug leads, wiggling them around, came back and said to Eliska, "There's so much room back there, so much empty space! Why the hell couldn't they have given us a bigger engine, can you answer me that? Six cylinders instead of a measly four, wouldn't that have made more sense?"

"And a lot more expensive gas consumption," Eliska said. And that, for the moment at least, was the end of the argument.

It started on the third try, and they drove on 'round to the headquarters of the regular police, where they were surprised—with Eliska worried, too—to see one of those infamous big black cars parked there, a sullen driver just staring at them as they entered the building. "Not for us," Zdenek said. "It can't be. We haven't done anything wrong. At least, not lately."

Inside, the desk officer looked a little uncomfortable, for no apparent reason, and Zdenek looked at his watch and said pleasantly, "Zdenek Zizka again, Comrade. You told me to pick up my passport at four o'clock. I'm precisely on time."

The man appeared to be confused, "Zizka, was it? Zdenek Zizka?"

"Yes. Is there a problem? Don't you remember me?"

"And I told you to pick up a passport? What passport would that be?"

"My own, of course! I gave it to you some hours ago. This morning you told me it would be ready at four, which is now. And are you saying you don't remember? That doesn't make much sense, does it?"

The officer said desperately, "I think it is lost, Comrade."

Zdenek stared at him, "You think what?"

"I think it is lost."

"Then what I think," Zdenek said coldly, "is that I want to talk to your Chief. Kindly pick up your phone and tell him that."

The officer hesitated, and then, plucking up his courage, he said firmly, "I cannot do that, Comrade. I will not do that."

Eliska said quietly, "That door over there, darling, it says Chief on it. Why don't we just barge in?"

"That's a very good idea," Zdenek said, and to the officer, "Either you call and announce us, or I'll break that damn door down if I have to. And I advise you not to try and stop me. I'm already in a very bad mood, my friend, so watch your step, or you'll find yourself in a whole lot of trouble".

The officer hesitated for only a moment, and then he picked up the phone. "We have a Zizka here who wants to see the Chief," he said. "Can I have your orders please? He has a very combative woman with him . . . Yes, will do." He put down the phone and gestured toward the door. But it was already opening, a uniformed guard of the S.P.S. there, signaling to them. As they moved towards it, Eliska caught her breath suddenly. The scent of cigar smoke was very strong. And there, sure enough, Mirek was sitting at the Chief's desk, and the Chief himself was seated on a hard wooden chair in the corner, his eyes cast down, looking like a schoolboy under punishment.

Eliska looked at Mirek and said coldly, "No, Comrade Captain. I will not speak with you again." She turned sharply on her heel and started to move back to the door, but Mirek said angrily, "No! Come back here! At once!" And immediately she felt the strong hands of the guard on her arms. Zdenek started toward her, but she said to him, "No, darling, no!" and he stopped.

"Sit her down," Mirek said, more calmly now, and the guard took her to another chair and gestured to her. She sat down and looked across at the Chief, but he would not meet her eyes.

Zdenek, too, was unsure of himself now, but he said, politely enough, "Comrade Captain Voitech Mirek, I believe? We have not met before, officially, but I do know who you are, of course. I came here to speak with the Chief . . ."

"Who is indisposed at the moment."

"It is about a missing passport. My own."

Mirek blew out a huge cloud of blue smoke, "Yes, I know about that."

It surprised Zdenek. "You do?" You know where it is?"

"Have you any ideas yourself on the subject?"

Zdenek said, very carefully now, "The desk officer seems to think it might be lost, but I myself find that hard to believe."

"Oh, really? And why would that be?"

Cat and mouse, Zdenek was thinking. No way am I going to be one of his damned mice. But he was trying hard to control the anger that was steadily rising deep inside him. He said quietly, "All that was required was for the Chief to put his stamp on it."

"Which I did!" the Chief said, blurting it out quickly. Mirek ignored him completely.

71

"A matter," Zdenek went on as though nothing had happened, "that could have been accomplished in just a few minutes."

"Unless, of course, it truly had been lost," Mirek said, and as though pleased with Zdenek's so carefully subdued anger and hoping to augment it, he added, "But I find this a very wasteful discussion. Would that be a good idea? What do you think?"

"Like what?" Zdenek asked, hoping his cold fury could still be contained.

Mirek pointed rudely to Eliska, "That rather sour-faced woman there, isn't she your concubine?"

"The lady is my companion," Zdenek said. He was visibly trembling now.

"Yes," Mirek said, "of course. Is she ever as rude to you as she is to me?"

"I'm afraid I don't quite follow you." Zdenek began, but Mirek suddenly rose to his feet and began pacing around, waving his cigar about.

"You saw her when she came in. You saw how she derided me, held me in the utmost contempt, did you not? You saw how she turned her back on me and tried to stalk out of my office as though I were some servile hireling of no quality! As though I were not the most powerful and widely feared man in the whole of this city! You saw it all, and said nothing?"

"A small onslaught of quite temporary anger," Zdenek said. "It's common enough in women and of very little importance. May I now have my passport?"

"Oh, your passport. We're back to that, are we? I thought we had decided that it was lost, so why don't you start searching for it?"

The anger was raging now, "Like where, for God's sake?"

"In the garbage, perhaps," Mirek said airily, "where you might also find this God of yours. Unless, of course, it's all been given to the pigs. Or you might, perhaps, find it floating somewhere in the river. Go now. I no longer find this exchange of ideas as personably enjoyable as it might have been. So go, both of you! Unless you want me to throw you both into jail where you can find the time to reflect upon your attitudes towards the police. Go!"

Zdenek turned on his heels, and Eliska followed him out. They went to the Skoda in silence, drove home in silence, and entered the apartment in silence. Since that awful encounter, neither one of them had spoken a single word.

The house was silent too, silent and empty. Martin had taken his young brother on a field trip into the woods to teach him what berries he could eat and what he should leave alone. "He's old enough to start learning now," he had said, grinning. "He shouldn't try to find out by trial and error."

In a little while, Eliska could tolerate it no longer, "Well?" she asked.

Zdenek turned on her. "Well? What do you mean by that?"

A little puzzled, Eliska answered, "I mean, what do we do now? We're back to square one, aren't we?"

"No, we are not," Zdenek said. "At square one, we both had invalid passports, plus the hope, the expectation, that we could get them both validated. What do we do now? You have yours, with the kids as well. And mine? Not a hope in hell that I can ever get that, any hope or expectation of it is gone down the toilet because of your damn stupidity! You hear me?"

"You don't understand! Yes, that's the whole problem! If you understood something just once in a while, it's highly possible we could have fixed the whole damn thing. But, no, you had to get on your high horse and insult this man Mirek's dignity, which he obviously prizes very highly."

"What dignity?" She asked. "You and I and the whole city know that he has none at all."

"Worse than none," Zdenek said, "but he imagines that he has a hell of a lot. The most widely-feared man in the whole of Ceske Budejovice, you heard him say that! And it's a hell of a lot that you insulted when you turned your back on him and tried to walk out of the room. For God's sake, don't you ever think before you start throwing your stupid weight around? It's like turning your back on a king or some mighty prince that holds life or death in the palm of his hand."

"And now it's you being stupid."

"I am not! And if you'd had enough common sense to know the difficulties that already lay ahead of us, you'd have tried a little restraint if you could ever find some. But no, that's beyond your capabilities, isn't it?"

"Oh, shut up, for God's sake! I'm mad enough at you already. Don't push me any further."

"So what the hell are you mad at me for, when it's you giving me this major headache?"

"For sucking up to this monster like you did!" She started mimicking him, 'Comrade Captain Voitech Mirek, I believe? I do know who you are, of course."

"You wretched woman creature, can't you realize that I was of necessity buttering him up, feeding his vanity while you were busy insulting him?"

White with anger, Eliska said, "What was that you called me?"

"I called you what you are, a wretched creature, and I should have added 'as stupid as they come.'"

Eliska raised a hand to strike him, but he seized her arm and easily pushed her away. He was shouting now, "Can't you realize what you've done, dummy? You have your damn passport, with the kids, and I can never get one again for as long as I live! It means that you can go, but I can't. I have to stay behind and rot here in hell! Just how much pleasure does it give you, will you answer me that? Less of your crappy ideas at the wrong time, and I could maybe have finished up with that passport in my pocket right now!"

"Idiot!" Eliska shouted back. "Are you so stupid you can't realize that your passport was destroyed, fed to the pigs, before we even entered that building? That nothing I did or said could have changed that?"

"So," Zdenek snarled, "just tell me where you got that price—less piece of information!"

"From Mirek himself. He told us," she began, and broke off, knowing at once the weakness of her argument, and Zdenek promptly took her up on it.

"Yes," he said, "that widely-feared man who never told a lie in his life, that God-fearing, righteous creature we all love so much!"

"Shut up!" Eliska screamed. "You've made your point!"

"No I haven't!" Zdenek shouted back. "The point is, you've screwed the ass off me through imbecility that passes all understanding! No thought at all for all the love I've given you. Just the hell with Zdenek, as long as I have what I want. Now I'm beginning to hate your guts."

Eliska felt the blood draining from her face; in her stomach, the seat of all emotions, there were vipers writhing, and she threw herself at him, her fingernails raking down his face, and as he seized her wrists she screamed at the top of her voice, "Then get the hell out of my house, you bastard! You hear me? God damn your eyes, I hate you! I never want to see you again! Ever!"

She broke free and struck him again, hard, and he swung around to save his face from those searing nails. His elbow caught her jaw and sent her flying, and she fell and lay there on the ground, staring up at him in a kind of stupor as he stood above her, staring down at her.

He stroked his cheek and looked at the copious blood on his hand, and he looked down on Eliska again and whispered, "Oh my God . . . God, what have I done? Oh, God almighty . . ." He dropped to his knees beside her and reached out to her. This tough and self-reliant man was actually crying, the tears streaming down his face, and he was inarticulate too, not finding the words he needed, knowing that they did not even exist. "What have I done? What has come . . . come over me? I can't . . . can't . . . can't have happened . . . you know . . . you know how much, oh, God, how much I love you . . . all that I ever want to live for . . . my love, my love, my love . . . I can't . . . can't think what came over me."

He was clutching her, holding her tightly, weeping his heart out, but she pushed him away, and said angrily, "A flashback, you damned Zizka."

It both surprised and angered him, bringing him suddenly to his senses, "A what?"

She said furiously, "The blood still running through your veins, blood from that ancestor of yours, the most famous of all the Zizkas, four hundred years ago."

"Five hundred."

"Yes, five hundred, a wild and courageous man of fearsome temper, but a savage, and sometimes a little stupid, too. And the blood . . . it's still there."

He stared at her for a moment, unsure of himself, "Well, I'll be damned." He released her and stumbled awkwardly to his feet, then reached down and took her hands to pull her up, too. Holding her again, his fingers lost in that silky hair he loved so much, he whispered, "I must have hurt you so very, very badly."

She shook herself free, "Yes, you did, disgracefully."

"And you think . . . you talk of some kind of deadly blood in my veins? No! It makes no sense at all!!!"

"Perhaps not the blood—yes, that's a little crazy, maybe—but the genes."

"Say again?"

"The genes," Eliska said heatedly. "What is it they call them? The units of heredity? Yes, that's what they are."

"But . . ." Zdenek was almost stammering now. "After what I've done, you can . . . you can find some . . . some way-out reason for it? For God's sake, just an unfortunate biological phenomenon?"

Eliska nodded, "That's exactly what it was, and I hate having to accept it." She laughed shortly, "Ha! Perhaps it's something in my genes. Perhaps all my own ancestors were very unforgiving people, who knows?"

"But can you . . . can you at least try to forgive me?"

She was quite unable to drive away her anger. "No! You think you can beat the hell out of me and just say you're sorry, and that's the end of it? You think you can rid yourself of those damned genes by pretending they're not there?"

"Biology! Philosophy! I'm way out of my depth! All I truly know is that I love you so much! Okay, I'm sorry." He gestured helplessly, "I lost my temper, and I'm ashamed of it! It's a shameful memory that'll stay with me for the rest of my life! But have you never heard of lovers' quarrels? The deeper the love, they say, the stronger the quarrel."

"Hey, that's great! You love me so much that you can beat up on me any time you feel like it!"

"Swear to God, it will never happen again."

"My turn to swear to God," Eliska said more calm now, "and I do. If and when it does happen again, you can call it the end of our long relationship. Do I make myself clear?"

The shock on his face was far beyond her expectations. Had she overstepped the limits of tolerance? She thought that perhaps she had, and she sighed deeply. But he was just staring at her as he wiped the blood from his face with a handkerchief. Then suddenly he turned on his heel, threw open the door, looked back at her and said coldly, "You don't want to listen to anyone else, ever, do you? Madame Eliska Kucera, the pinnacles of wisdom, always right! And everyone else? Always wrong! So I'm going out. I think a few drinks will do me a world of good."

He went out and slammed the door behind him.

Eliska sat down on the sofa and leaned back, finding that her thoughts were very confused and searching for a way to sort them out properly. This was not, for her, just a threatened breakup with Zdenek, it was far, far worse than that. It was a risk for the whole family. She knew that she was not, by nature, introspectively inclined, but was this the time for a certain amount of self-examination? Should she truly have controlled herself better in that awful meeting with Mirek? Was Zdenek possibly right in his accusations after all? Should she have attacked him physically in a fit of unrestrained temper? And, for God's sake, what was happening to her? What should she do when he returned, almost certainly drunk, to whatever extent? No, the question was not what to do. The inner recesses of her mind told her the answer to that—she had to make up! The question then was how? To beg his forgiveness? No! That was impossible! To pretend that nothing had happened? Well, maybe, and would that not depend on his condition upon his returns? With a sudden shock, she thought: 'should that be, if he returns'? The idea terrified her, the cohesion of the family was at very grave risk here, Martin and young Michal, would that not be a dreadful threat to their well-being also? She said aloud, "Dear God, no!" and found that she was trembling and close to tears.

She rose from the sofa and went out onto the veranda, his favorite place, and she was wondering, would she ever laugh again? Would they ever laugh together? Her hands were at her face, and she took them away and leaned onto the railing, looking up at the brightness of the rising moon, feeling the gentle softness of the breeze.

Time was passing, inexorably, and she could only wait.

There was the sound, then, of the opening front door, and her heart missed a beat, but it was only the two boys. Martin's voice was crisp and cheerful, "Mom? Mother, everything all right?" And was he staring at her?

"Fine," she said, and forced a smile. "Just fine."

They went to their room, and went about their own business, and Eliska went to the bathroom, took a shower, and put on a dressing gown. Quite soon, there was the sound of the opening door again, and Zdenek was there, moving toward her with the walk of a man who is drunk and doesn't want anyone to know it. His arms were outstretched to her, and she ran to him and took his fervent embrace and hugged him tightly, too, and neither of them spoke a single word.

Both of them knew with certainty that the trouble was over. They knew it would never happen again. They knew that fortunes of the family were secure.

CHAPTER FIVE

It was a Saturday in early July, and the weather was cool and refreshing with the sun coming and going at the whims of the clouds. The children had gone off to camp in the woods, an endeavor that Michal was beginning to think he was stuck with now, though when he wasn't actually at it, he sometimes thought there was a certain pleasure in it. And for his part, Martin was sure that, sooner or later, he'd turn this child into something of a woodsman.

"A beautiful day out there," Zdenek said.

Eliska nodded, "Yes, and here I am cleaning the house. I can't think how it always gets into such a mess."

"But today, sweetheart, I have a much better idea, so forget the house. We're going boating."

"We are?"

"We are. It's been too long since we did that."

It pleased her, but with so much work to be done? "Can I have an hour to finish off the living room at least?" She asked.

"Nope. We're going now," Zdenek said cheerfully. He took her broom away from her and brandished it, "YOU can trade this in for a pair of oars."

"What? You mean I have to row? Me?"

"You! I'll be too busy talking, and maybe thinking as well."

She sighed, "Fifteen minutes to pack a picnic basket?"

"We have some cold sliced lamb and some pork. Which would you prefer?"

"Both, I think. And didn't I see some boiled new potatoes in the fridge? And some apple pie?"

"You got it."

"I'll give you ten minutes."

Half an hour later, they were on their way, and even the Skoda was driving well today. More seriously, Zdenek said, "We have so much to discuss now. I laid awake half the night and came up with a few ideas, some of them good, I think. We'll take all the time in the world to talk about them. Safely."

They drove to the river and found the boatman, a grizzled old man with a thick gray beard and an unfortunate habit of scratching it furiously all the time, as though a myriad of insects were nesting in its comfortable thatch. "Mr. Zizka, I do believe?" he said. Zdenek took the proffered hand and shook it. "How are you Tomas?"

"Getting a few days older every month," said the old man, "but that's the way things are, isn't it now? And what kind of boat would you like today?"

Zdenek pointed, "That one."

Tomas nodded, "Ah, yes, you always did have and eye for a good boat, didn't you? That's a carvel-built beauty I bought just a few weeks ago, solid elm lumber; she's deeper than most, the best there is."

He hauled the little boat in and graciously helped Eliska aboard, saying, "Two pairs of oars aboard, Ma'am, in case you want to do some rowing yourself, but I always tell the ladies to make themselves comfortable on them cushions there, and let the man do the work."

"That, Master Tomas," Eliska said, "is exactly what I intend to do . . ."

He looked to Zdenek, "Not important, Mr. Zizka, sir, but you know what time you'll be back?"

"Not yet," Zdenek said, settling the oars, "but I'll know, I guess, the moment you see us coming 'round the bend in the river, if that's all right with you."

"It certainly is," the old man said, and he was still furiously scratching at his beard as Zdenek headed the boat into mid-stream and started pulling heavily on the oars. Eliska was stretching herself out on the cushions, making herself as comfortable as she had ever been in all her life.

"Heaven," she said. "Absolute Heaven."

In a little while, they had gone quite a way, into far more open country, and Zdenek rested on the oars and flexed his muscles. "Now," he said, "we can talk our hearts out, undisturbed and unheard. Are you ready?"

"More than ready," Eliska said, "I have things to say, too. But you first, darling."

"Problem number one," Zdenek said, "I have no passport for this journey. Without it, I stay home, which I don't want to do—and will not do."

"And I won't tolerate it either," Eliska said. "We go together, all of us, or not at all."

"So do you have any ideas on the subject?"

"Tell me yours."

"The solution is—we have to buy a forgery. A phony passport, skillfully put together by an expert. I wonder if that can be done?"

Eliska shook her head. "I doubt it very much. I don't think there's anyone in town who could do that. In Prague? Bratislava? Maybe."

"I think our own underground is better by far than theirs."

"But it's not a matter for the underground, surely! Isn't it more black market kind of stuff? That young man who likes cats . . ."

"Huh?"

"The one who stole my purse. It's the black market where he'll be selling my passport, I have an idea that there must be quite a lot of that going on these days."

She was right. In 'these days,' as she called it, the number of people trying to leave the country was growing month by month, as was the strength of the regime's efforts to prevent it. Week by week there were more riots in isolated areas, for the most part quite uncoordinated, that were a rising indication of how strongly the decent citizenry felt about the oppression. But this was a matter only of furious groups—sometimes several hundred strong—setting fire to Russian tanks, assaulting Russian soldiers, sabotaging Russian supply vehicles, venting their anger in every possible way, and often losing their lives as a result."

But there were others—perhaps hundreds of them, too—who preferred the more devious route, sneaking quietly out of the country against considerable odds, just as Eliska and Zdenek were trying to do now. And this meant, for the black market, a very profitable trade in stolen passports for alteration to suit the buyers.

But this, too, was extremely hazardous; Czechoslovakia's quota of skilled forgers was desperately small, and they were not, on the whole, very expert.

Frowning, Eliska asked Zdenek, "A couple of times last year we bought some dollars we needed from a skinny little guy on crutches. You remember his name? And didn't he sell us that copy machine that your group finished up with?"

"Yes," Zdenek said, "and I think that's the man we need. His name's Ctibor—at least that's the name he goes under. Supposed to be the top black market man in town, and he might well be; he's very, very sharp.

"Question, then. How do we get in touch with him?"

"The easiest thing in the world. It's like he has an office where he can always be found. An outside table at the Deminka Cafe over innumerable cups of espresso, seven days a week from nine till twelve. The cops know about him, but they leave him alone. Too many of them find him useful."

He laughed shortly, "Although they did beat him up one time last year. They wanted information on the other dealers, but apparently he told them he couldn't do that, said it would be bad for business. They just broke one of his legs and let him go."

"Poor devil," Eliska said. "So that might be step one."

"And best if you approach him rather than me," Zdenek said. "He's almost certain to know that I'm underground and won't want to be seen talking to me."

"Besides, I'll get a better deal from him than you ever would. What's a fair price for a stolen passport, do you suppose?"

"At a guess, about half of what he asks."

"More like a quarter. You can leave that to me."

"It should be in good condition, but not too new."

"I know."

"And not too old either."

"I know."

"And he'll have to stamp it with the Yugoslav visa and the police permit, but that should be easy; they're just regular rubber stamps."

"I know, I know, I know . . . what do we do about the photograph?"

"If we can't find a decent one of me lying around," Zdenek said, "you can take one that we can cut to regulation size. We'll find out what that is from your passport; he'll have to erase the original signature, which I'm sure he knows how to do, and then . . . that would seem to be it."

"Erasing the signature," Eliska said, worrying about it. "I hope he knows how to do that without bleaching the page color out which is possibly what could happen."

"That's why he has to find a really skilled, professional forger for the job. Once the space is clean, I simply sign, and there we are: the new Zdenek Zizka passport. And may the devil take that bastard Mirek!"

"Amen to that," Eliska said. "What's next on the agenda?"

"Now," Zdenek said settling his oars again, "we move on a little. I want to reach way beyond the bend in the river. You remember that beautiful stand of oak trees?"

"This time of the day, the sun almost overhead, they should look marvelous. And we might have our picnic lunch there, what do you think?"

"I think that's a great idea. I'm ravenous already."

He started rowing again, very strongly. "I like this little boat," he said, "Tomas was right, she's a beauty, handles like a dream."

"The first crossing," Eliska said, "into Hungary. "I don't know how many crossings there are."

"We can find that out easily enough. After all, everyone knows we're just on a ten-day vacation. I'd say we should try somewhere around Komarno, if the customs offices there are not too big. Where did we cross the last time, do you remember?"

"Yes, I do. It was Komarno. Don't you remember they were building the place up, a whole lot of traffic there? It took us forever to cross."

"Ah, yes, I remember now. But that was in the middle of the day, and I wonder . . ." He broke off, and then, "That's something else we should think about. Let's suppose that there might be some little discrepancy in my nice new passport, too small for us to notice. I hope that won't happen, but to be sure, we don't want the biggest and most important of the crossings, because that's where all the prestige customs people will be. I'd rather we find a run-down sort of place if we can, where the staff, hopefully, might be—if not exactly rejects—at least not up to the standards of the main station officers. Is that good thinking?"

"And maybe late at night too, when they'll all be tired."

"Yes, I think you're right. And wait 'till you see those oak trees."

He was pulling mightily one oar as the little craft took the bend. He rowed on and on and on, and there they were, four very old and quite splendid oaks, with a score or more of other trees close by, and what were they? "Oaks?" Eliska asked.

Zdenek nodded, "I think so, I can't be sure."

"We'll take a twig or two home with us," Eliska said, "and ask Martin. He'll know."

Zdenek just grunted, and then rammed the boat into the bank. He jumped ashore and reached out to help Eliska with the picnic basket, and in a very short while the red-checkered tablecloth was neatly spread out on the grass, and Eliska was setting out the food. A clutch of very young quail, six of them, were strutting around, paying no attention at all to the raucous screeching of their mother, up in one of the trees warning the chicks of danger as they pecked happily away at the insects they found.

"Beautiful," Eliska said. "They're babies, and they don't have a care in the world." And indeed they were, the brown of their backs just darkening against the soft light buff of their breasts. A little further away, there were a few cows lying down, and a dozen or so horses tugging at the long grasses, and there were white and pink and red and blue and yellow wild summer flowers everywhere."

"Marvelous, quite marvelous," Eliska said, watching them all.

Zdenek, his mouth full of good meat, said, "And so is your roast lamb, darling. It's terrific."

"So quiet and peaceful. Why can't it be like this always? It was once, remember?"

But Zdenek was looking up at the bright blue sky and studying the horizons too. "Strange," he said, "not a cloud in sight, not one."

Eliska looked at him, puzzled, "So what's strange about that?"

"The cows," Zdenek said, "all of them lying down on the grass, none of them on their feet."

"How very interesting."

"You mean you don't know?"

"I can't wait to hear . . ."

"I thought everybody knew. Cows lying down is a sure sign of rain."

"You're joking."

"Nope. It's gospel truth."

"Who said so?"

"Ah, that I don't know, but it's as age-old as the ages."

"So just tell me where the dark clouds are."

"Over the horizon," Zdenek said affably. "Unless, of course, those cows are completely screwed up—like so many other of our friends. And would there be any more of that pork? It's quite fabulous. I take my hat off to you."

"You know darling," Eliska said, sorting out more meat, "you're nuts. I'm sometimes—quite often I'm afraid—driven to the conclusion that there's no hope for you at all."

"Tell me that," Zdenek said, "on the way home. When we're both drenched to the skin in an open, carvel-built boat. Ah, that roast is so good."

"Finish it up," Eliska said. "I just hope you'll still have room for some apple pie."

"I will," Zdenek said, "never fear." And only a little while later, he had finished off the last morsel of pie and was actually licking his fingers. Eliska watched him, sighed, and shook her head slowly.

"I was thinking," Zdenek said, "about the car. Our route . . . first to the Hungarian border, which is about three hundred and fifty kilometers, then clear across Hungary to the Yugoslavia border, another two hundred or so, and then, what, a further hundred, maximum, to the Austrian line? That's a total of about six hundred and fifty. Not a great distance, really, but I'm wondering if the Skoda will get us there without a breakdown or two on the first leg of the journey, which could be a really major calamity."

"It got us to Yugoslavia and back the last time without much in the way of trouble except that problem in Budapest."

"Yes, three days to get the car fixed: that's fine in Hungary. But if it were to happen again, only here, before we cross the border . . . it's not a bad little car, but it's really showing its age. We all know, surely, that within our own borders, any mechanical problem, even the smallest, takes forever to fix. And suppose it were something that required replacement parts! How long would that take?"

"Months, perhaps," Eliska said, "certainly weeks, yes, I get your point."

"Hanging around in today's Czechoslovakia for weeks on end with uncertain papers? It's not a situation I would relish in the least."

"Well, it simply means that we have to make sure it's in top condition before we start out! You always say that, what's his name, Kornel?—is such a good mechanic, let him have the car for a day or two, go over it with a fine-tooth comb, fix what has to be fixed."

"Yes, that's right," Zdenek said, "he's excellent, certainly the best at his job in town. And a very nice guy, too. I always wish we both knew him better. But you have met him, I think, a couple of times, no?"

"Sure, several times, I liked him a lot."

"Good. I'll give him the car tomorrow, and that'll be another step behind us." He went on, musing, "Ctibor for the passport, Kornel for the car. In another week—two at the most—we could quite possibly begin discussing a date for our actual departure."

"Something I can't wait for," Eliska said.

But then, she suddenly raised her eyes to stare beyond and behind him, "Oh, my God," she said.

And Zdenek swung 'round to see. There on the far horizon was a long thin line of a very dark and thunderous cloud, and Zdenek echoed her thought, "Oh, my God, is right," he said. "Let's move it, and fast!"

They hastily bundled everything up and tossed it into the boat and jumped aboard. Zdenek seized the oars and began rowing furiously. "We'll make it," he said, "but only just."

Eliska was kneeling on the cushions, watching, and she asked, "Will it be faster if I take the other oars as well?"

"Well, it would," Zdenek said, "but are you sure you can manage?"

"You know I can."

"Okay, come sit beside me and grab my oars, I'll take the other pair up front. I want you behind me."

The change-over was quickly effected, and the dual rowing began in earnest, but Zdenek was worrying about it, wondering if he should temper his timing, slowing down to make it easier for her. But wouldn't that defeat their effort? He kept up the grueling pace, but in a while he called to her, "Are you all right back there?"

"Of course I am," Eliska answered.

"Not too fast for you? We can slow down just a trifle if you want."

"No!" she said, "I'm a very tough lady. It's time you knew that! So row on! Don't talk so much!" He looked back to grin at her and saw that the ominous black cloud was wider now, much wider, and still spreading from horizon to horizon.

"We'll make it," he said.

They came to the bend in the river, and the dark cloud was almost overhead now. There was a sudden clap of furious thunder, and an instantaneous lightning bolt hit a tall elm on the river's bank close by; they saw it's top-most branch smoldering and then catching reluctant fire.

It was only a very few minutes later when the sky darkened almost completely, and the rain came down on them with enormous power, the drops hitting them hard, like watery pebbles.

"Well," Zdenek shouted over the storm blasting racket, "how about that? Those cows were right . . . ship your oars, darling, I'll take it now."

"Why?" Eliska shouted back. "The less we get of this, the better! It's faster if we both row."

"It's a half-hour to the boathouse; saving five minutes won't make a blind bit of difference! Ship your oars!"

"No, I don't want to do that! I want to row! Only way I'll keep warm!"

"Okay, okay! But we'll take it more easily now, we're already soaked to the skin and wringing wet. It can't get much worse however long we take!"

"True, true," Eliska said, resigned to it all, as they both applied all their strength to the oars, saving the chitchat for a better occasion. And twenty-five minutes later they were in sight of the boathouse.

Tomas was standing there, with an oilskin cape over his head and shoulders, and as he helped Eliska up onto the deck, he slipped it off and threw it over her, quite uselessly. "Too late to do much good," he said, "but we mustn't forget our manners, must we now? Come inside, fast as ever; dry you off in no time at all. And I've got some coffee brewing in there, too."

They all went into Tomas's office and stood in front of the big casting stove there, and their host asked, "How far did you nice folks go? You reach that bend there?"

Way beyond it," Zdenek said. "You know that stand of oak trees?"

"That's real pretty countryside there, yes, I know it." He was frowning suddenly. "There's always a small herd of cattle there. They weren't lying down?"

"Well, yes, there were," Eliska said, "and I know what that means, of course, I just figured they were mistaken. The sky was so clear and blue."

"Hey," Thomas said, "I have seen the cows sometimes telling us all about the rain ten, twelve hours before it comes. They know. They always know."

"And next time," said Eliska, "we'll know better."

They hung around the hot stove for a while, making friendly small-talk and drinking scalding hot coffee, till at last they figured they were partly dry—at least, dry enough to go home. And on the way there, Zdenek said, "This little scheme of ours is going to cost us a bundle. How well off are we with money?"

It was a legitimate question. Both of them were in the highest paid ranks of the Administration as what used to be called public servants. Pity the poor junior typist with no real responsibility; she earned little more than a starvation wage. But the regime had always thought it advisable to build up a separate class of workers, paid from government rather than private funds,—the doctors, the nurses, the dentists, the hospital staffs, the departments—as a sort of counter to the common citizenry.

And for these two honest citizens, Zdenek's and Eliska's salaries were far more than they needed for a relatively comfortable existence, at least, financially.

It had long ago been decided that Eliska would handle all their money matters (this gave Zdenek a great deal of pleasure) and she had become, with constant practice, quite an expert. She knew when the black market dollars were falling drastically in price and the really rich people here were anxious to unload them against further depredations, and at just the right moment, she would make her bid. A month later—or two months, or three or even six—when the price skyrocketed again, she would sell them again for korunas. It was a practice that she did not like at first, but she soon realized, with what she liked to call her well-informed woman's wisdom, that sooner or later, surely, they would both stand in need of much ready cash if ever the opportunity arose for them to flee the county. And now the time had come.

"Well off," Eliska said, "is probably the right phrase. We have two hundred and seventy thousand korunas in the bank, and roughly the same amount in black market American dollars, call it ten thousand, safely hidden away, you know where. Yes, we're in very good shape."

The 'you-know-where' was an undistinguished-but very strong-storage place only a fifteen-minute stroll from the apartment. She went on, "And we mustn't forget all that jewelry I've chosen not to wear in recent years. We can always sell that too if it becomes necessary."

He reached across and patted her knee. "Just like the old days, isn't it? When a lot of money meant a lot of comfort."

"Except," Eliska said, "in the old days, we didn't have to be so sneaky about it."

"True, true," Zdenek said. "Unhappily, that's very true."

They drove on, and soon he dropped her off at the apartment and drove on to his office for the last hour or so of the workday, just to show himself and to make sure that his deputies were doing what they were supposed to do. And Eliska was delighted to see that both the boys were there, pleasantly exhausted after a long session at the swimming pool, where Martin was still teaching Michal how to improve his swimming.

"The kid's coming along great," he said. "I have to be the world's best coach! How long is it since we first started? A couple of months? And his back stroke now is almost as good as mine!"

"Better," said Michal.

And Martin lightly boxed his ears for him, "Shut up, kid," he said. "You can't talk to your teacher like that."

"I can, and I will," Michal said, and marched off to their room. Martin sighed, and turned to his mother, "You see what I have to put up with?"

Not waiting for an answer, he went on, "How's the vacation planning coming along?"

"Fine, just fine," she said. "My passport is all in order, you two are on it, as you know, and all we're waiting for now is Zdenek's. A small problem there . . ."

"What kind of problem?"

"Well," Eliska said, "it's all very simple. It seems that the police have to put a final stamp on it, though I don't quite understand why they should have to do that."

"It's their job, that's why."

"Darling," his mother said, "please don't interrupt me. If you'd let me finish what I'm trying to tell you."

"Sorry," he said, interrupting her again, "please go on."

"What I don't understand is why Zdenek needs that final stamp and I don't."

Martin spread his hands wide, "It's because Zdenek is technically the head of the family, so he's in a quite different control-factor. That's perfectly normal! Isn't it the same over the whole world?"

"Technically?" Eliska let it pass. She said instead, "Martin, if you had been born just a handful of years earlier, you'd know that since the time you were in diapers, we here have not been like the rest of . . . the whole wide world. But can we not talk about that? Please? It might make both of us angry."

"And I wouldn't like that!" Martin reached out and took both hands in his. "And neither would you! Do you know that you just happen to be the best mother ever? Honest, the greatest."

She drew him to her and embraced him, "And the greatest son a mother could ever wish for."

He said, pressing on, "So why won't the cops stamp his passport? They got something against him?"

"No, it's not that at all. They've lost it."

"What? He drew back, "How on earth could they do a thing like that?"

"Perhaps I should have said 'misplaced' it. It's the kind of thing that can happen in any bureaucracy. And ours is pretty heavy here. We just have to wait and see."

"Not too long, I hope," Martin said. "I can't wait to catch up with those three monsters . . ."

"Huh?" Eliska asked, "Say again . . ."

And Martin explained, "Those three Yugoslav kids I sent my chess problem to, I want to find out if they've solved it. I don't think they could have done it; they'd have written to me, just to show how clever they are."

"Ah, yes, you told me about it, but I didn't understand word one, I'm afraid."

Martin laughed, "Good. It's a real tough one, based on what Dubrovsky, one of our own Bohemian chess-masters, used to do with his knights in the middle game, but switching over to Adolf Anderson's ideas about his four remaining pawns . . ."

"Martin! Please!"

The wide grin was still there. "Of course you wouldn't know about Anderson. He was like a couple of years before your time." He paused for effect, and then added, "He was world champion in 1858."

"Martin . . . I hate you!" she said, laughing with him.

"So tell me what happened to Zdenek. You went out with him and came back alone. Is he leaving you at last?"

"He's gone to his office," Eliska said, "just to make sure it's still there."

But it was not quite true. On his way, Zdenek had passed the rundown garage, which his friend, Kornel, owned, and he had changed his mind, telling himself that he had more important things to do. He was in the right mood for a chat with him, whom he regarded as a strange and unconventional man, which, indeed, he was.

This was a strange friendship in itself, which had started more than two years previously, at a time when Zdenek had found that Kornel was a mechanic of extraordinary ability and had used him and no one else to fix the constant troubles with his Skoda. He was a big, bluff giant of a man in his middle fifties perhaps, with quite startling, deeply set brown eyes, a mass of unruly mouse-colored hair and a very large mustache—and muscles of formidable strength.

And then, much later on, they had run into each other at one of the butchers' stalls near the famous Black Tower, both looking for the best cuts in beef that had been hung for a while until they were beginning to turn a trifle blue. They had chatted there as they bartered, and had then moved on into the city's main square, to down a tankard or two of Budwar in a bar called the Buffet Zvon; and there, Kornel had told his newfound friend what he called a terrible secret.

"No one knows," he had said, spreading his arms wide, "where I come from, that I am not, except in spirit, a full-blooded Czech from the center of Bohemia. I am not even a foreigner."

"Kornel," Zdenek had said, "sounds like a German name. But I'd never take you for a Bosche."

"And I'm glad of that, at least. But Kornel is not my real name. I changed it some years ago now, twelve years ago. It was necessary; they were hunting me like an animal."

He had risen, abruptly and violently, to his feet, "And why do I tell you these things? Can you answer me that?"

"I think," Zdenek had said clearly, "because we are friends."

"No! We are not! How could that be? You are Zizka, the most famous man in Ceske Budejovice, the most famous name in the whole of the country! And who am I? Will you answer me that?"

"A friend," Zdenek had said, whereupon Kornel had turned on his heel and had stalked out.

Well, this was the kind of misadventure that could easily be remedied. The next day, he had taken the car 'round for an imaginary problem with the gear-shift, and when it had been handed back, Kornel had said, smiling, "Nothing wrong with it at all, my friend. No charge." And it was as though the previous day's encounter had never happened.

And then, in meeting after meeting, more of this extraordinary man's 'terrible secret' had seeped out in little driblets, until Zdenek figured that he knew more about Kornel's inner workings that he knew about his own. And not one word of these secret confessions has Zdenek told to Eliska. Some of them, notably the Bratislava horrors, were just too dangerous for anyone to talk about.

But this day, today, it was necessary to get the Skoda into shape, and on arriving at the garage, which said in big letters: 'Mechanic' Zdenek said brightly, "We're off to Yugoslavia for a ten-day holiday. You want to go over this damn car for me with a fine-tooth comb? Fix what has to be fixed?"

"Sure, can do. When do you want it back?"

"How about yesterday? All I really need is to know that I can get there and back with a fifty-fifty chance of making it."

"What you need," Kornel said, "is a rebar. Your pistons are flapping around in the block like they don't know where to go. No problem, I do have some oversize pistons for this car, but if I need something else . . ."

He picked up a half-empty bottle of Bud, the famous beer that had named itself after this town, drained it, and said, "Four hundred and eighty-two Skoda factories in this country more than half of them for automobiles. Did you know that? Back in '68, the Russians took them all over, switched them back to armaments. Then they discovered that those crummy trucks they brought down from Ukraine—they found out that our Skodas were a hell of a lot better, so they switched some of the factories back again to manufacture parts. But if I need something for this wreck, some part they don't manufacture anymore, give me three days and check with me. You want to leave it with me now? I can shove other stuff onto the back lot and start on it first thing tomorrow morning?"

"Great. But how do I get home?"

"I'll drive you."

"So how do you get back?"

"You drive me, what else?"

"Great again. You have any other brilliant ideas?"

"I've got this nice little car here—we call it a 'loaner'—I just might try to sell it. It's in terrific shape. Bring it back in three days, and keep your fingers crossed."

Finally, Zdenek drove home, and he told Eliska—out on the balcony for safety, "We have for a while at least, a very nice little car. It even starts every time you turn the key."

"Kornel?"

"He's giving ours a rebore; should make a very big difference." But there were more urgent matters on his mind now. "Are you planning on seeing this black-market guy tomorrow morning?"

"Yes, I am," Eliska said, "and I'm taking some American dollars with me. He's sure to want something up front." She grimaced, "I hope to God it works out, because what do we do if it doesn't? Do we have a plan B?"

Zdenek grunted, "That's something worth thinking about, certainly."

"I have thought about it," Eliska said heavily, "and I've come up with the answer. Quite simply—there is no plan B that's going to work. I don't know, we have to stake everything on what Ctibor can do for us. And if he can't give us what we need . . . I guess we'll have to look around and find someone else. How? Don't ask me that."

"Lenka's people? The Intelligence cell?"

Eliska shook her head slowly. "No," she said, "it's too risky. She's my best friend, I love her dearly, and I know that she's no fool. All this trouble we're going to just for a ten-day vacation? She'd suspect at once that we're not coming back and, smart as she is, she's not quite as secretive as she ought to be. She's a bit . . . what's the word?"

"Capricious, maybe?" Zdenek asked.

And Eliska agreed, "Yes. She has so many boyfriends, and she's madly in love with each and every one of them. I like to think that I'd trust her with my life, but that's simply not true if it ever came down to a case in point."

"Dangerous, then. I agree."

"Somehow, I can easily imagine her telling one of those lovers—call him the lover of the moment—'Honey, do I have news for you! I'm helping some friends defect, but don't tell a soul.' And there goes all our secrecy, right down the toilet."

"No plan B then," Zdenek said, quiet placidly. "We'll put all our cards, such as they are, on Ctibor, and then . . . we'll wait and see."

Eliska sighed, "As usual." But she smiled suddenly at a memory. "They do say that, historically, 'wait and see' is a kind of national philosophy, part of our diplomats' thinking for hundreds of years."

"Bohemia!" Zdenek said. "Never forget that we are part of a picture-book fairy-land, most of it not quite real. But the sad thing is that the Soviets, quite unwittingly, of course, dragged us out of never-never-land and laid all their stern and sullen practicalities on us. I hate them for it."

"If we were to tell the children that we want to leave the country because there's no Santa Claus here, who lives forever . . ."

"He was Bohemian, too . . ."

"They'd think we were nuts."

In a moment of alarm, Zdenek said, "But they don't know, for God's sake . . ."

"Of course not," Eliska said. "You and I, no one else. The boys get to be told when we both decide that the time has come to tell them, not before."

"What if Martin then wants to turn 'round and go back?"

"I've thought about that, too," Eliska said, "and I've dismissed it as highly improbable. So unlikely that I don't think it's even worth discussing."

"But if he does?"

"You don't listen to me, do you? I said it's not worth discussing."

"Do me a favor, sweetheart, answer the question."

"And I wish you'd call me sweetheart sometimes when you didn't actually want to get something from me!" Eliska said. But her tone was very affable, and she was smiling to take the edge off it.

"Touché," Zdenek said, and he, too, was amused now. "So tell me."

"Well," Eliska said, "Martin is too tight a part of this family to allow it to break up. But let's suppose that I'm wrong there . . ."

"Which you know you're not. But in a few months' time, he's going to be eighteen years old, for God's sake; he already has a mind of his own.

And if he should insist on going back, leaving the rest of us to go on, I would have to let him have his own way. But he'd know that it would break my heart. He'd never, ever, do that. No. I have no anxiety there at all, not the slightest. My only concern at the moment is about your passport. If something goes wrong there, we're back where we started."

"And in my opinion, for what it's worth," Zdenek said firmly, "we're worrying for no reason at all. This man Ctibor is known to be the best in the business, the virtual king of the black market. He's never let us down before. There's no sensible reason to suppose that he'll do that now."

"But if he should?" Eliska asked.

Zdenek answered at once, shooting from his hip, "That, my love, is something that I personally do not consider worth discussing."

And then Martin was there suddenly, coming in from the boys' room, "So that's where you are," he said. "I've been sniffing the air, and there's no scent of dinner anywhere. I went into the kitchen, and the stove's not even lit!"

"I plead guilty," Eliska said, looking at her watch.

So how about stuffed green peppers, dripping with tomato sauce? With pancakes and ice cream for dessert? Any takers?"

"Maybe some dumplings, too," Zdenek said, "and for me, a glass of rum would go down very well also."

"Coming up," Eliska said.

The dinner was a very satisfying end to a fairly satisfactory day. Tomorrow, Eliska was thinking, tomorrow is going to be the day that really matters.

CHAPTER SIX

It was a quarter past ten when Eliska arrived at the Deminka Café and saw her formidable quarry sitting there at a sidewalk table, the same thin and sharp-looking kind of man she had met before, dressed in the same gray suit with the same red tie. The crutches were missing now, though one leg was a little twisted. He was reading a magazine, and there was a large espresso there too, with three empty saucers neatly stacked there beside it, which meant that he was now on his fourth coffee. It astonished her; four double espressos in a little over an hour? Was he crazy? She saw that there was hardly anyone else at the sidewalk tables just now.

She dropped her purse close by him and when he was crouching down to gather up its contents, she said, very quietly and not looking up at him; "I need a long talk with you. Tell me when and where."

He was turning the pages of his magazine, and his voice was a zephyr, "Twelve-thirty, top of the Black Tower."

"Yes," she said quietly, and finished with her purse and went on her way, which was back on the bus and a long walk to the apartment. She found the vacuum cord was coming loose and repaired it, then went over all the rugs and carpets whether they needed it or not, not thinking too much about what she was doing. And when there wasn't a speck of dust left in the whole apartment, she found some glasses she could polish.

But the time came at last, and she made her way to the city's main and most important square, which was named after King Otakar who, way back in the thirteenth century, had built this city, had fortified it, mostly against his own populace, and had named it Royal Town.

But today, more platonically (and perhaps unhappily), Ceske Budejovice was better known for its pencil factory and for the brewery where its famous beer, Budweiser, was made. (In the old days, when German was the predominant language, this city was known as Budweiss, but with the arousal of Czech ethnic aspiration, the name had reverted to Otakar's own, its equivalent in the remarkably convoluted Bohemian language.)

Eliska was ruminating on these things, on Zdenek's talk about never-never-land, as she walked 'round to the tiny street behind the square where the Black Tower was. She paid her six korunas to the cashier there and began the long climb to the top, counting the steps as she went. At one hundred and fifty she rested for a few moments, silently voicing a few carefully chosen obscenities about this man Ctibor, and at three hundred she had to stop for a little while longer, wondering how come she wasn't getting as much exercise as she needed these days. She knew the number; sixty more to go, and at last she was there, leaning against the iron railing and trying to get her breath back. From up here, the view of the whole city was wonderful, and in the far distance even the Alps were visible. Down below her she could see all the beautifully arcaded houses that lined the immense square and the Samsonova Fountain, a very satisfying piece of Romanesque statuary, though now dry.

She looked at her watch; it was twelve-thirty exactly, and the door to the Galleria behind her opened, and there was Ctibor, moving toward her. There was no one else around.

He said quietly, "'A long talk,' you told me. Here we can talk safely, unheard, for as long as you wish. You are Eliska Kucera, I think, no? We met once."

"Twice, actually," Eliska said, "yes, we did."

"And you are Zdenek Zizka's lady."

"Yes."

"A good name, a good man."

"I think so, too."

"And what is it you want from me this time? If it's dollars, I would suggest you wait for a week or so. Today's rate is very high. If you wish to sell me some, then I must wait also."

Eliska took a long, deep breath. "No, we're not talking dollars now. What we need is a passport to replace one that has been confiscated by the Secret Police."

He was silent for a moment, and then, "I see. Would that be for you?"

"For Zdenek. Do you think you can find us one?"

"Tell me first what borders you will be crossing."

95

"We're going to Yugoslavia by way of Hungary. We're taking a ten-day vacation."

"Yugoslavia will not present much of a problem," Ctibor said. "They are very easy going people down there and they rather welcome us, even if the passport is perhaps a little dubious. But the Hungarians don't like us in the least, and you must understand that yours will not be an isolated case. Their immigration staff has to process hundreds of our people every day, many of whom are refugees who, like you, are hoping to leave the country permanently on passports that will not bear inspection."

"No!" Eliska said quickly, "we are returning home in ten days. There's no refugee problem here at all."

"Ah, yes, of course. Forgive me. That was just a slip of the tongue."

"And you were telling me about the difficulties at the Hungarian border."

"Quite recently," Ctibor said, smiling, "a Czech lady from a very high-class family here, very rich, was escaping to France, where she has family. Her passport had been confiscated by regime because of some unfortunate comments she had made about them. I gave her a new one. They spent—can you believe this?—more than two hours examining every aspect of my work. But at last, they were obliged to let her through." He added, a little smugly, "It was not even one of my best endeavors."

"In terms of practicality," Eliska asked, "can you tell me how much this cost her?"

"No, I cannot. Cost is a matter we will discuss when the time comes, not now. What is Zdenek's height? A smidgeon under two meters, I think, no?"

"A smidgeon over."

"Eyes brown, right?"

Eliska nodded.

"His date of birth?"

"November ninth, 1949."

"Do you have a recent photo of him? A close-up?"

"I do have a camera. I can take one."

Has he ever been to Warsaw? To Budapest? To anywhere in East Germany? Or Bulgaria?"

"No, never," Eliska said, wondering why this should be important.

As though reading her mind, Ctibor explained, "The lack of stamps for these countries would suggest to the Hungarians that Zdenek is not a communist, which could be an advantage. Because although Hungary is a member of the Warsaw Pact, they are not true communists; they call themselves a Republic, not quite the same thing. It means that I have to find a passport that has not much been used."

"And is that difficult?"

"No. It just reduces the choices. And I would like you to realize that this is not just a matter of taking the first stolen passport that turns up; it is a matter of careful selection."

"And therefore," Eliska said dryly, "of high cost."

"Precisely. Since you are using it for just a short holiday, you will not want to pay very much. But I cannot take this into account, I'm afraid."

"Of course. Can you give me a figure now?"

"What kind of figure did you have in mind?"

"It's a question, really, of how much we can afford."

"You are both government servants, are you not?"

"Well, yes."

"And therefore highly paid."

"I suppose that by some standards that would be true. But I don't want to empty my bank account for just a short vacation, a very valid point that you yourself made just now."

"I understand. Tell me then, what you find you can afford to pay."

"I was thinking of two or even three thousand American dollars, or a tiny bit higher in korunas."

Ctibor seemed to be quite shocked, "Dear lady!" He said, "I find that quite impossible to accept!" Not letting her speak he went on. "There are three things that I believe you do not appreciate, the first being that I am the only man in Ceske Budejovice who can get for you what you want. The second is that in Prague or Bratislava they would take from you every penny you have. And the third . . ." He paused for a while as though thinking how to explain this to a woman of limited understanding, and then, "Removing the original signature so that Zdenek can put his own in the allowed space is a forger's nightmare because none of the underlying color of the paper, obviously, can be accidentally removed too. Fortunately, I have access to a forger of incredible expertise."

"And he can do that?"

"She can," Ctibor said. "My pet forger is a woman. She is an artist, a Russian, who works only in the ancient Persian art of hair painting. You know what that is?"

Eliska shook her head, "I've heard of it somewhere, that's all. No, I know nothing about it."

Ctibor took her arm, and said, "Walk with me for a while, north, east, south and west; there are so many splendid views from up here." They casually strolled around the iron railing while he told her how this lady used, not a fine brush as one might have expected, but a single human hair, just as the Persians—and sometimes the Russians, too—historically did to execute their masterpieces of unbelievable delicacy, touching the hair to the work iota by iota, and in this case spending eight, ten, or even twelve hours to erase a name and nothing but the name.

"And you cannot believe, surely," Ctibor said, "that a lady of this competence works for peanuts! And this, without a doubt, is the most essential part of the whole operation. If I were to employ a forger of lesser capability, which I could easily do, we would be running a terrible risk. There would be grave danger to you—and also to me. My reputation is at stake. No, I need this artist, none other, and I would have to pay her more than you suggest for just this one necessity."

And then the haggling began.

"I think," Ctibor said, "that fifteen thousand dollars would be a very fair price. I would ask for more, but my high respect for you and your Zdenek is a consideration here, too."

It was Eliska's turn to look shocked. "Far too much," she said. "But as you say, there's no one else we can turn to. I suppose I could go as high as five, and even then, I'd have to find something that we could sell."

"I could not, in all conscience," Ctibor said, looking very worried, "put you to that kind of hardship. Very well, then, my final offer. Thirteen-five."

"So why don't we make a quick and sensible deal and call it six? No, I don't wish to take advantage of your kindness. Six thousand five hundred."

Ctibor spread his arms wide, "For such a paltry figure, how do you expect me to feed my family?"

"Six thousand, seven hundred and fifty," Eliska said firmly. "That is my absolute maximum."

Ctibor sighed heavily. "I see that I face defeat," he said, "and one of my finer qualities is that I know when I am beaten. Very well. Let us agree at last and shake hands on it. Will you do that?"

"Of course."

"A straight twelve thousand, and no more discussion, good."

"No," Eliska said firmly, and she turned away from him. "No. I will excuse myself now and go home, to tell the good Zdenek that we were unable to come to an agreement. But it was nice to have met you again. I really do find your company very stimulating."

"No! Wait! We cannot part like this! You must know how fond of you personally I have always been . . ."

"So?"

He pulled himself up to his full height and said, with great dignity, "For the sake of such a lovely lady, I am prepared to face ruin and even disgrace. Ten thousand dollars, and the passport is yours."

"And seven thousand is yours."

"I cannot possibly accept."

They argued on and on and on, and in the course of another half hour, the matter was settled. At eight thousand five, Eliska shot out her hand and took his. "At last," she said, "Eight thousand it is."

"Eight twenty-five. With four thousand up front."

Eliska reached into her purse and took out an envelope. "The down payment," she said, "three thousand dollars, and the rest on delivery, the final five."

"The final five on delivery, agreed."

"Five twenty-five. And how long will it take?"

"I believe I know where I can find the right passport, and I think the artist is free now. It should not take her more than two or three days. How can I get in touch with you?"

"I have a phone at home."

"Ah, what luxury."

"The number is 038/27948. Call me in the evening, around seven o'clock. You know even the government phones, like mine, are monitored."

"Yes, I know that."

"So say: 'I'd like to speak with Zdenek, please, and then promptly hang up. Then, at nine the next morning, I'll come to your cafe."

"No! There's danger there! Once in a while, quite rarely, the cops do pick me up there for some stupid reason or other, and I don't want to visit them with a phony passport in my pocket! No, make it here at twelve-thirty again."

Eliska sighed, "All those steps?"

"It's the safest place in town. The Galleria here has almost no visitors. It's those steps that keep them away."

"Very well. I'll bring the rest of the money with me, and our business is over."

"The rest of the money," Ctibor said, "the five thousand five hundred."

"Five thousand," said Eliska. "And it will be with my thanks and our best wishes." He sighed, but he was smiling too, knowing that the deal he had made wasn't too bad at all. He could find a fairly good passport for six or seven hundred dollars, pay that damned Russkie woman another five or six, and the rest was all his.

He hurried off to start the ball rolling; the sooner he put all this behind him, the better he was going to like it. And for her part, Eliska hurried home, too, anxious to let Zdenek know how well she had done. That morning, he had told her severely, "I've been doing some guessing, sweetheart, even a certain amount of thinking, and I'm convinced that His Majesty the King of the Black Market is going to ask an impossible sum. Don't go over ten thousand."

"And if I have to?" Eliska had asked.

His reply had been typical, a long sigh, followed by, "I'll be so mad if he wants more . . ."

"Now," she said happily, "He wanted fifteen, darling. I beat him down to eight, how about that?"

He got up from his table and hugged her, "Do you know, I honestly believe I couldn't love you any more if I tried. Good work, sweetheart, we're on our way. How long before we get it?"

"Three days. I had to meet him at the top of that confounded tower."

"The Black Tower? What's so confounding about it?"

"Three hundred and sixty steps are what's confounding about it! I'm not as young as I used to be."

"But you don't look a day older than you are," he told her gravely.

"And I have to do it again in three days' time, if it's finished by then. Whenever, at around seven in the evening he's going to call and ask for you and promptly hang up. That tells us it's ready. The next day, at half after twelve, I have to do it again to pick it up. He says that's the safest place to do business in the whole town, and he's probably right. There was nobody up there! The Galleria was empty!"

Zdenek grunted, "It figures." Eliska looked down on the huge scattered pile of photographs on the table, "Did you find something suitable?" she asked.

He nodded. "I think so. Where did I put them?" He shuffled them around. "Ah, here they are, four of them, all more or less head and shoulders. We can cut one to size as needed." He handed them to her to examine.

She discarded the first immediately, "Well, we can't use that one, you look a little bit like Dracula."

"I do not," he said indignantly. "Matter of fact, that's just about my favorite mug shot. And let's move outside; it's a wonderful evening."

"Ah, yes, of course." She took the essential photos, and they went together out onto the cool and now breezy veranda. She liked number two, but it was too much of a close-up, not enough shoulder showing. And for number three she said, "This is the one, though you never looked quite as handsome as that."

"And number four?"

"Not bad, but three's the best by far."

"Very well, that's the one we'll use. But tell me something that's quite important. Martin. How much does he know about the loss of my passport? Are we going to try and persuade him that the new one I'm getting is, in fact, my original one that the police took?"

"No," Eliska said, "I was very careful about that, telling him just enough, but no more. I told him that the police had 'mislaid' yours, and he's bright enough to know that if that's the case, it's gone forever. You agree so far?"

"Yes, I agree so far. But . . . ?"

"Sooner or later, like it or not, he's going to see this new one and he'll recognize it as not yours."

"And he'll know at once that we must have bought ourselves a forgery. So?"

"It's making him a party to top of the line deceit," she said, "and I don't really like that."

"Just coming with us makes him a party to the deceit. You want to leave him behind then?"

"Of course not!" Eliska said, quite angrily. "You know that!"

"Then what's the problem?"

"Motherly love," she said flatly. "Bringing up a child with the knowledge that his parents will cheat when it pays for them to? I honestly don't like that too much."

"That's admirable thinking," Zdenek said, meaning it, "but cheating the damn government is part and parcel of the way we live here. He must know that!"

"No, he doesn't. You want the most instructive piece of information ever?"

"Tell me."

"I mentioned the fact that your passport was getting all the attention, mine very little. He said, quite unfazed, that it was because technically—you like that word?—technically, you were the head of the family and therefore there was a more rigid control factor for you than there was for me."

Zdenek stared at her. "He said what? A more rigid what?"

"Control factor, his term precisely."

"My God . . ." Zdenek said.

"He said the police were merely doing their job. He was defending them."

"I can't believe this." He was in a kind of shock. "Are you saying that we're bringing up a young communist without even knowing it?"

"No," Eliska said patiently, "it's not that at all. He hates the way we're all ordered around: do this, don't do that. But he doesn't realize, won't believe, that it's only here in Czechoslovakia that the citizenry has to put up with all this crap! He has nothing to compare it with! He thinks it's all perfectly normal everywhere, in what he calls the whole wide world, and therefore he accepts it."

"It seems I don't really know that boy as well as I thought."

"If you'd only talk with him more often . . ." she began, and then broke off when she saw the hard look on his face. But he sighed, and nodded, and said, with a touch of resignation, "Yes, I do know what you're driving at. It's no secret, surely, that I've never liked him very much; but perhaps that's my fault more than his."

Was it a small victory for her? She said gently, "It's not really very hard to get along with other people if you set your mind to it." She smiled, "You may find that you'll need a little patience at first. Just for a while."

"I'll try," Zdenek said. He thought about it for a moment, and then he asked, curiously, "Tell me something I've never quite known, never really thought about, actually. Whenever we do talk together, he's always respectful, doesn't try to force anything on me, always listens to what I have to say. And he's always a little withdrawn. So what does he really think of me? That's a very important question, sweetheart."

Eliska said,

"Well, he respects you very highly."

"He does?"

"Oh, yes, very much so. And he's proud of you, too."

"What?"

"It's true. When we first started living together."

"Did he mind that?"

"No, why should he? That was a long time ago, he was just a child. But even then he knew the name Zizka, had read and heard about the Hussites in school, and suddenly to find one in the family . . . Yes, he's always been very proud of you."

"You mean he never knew that I wasn't particularly fond of him?"

"That is not what I mean," Eliska said, "and it's by no means true. He knew that very well, and it puzzled him, because he never knew the reason for it." She hesitated briefly, and then asked the critical question, "Are you?"

Zdenek started prowling along the veranda, rubbing his chin, stroking the back of his neck, even mussing with his hair, and she waited for a very long time, saying nothing, just waiting. He said at last, "That is something I've never asked myself, never even thought about it until this moment. And that I truly must . . ." He broke off, and there was another long silence.

He went to the railing, gripped it hard and stared out at nothing, where the streets and the cars and the pedestrians were.

"And?" Eliska asked.

He turned to face her. "It's not often," he said, "that I try to analyze my own mind." He was gesticulating broadly now. "That's not something I'd ever be any good at, but I think I know the reason you're looking for it. No. I know it! And it's hateful."

Eliska shook her head, "No. That's one thing I can vouch for, darling. There's absolutely nothing in your character that can be called hateful."

"So let's call it despicable."

"Not that either."

He moved to her and put his arms 'round her, holding her tightly. "I've just found out, sweetheart, and I know it's the truth. It's jealousy."

"What?"

He said it clearly, "I've found out that I'm jealous of him. More correctly, of the great love you have for him. Deep inside me, and I knew it, there's this . . . yes, this despicable feeling that you love him more than you do me."

"Dear God . . ." Eliska whispered. "Dear God."

"The better part of me," Zdenek said wearily, "knows that this can't be true, or—if it is true, it should be perfectly acceptable."

"If it were true," Eliska said, and there was a touch of desperation in her voice, "and it isn't, it would not be acceptable either. I love you both, darling."

"I know it, and God knows I have love enough for you both. That wretched lesser part inside me . . ."

"Then get rid of it! Please! Darling, please! You must!"

"And I will," he said. Believe me, I will." He laughed shortly, without much humor, "Get thee behind me, Satan! Give me a little time, and I swear to God, it will be gone."

"Forever?"

"Forever and ever, you have my word."

She believed him implicitly, for this was the nature of their relationship. And she was pleased to see that the change was beginning to take place almost at once.

Martin came in with a chessboard set under his arm, and Zdenek asked affably, "Been looking for someone who could beat the pants off you? How did you make out?"

For Martin, there was the briefest moment of surprise, and then a quick recovery. "I made out very badly indeed," he said, "five games, and I couldn't manage to lose a single one of them."

"I often wish I hadn't let my own game get forgotten," Zdenek said. "I was pretty good in the old days," he laughed. And was that astonishment or only pleasure on Martin's face? He went on, "Never up to the standard that I'm told by all and sundry you've reached."

"All and sundry? You mean you actually talk about my chess with your friends?"

"Well, yes. Once in a while. Not very often, but . . . yes, when I do, they're very impressed."

"Well, I'll be damned," Martin said, and Zdenek instantly dropped back into character, "Watch your language, boy—I mean Martin."

"The word damn," Eliska said, "is permitted at age eighteen. Four months to go."

But Martin was already apologizing, "Yes, of course. I'm sorry. What I meant to say was, well, something like Good Heavens. I'll watch it. Yes, I'll do that. And why don't we play a game one day?"

Zdenek was more amused than ever. "Are you crazy?"

"There's a thing called handicap. The better player gives up a pawn."

"I have no desire to make a fool of myself in front of any member of my family," Zdenek said. "You could give up your queen and still win. No. Suggestion refused, though I thank you for it."

"Oh, shut up!" Eliska said genially.

But Martin was getting ideas of his own. "One day," he said, "in the course of time, maybe I can coach you. We'll play a couple of games and if you'll allow me, I'll tell you when you make a bad move and explain what's wrong with it. The knack, of course, is seeing two or three or even more moves ahead, and that needs a lot of practice."

"Well," Zdenek said, "let me think about that for a while. One day. Yes, one day."

"Good," Martin said, "I'll look forward to it."

"Right now, I've rather too much on my mind."

Martin asked politely, "Your passport problem?"

"Oh, you know about that?"

"Mother mentioned it to me, like the cops have confiscated it or something."

"They say they've lost it."

"Which is not very likely," Martin said. "I'd say they've decided to make sure you don't ever have one."

"Which is what your mother and I both think, too. In fact, we're quite sure of it."

"Well," Martin said, and stopped to think for a moment. He went on, "One of my friends at school, his dad never had a passport, never needed one. But then he wanted one in a hurry, because he had a sister in Bulgaria, where his family came from, and she was getting married or something. The passport people told him to come back in a year's time, can you believe it?"

"Yes," Eliska said, "I can believe that. So?"

Martin shrugged, "So he went out and bought himself one, on the black market, said it was the only thing he could do."

"The ethical question here," Zdenek said, pontificating a little, "is when may the law be broken by reasonably law-abiding people?"

"Always," Eliska said. "The nicest people do it all the time."

Martin nodded. "I'd say that's true. But Zdenek is making an ethical question out of it, and 'always' is quite the wrong answer."

"Then what, in your opinion, is the right answer?" Zdenek asked.

And Martin answered him at once, "When the law seems to be a foolish one, as in the case of my friend's father being told to wait for a whole . . ."

He broke off, and a harsh look spread over his handsome face, still more child than man. "Oh," he said, "you set a trap for me and I walked right into it, didn't I? Am I being asked to believe something I really can't believe? Are you going to tell me that you are going to the black market, too? I can only hope that my guess is absolutely wrong! Though I'm flattered that you worry about whether I'd approve or not."

Eliska held his look. "There was a time," she said, very carefully, "that some such idea crossed our minds for a while. If we had pursued it, would you worry about that?"

"Absolutely and emphatically," Martin said. "A couple of criminals in the family is not something I could easily live down if the guys at school ever learned of it. It makes me feel just awful! The infamous knock on the door any day now! No, that's not right; they don't knock on the door any more, do they? They just bust it wide open! And do you even know how to contact the right people? I have this idea that you probably don't."

"Watch it, boy," Zdenek said.

"How nice it is," Eliska said sarcastically, beginning to dislike this trend in the conversation, "that you think so highly of us! But we were thinking of dealing with a man who calls himself the King of the Black Market, who, we've been told, can find us exactly what we need."

Martin was staring at her, "A man named Ctibor?"

"Oh, my God! Don't tell me you know him?"

"Not personally," Martin said, "just the name. A couple of the kids in school buy phonograph records from him. Kids who get tired of listening to all those Soviet marching songs, which is about all you can legally buy here. But they've no idea of the trouble they can get into. That's breaking the law, too."

"I did hope," Eliska said, "that you would approve if we went ahead with this."

"You must think I'm nuts."

"No!" Eliska said angrily. "Put it down to parental overindulgence, but it's actually none of your damn business, is it? So will you shut up? You hear me? Just shut up!"

Martin was visibly upset, and he turned away in silence. But in a moment, he turned back to her, deeply concerned. "I guess I was a bit rough there," he said. "I'm sorry. So can we talk about something else instead?"

Eliska looked to Zdenek and saw that he, too, was disturbed. But he nodded, "About something less argumentative? I think that would be a good idea."

"About Michal," Martin said, and it seemed that his good humor was slowly coming back.

"Michal?" Eliska asked. "Well, he's with the Stransky children again, for their favorite game, which is called Cops and Robbers. Only this time, they have a new slant on it."

"They do?" Martin asked politely. "I can't wait to hear."

"The kids who played the cops last time are now the robbers," Eliska said, glad that the fight was over.

"And the kids who played the robbers before . . . don't tell me!"

"Yes! Believe it or not, the ex-robbers are now the cops."

"Wow!" Martin said.

"Mrs. Stransky tells me that it's a very healthy exercise for what she calls their imagination capacity."

"And they'll all grow up," Zdenek said, "to be the one or the other. Of course, there are some of us who believe that the two words are synonymous."

"Not true," Eliska said. "The cops make a lot more money."

"But I have news about Michal, too, news you both will be pleased to hear."

"Do tell." Eliska said.

"Swimming stuff," he went on. "In a couple of weeks or so, there's a race for the under-tens, and the first prize—are you ready for this? It's a solid silver medal the size of your fist! I've checked Michal out, and he's four and half seconds ahead of the nearest competition! And if he wins this, it will put him into competition in the Internationals with Russia, East Germany, Hungary and Bulgaria! Can you imagine what this would mean for a seven-year-old kid? With, admittedly, the worlds finest coach. Solid silver! And he'll win it! But I want every hour of his time now for intensive training!"

"And you both have our very best wishes," Zdenek said. "Let us hope that all of your expectations are fully realized. I hope you understand that they might not be. A seven-year-old in competition with others three years his senior? It may be a very uphill battle."

"I'm sure it will be," Martin said, "but that kid has what it takes. Nothing much in the brain department . . ."

"I beg your pardon," Eliska said indignantly.

But Martin pressed on. "But what he has is guts," he said, "and it's guts that's going to give him this race."

"You may be right," Zdenek said. "Possibly."

Martin sighed, "So let's change the subject once again. I saw a different car in your parking space. Is that our new one?"

"No, that's a loaner," Zdenek said. "Kornel is giving ours a rebore. You know Kornel, don't you?"

"Sure, I was with you a few times when you took the Skoda there. A nice guy; I liked him. A mystery man, right?"

"Mystery man?"

"One time I was there, you were fixing things with that nice cashier lady, and I asked him where he was from, you know, just being friendly. And he said: 'I was born in heaven, and I was brought up in hell,' and, I mean, that's a very funny line, but he wasn't joking, he was dead serious. I have to say it gave me the willies, the real heebie-jeebies. Like I said, I really like him, but . . . yes, a mystery man."

"But he'll do a very good job for us on the car, and that's all that matters."

"Sure. And I guess I'll excuse myself and go figure out a few calculations about the various end games in championship chess." He looked to Zdenek. "That was a nice talk we had. I greatly appreciate it. I have to thank you, sir." And he was gone.

Zdenek started after him in acute astonishment, and turned to Eliska. "Sir?" he asked incredulously. "Did you hear that? He called me sir! Maybe that kid's got something going for him after all."

"I'm glad you think so," Eliska said calmly. And there was a deep satisfaction there, because in spite of that momentary quarrel, this was nonetheless a satisfying end to yet another of the days they were so anxiously counting.

CHAPTER SEVEN

The waiting time was murderous for her. There were so few days ahead for the next important step to enter its fruition, but they were nail-biting days, and she found it necessary to do little jobs that were really not that important, like sorting out the jewelry she had never worn since the time when precious stones had come to be regarded as 'capitalistic ostentation'. There was money enough for their endeavor, she was sure, but she also knew that emergencies could easily arise that might demand instant access so more ready cash. And to make doubly sure, she transferred most of their korunas from the bank where she had always kept the account to another much smaller bank, under another name, Comrade Sarka Matej. The 'Comrade,' she knew, would guarantee the funds certain privacy.

When six-thirty on the crucial day came, Eliska was already sitting by the phone, waiting for seven-o'clock. When the clock struck the hour, the phone rang, precisely on time.

"That's him," she said to Zdenek.

He nodded, almost as impatient as she was. "Let's hope," he said as she picked up the handset.

"I'd like to speak with Zdenek, please," said the disembodied voice, and the line went dead. For good measure, she tapped on the phone a few times and said loudly, "Hullo? Hullo? Hullo . . ." and then, "It's gone dead again, what a nuisance." She placed it back on its cradle and said, "Well, all we have to do now is wait just one time more. Tomorrow, soon after midday, it's a climb up those damn steps again. But this time, I really don't mind."

The time passed so very slowly. Michal returned from the Stransky's place, still wearing his paper cops' hat, and went to his own little world in his half of the boy's room, and then Martin turned up and chatted with them, strengthening a relationship that was slowly evolving along somewhat better family lines. Then there was dinner and a few glasses of rum for Zdenek, just one for Eliska. Finally, there was bedtime, eight o'clock for Michal, ten for Martin, and midnight for the adults, with all the relief for the two of them that bedtime could sometimes offer.

She left the next morning a good half-hour earlier than was needed, took her time on the punishing steps, and looked at her watch when she reached the top; twelve-fifteen, not long to wait now. She peeked into the galleria and saw no one there except the lone attendant, dozing at his desk, and then strolled slowly around the square, gazing out over the city and wondering how Ceske Budejovice had lost almost all of the past glory which the great King Otakar had given it; how even as Budweiss in the days of the Empire had flourished nobly, had become at last nothing but an ordinary industrial town of factories and high-rises.

What are we known for today? She asked herself, and gave herself the grunted answer, 'Beer and pencils, for God's sake!'

But as she saw Ctibor taking the last of the steps quite laboriously, suddenly the impatience was gone, replaced by a certain sense of well being. He was smiling broadly.

She took her proffered hand and said gently, "I know what it was they did to your leg. I think a whole lot of people know it and sympathize with you. And still, you climb up here whenever you feel like it?"

He was still smiling. "It was a long time ago, the pain and the indignity have long gone away. I did see a doctor once, and he told me, 'Exercise, and more exercise.' A question of repairing the bone by strengthening the muscles. So that's what I do. And I have a splendid passport for you, one of the little gray ones that are only good for Yugoslavia."

"Like the one I have."

"But should you, by chance, wish to go from Yugoslavia into, perhaps, Austria or Romania or Italy, they will recognize it and allow you through. They say Bulgarians will too, but who in their right mind wants to visit Bulgaria? And how long have you been waiting for me?"

"Not long," Eliska said, "about ten minutes or so."

"Did you see if there's anyone in the galleria?"

"Just the attendant, half asleep."

"A government job," he said. "Government servants always have plenty of time for sleeping. Ah, forgive me, you work for the government, too. I should never have said that."

"But never a truer word spoken," Eliska said.

110

He took the passport from under his belt at the back and showed it to her, turning the relevant pages. "Height two-zero one, almost exactly correct, we got lucky. Eyes brown, that's the original too, good. Date of birth—we had to alter that, but can you see how expertly it's been done?"

She studied it carefully, even holding it up to the light, "Yes, I'd say that was original, nothing at all to show that it's been altered." She held it up to the light again. "Yes. It's perfect."

"And the space for the signature, just a blank space now, Zdenek has to sign it. And the photograph, we've removed the original, all you have to do is cut a head-and-shoulder shot to size, and paste it in the square there. Ordinary glue. And then . . ." He smiled broadly, "Then your Zdenek will have a new passport that will easily survive even the most thorough inspection. And all I will do is wish you good luck on your journey." But he was holding out his hand expressively.

Eliska took the prepared envelope from her purse and handed it to him. "Five thousand, two hundred and fifty, as agreed."

"As agreed, and I thank you for it. It is best if we are not seen together on the street. Will you go first, or shall I?"

"If I could go first?" She asked. "I so much want to get home and show this to Zdenek. You've no idea how pleased he'll be!"

"Of course. I'll wander around for ten minutes, maybe even visit the Galleria and see if the attendant wakes up, as he might just to make sure that I don't steal something."

"Good. Thank you again."

She took the steps down with a jumpily-jump, and in less than half an hour she was back in the apartment.

"Well?" Zdenek asked.

She held it out for him, feeling on top of the world. "All it needs now is the photograph and your signature."

"I have the photograph, already cut to size."

"Show me."

He gave it to her, and she said, "Ah, yes, that's the one I like best of all, even though you look a little bit like a rather severe Party Chairman."

"Which is all to the good. You like the grim look? I thought that might be a rather nice touch."

"It certainly is. When I look at this picture, I find myself thinking, 'Well, there's a man I don't want to tangle with.' I think that might be a miniscule advantage for us."

"Do we have some glue somewhere?"

"Sure we do."

"Tell me where and I'll go get it." She was thrilled to see how genuinely excited he was, this normally calm and solid sort of man.

"Yes," she said, "the glue, I wonder where it might be? Try the top drawer in the kitchen cabinet, left-hand side."

He went off to search and was back with it in a very short while. "Bottom drawer", he said, "but it was indeed the left-hand side."

He gave it to her, and slid the photo over. "You do it. I'm not sure I can cope with it."

She laughed and went to work, bent over it very seriously, and in a moment she had it done and showed it to him. "Perfect," he said gravely, "a true artist at work."

But then there was the sudden beep-beep of a car horn outside, and Zdenek said, "Hey! That's our Skoda! It's Kornel! This is a great day, sweetheart. Can I invite him up?"

"Why not? Yes, that's a good idea. I always wanted to know him better. Yes, invite him up."

Zdenek went to the veranda and looked down on the street, and there was his old car being expertly squeezed into a small parking space. He waited till the driver got out, and then he called down, "Hey there! Kornel! Come on up! Top floor, turn left!"

Kornel looked up and shouted back, "I thank you, friend! I come!"

Zdenek turned back to Eliska. "A good chance for you to get to know him better. But be warned, this is a very strange man. Don't try to get close to him." He sighed. "There's so much I know about him that I've never wanted to tell you. Maybe I will one day."

And then he was there, knocking on the door, and Zdenek said quickly, "Well, at least he didn't just knock it down."

Eliska opened the door for him and put out her hand, which he took, this giant of a man, surprisingly gently. "Mr. Kornel," she said, "we have met before, or course, but I'm happy that now it's on a more personal level."

"Not Mister," he said. "I am Kornel."

"My pleasure," she said; but she was thinking, . . . wow . . .

He strode past her and crushed Zdenek's outstretched hand. "The Skoda," he said, "a good car now. You have oversized pistons, which are like new gloves, very stiff until they are worn in. Do not drive at high speed for at least two hundred kilometers. After that, you will see how good this old car is."

Eliska asked, a little desperately, "Can I make you a coffee, Mr . . . er, Kornel? An espresso perhaps?"

"I thank you, but no. I would like a Budwar."

"Ah, yes, I'm sure we must have some." She looked to Zdenek for help, and wondered what it was that he found so amusing.

"In the broom closet," he said, "but don't ask me why."

"What about you?" she asked Zdenek.

And he replied, "Why not? Help keep our brewery busy."

She went to find it, and Zdenek said, "I'm very grateful you did that so quickly. So how much do I owe you?"

Kornel shrugged broadly, "How should I know? He asked. "The next time you come around, my lady cashier will tell you."

"Fine. And I liked the one you lent me, a terrific car."

"It was a wreck when I found it. It had rolled over three or four times down a mountainside. Good engine, good gears and brakes. I rebuilt the body completely, took off every single panel till it was just a barebones chassis, pounded them back to their proper form, gave each one of them a quality paint job . . ."

He broke off as Eliska came back with two steins of Budweiser brew. She handed them to the two men. "May it always be good."

"I second that," Zdenek said cheerfully, raising his stein to her too, and they were both astonished to see that Kornel was draining his, down to the very last drop. He jumped to his feet then, seemed to tower over them, and he handed a key to Zdenek. "And you give me mine, please, no?"

"Of course." He dug into his pocket and handed it over, and Kornel said, "I go now. I thank you." He looked at Eliska and added, unsmiling, "A very lovely lady. Good day."

Without more ado, he turned on his heels, opened the door, closed it silently behind him and was gone.

Eliska looked at Zdenek and said, "Well! Can you please tell me what all that was about? And why I like this extraordinary man so much?"

"I wish I knew. I wish I knew why I like him so much too. There's not very much that's lovable about him, is there?"

"And he's a Czech?" Eliska asked. "His use of language . . . it seems very, very strange."

"He calls himself a Czech in spirit," Zdenek said.

She took him up on it at once, "And what on earth is that supposed to mean?"

He sighed, "He wants to be a Czech, but he's not. He's a Gypsy."

"What?"

"A Gypsy," Zdenek said again, "born and bred a Gypsy."

"Oh, my God! I thought the Nazis had slaughtered them all."

"They tried. They missed some of them and he got lucky. Well, sort of."

"I don't understand that comment either. Sort of?"

"Can we leave it at that for the moment?"

Eliska did not like it very much, but her love for Zdenek . . . she smiled to hide her frustration. "Of course, darling. It's not important. And I hate to be thought of as overly inquisitive; it's an abominable characteristic."

"Not really. Let's go on with my passport, the gateway to heaven for us, and a far more important subject."

"Good."

She picked it up and studied it some more, and said, "This Ctibor fellow, he's done a wonderful job! Or rather . . . did I tell you about the forger he hired?"

"Nope."

"A Russian lady, an artist working in hair-painting. You know about that?"

"Sure. That's how they did it?"

"Yep, that's how they did it."

"Fantastic! I don't care what it cost—a very good price, actually. It's worth every penny of it."

"And do you realize," Eliska asked, "that there's nothing left for us to do now? Nothing to keep us here even a day longer?"

"A few days to tidy up," Zdenek said. "What about all our personal stuff? That's something we've never even talked about."

"We only carry with us," Eliska said, "what we would normally take on a ten-day vacation."

"Leave everything else behind? All our furniture and stuff?"

"What, you want to carry a washing machine on your back? That's great, just great."

"How come we didn't even think of discussing this before?" Zdenek asked.

"Because," Eliska said, "I just took it for granted that we'd have to leave everything behind! It never occurred to me that you might worry about it. We rent this place from the government, the furnishings are ours. We abandon them."

"My favorite armchair . . ."

"On your back with the washing machine! No, the only thing we have to worry about now is just how to smuggle stuff that must be smuggled. Like a whole lot of cash. We can't be caught with a thick bundle of America hundred-dollar bills in our pockets."

"We'll go over the car very carefully," Zdenek said, "and find ourselves some good hiding places. I'm sure that won't be very difficult."

"I think you're right. But let's not leave it till the last minute."

"And meanwhile, suppose I sign my passport? Can I sign with a bit of a flourish?"

"Just your usual signature, if you don't mind" Eliska said, and she was quietly wondering if, between them, they were treating this matter with far too much flippancy. Was it not, surely, the most important decision they had ever had to make together? Did it not deserve a great deal more of resolution—even, perhaps, of solemnity—than they were giving it? It was a question that disturbed her greatly, and she broached it with Zdenek, very carefully. "Are we being a little too light-hearted about this, darling? Are we serious enough about it? What do you think?"

He signed the passport first, and then looked up at her. "Why do you ask? Because we feel we can joke about it now? We can! Of course, we can! All the serious stuff is behind us now; we're practically on our way. And if we both find ourselves in a very good mood, hey, we deserve it!"

"Good," said Eliska. "Just as long as we agree on that. As we do."

It was a very good night for them both, and the next morning, not surprisingly, it was Monday, a day that Eliska had always regarded as the best day of the week for her, even though under normal circumstances it meant the beginning of a week's nothing kind of work in a rather dull and boring office. There was always the professional nice guy Peter Tuka there to do nothing with her. It was on a Monday that she'd first met Zdenek, a Monday when they'd first decided—so many years ago, to live together. It was on a Monday, too, that she had first met Vaclav Cubirica, and the thought of him made her laugh a little, silently, and only for herself. Poor Vaclav! Well, he'd fought a good fight as long as it lasted, and bore no ill will whatsoever against Zdenek, the victor, or even against her, accepting defeat merely with a shrug of his elegant shoulders. She looked at her watch; what, nearly eight o'clock already? What happened? She struggled out of her bed, put on her dressing gown, and went to take a shower. The water was only warm, the heater not working very well today, a common enough occurrence. When she was through, she sprayed her body liberally with perfume, a little luxury she always thought was well worthwhile. She chose her clothes for the day with unusual care, and looked at herself in the full-length mirror, and decided that peacock blue suited her very nicely, and why, then, did she not wear it more often? As she left the bathroom, Zdenek was standing there in his pajama bottoms, taut-stomached and muscular, waiting for his turn in the shower. "All yours," she said, kissing him briefly.

"G'morning," he said, "sleep well?"

She nodded, "Overslept, though."

"Me too. A busy night, I guess."

"Where did you put the new passport?" she asked. "I want to take another look, it makes me feel good."

"It's on the desk somewhere, where all the bills and stuff are."

"Got it."

She could hear him singing in the shower as she shuffled the papers around. There it was, the little gray passport that was their ticket to paradise. She opened it at the first page and felt the blood leaving her face. She screamed at the top of her voice, "Zdenek! Zdenek!" and he came running out of the bathroom, his beard dripping soapy water, a towel around his wet body.

"What is it for God's sake?"

She could hardly hear herself speak. "Look . . . look what's happened . . . the bleach . . ."

He dried his hands quickly on his towel, took it from her, and stared in shock at the space where he had signed it. On the once-pale color of the paper there was now a dead white, and as he touched it with his finger tip, it disintegrated, and a little shower of desiccated paper fell to the ground. He turned the shattered page, and there was the patch where his date of birth had been. It, too, had been bleached out of existence.

"Dear God," he muttered. "Jesus Christ . . ."

Eliska put her hand to her face and screamed as the tears came flooding out, and suddenly Martin and Michal were there, and Michal was running to her to clutch at her 'round the waist. "Mommy, I don't want you to cry," and he was crying, too.

"Mother!" Martin said, staring at her in shock, "what is it, what's wrong?"

"My nice new passport," Zdenek said, "the forgery we told you about. Look at it."

Martin took it from him and looked at it in bewilderment, "Jeez! What happened?"

"They bleached out the original signature. Either they used too strong a bleach or too much of it, who knows? That's only a guess, of course."

Eliska had ceased her crying and was even ashamed of it. She hugged Michal, and said quietly, "It's all right now, baby, all over. Just . . . just don't worry about it anymore." And to Martin, "Irreparable damage, without any doubt at all. So I have to find a way now to fix it."

She looked at Zdenek and echoed his question, "Who knows? There's one man who might, and I'm going to have a word with him right now. That bastard Ctibor."

Zdenek sighed heavily, "You think that will do us any good? I'm not sure that I do."

"It'll do me a lot of good," she said, "just to get my hands at his throat and strangle the life out of him."

"I have this feeling that I ought to come with you."

"No," Eliska said. "Let me yell my head off at him and see what happens. I might just be able, one way or another, to force him into starting over, this time with far better control than he's exercised so far."

"Not easy . . ."

She was trying to subdue the harsh anger that was on her. "He mentioned, when we met, something about protecting his reputation, and maybe there's a starting point tucked away there someplace. His living depends on satisfied customers, right?"

"Yes, I'd say so. I still think I should come with you."

She was very firm about it. "No, darling, no! Once I've finished yelling my head off, I don't quite know what kind of attitude I should take. I'll have to play it by ear. And I'm much better at this kind of duplicity than you are! You're far too honest and straightforward man, did you know that? You'd just be in the way."

"I'd be more likely to beat the daylights out of him. I feel like hell about it, too."

"So there you are," Eliska said, "you see what I mean?"

She checked her watch; nine-forty. She went to the bathroom to fix her face. She decided that peacock blue was not a lucky color for her, not a good color for a fight. She changed into a gray skirt and a rather severe-looking purple blouse.

She went back into the living room and slipped the offending passport into her purse, and said to Michal, "Everything's all right now. But there's something I have to do, darling, back in a little while. You look after your father and Martin, too. Will you do that for me? Can I trust you to do that?

"Sure will," Michal said. "Sure can."

"It's a calamity, I know that. I also know that I'm very good at calamities.

"I guess that's something we'll find out about very soon now," Zdenek said. "But for what it's worth, I do have confidence in you, sweetheart. I don't suppose that he thinks for one minute in terms of money-back guarantees, but . . . well, do what you can."

"Of course."

"Why don't I drive you over there and just drop you off and wait around the corner, so to speak?"

"Well, it would be quicker," Eliska said, "than waiting for the bus, and the faster we can get this thing behind us, the better."

"Just a few minutes, then, to put some clothes on."

"If you insist."

He was smiling now as he went to get dressed, and he was back very quickly, dressed in light gray slacks and a yellow turtleneck sweater. "Let's go," he said.

On the way there in the car, Eliska told him, "I don't want him to see you. It's best if he thinks he's dealing with a weak and helpless woman . . ."

"Ha!"

"So don't drop me off at the café, just nearby. Then find somewhere to park and wait for me."

Zdenek nodded, "We'll go to the parking lot of the department store there; that's well out of his sight from the Deminka. You wander off and I'll just sit and wait."

"Good."

The traffic was heavy this beautiful spring morning, just a few cumulus clouds scudding slowly across a robin's-egg blue sky, but they were there in twenty minutes or so, and Eliska stepped out of the Skoda and said, "Wish me luck. I'm going to demand a replacement in two days, no more. I don't intend to pay him a penny for it."

"Then I wish you luck, indeed."

"It might be quite a while."

"I'll wait. Don't worry about it."

She went on her way, just a few minutes' walk, and as she came into sight of the café, she felt her anger rising. As she drew closer, and she was in the vilest temper ever. There he was, the wretched Ctibor, reading one of

118

his magazines, a large espresso beside him. He saw her as she approached, frowned darkly, and looked around to see who might be watching. But there was no one there except the usual waitress standing in the doorway.

Eliska walked up to him and slapped the passport onto the table and said, not modifying her voice in the least, "You want to take a look at that?"

His face was contorted with his own anger and with a single, very fast movement he swept it into his pocket. "Are you mad," he hissed, "quite mad? We are watched here, can't you realize that?"

Not lowering her voice, she said, "We have a great deal to talk about, here and now."

"No, no!" he whispered, "not here, the waitress . . ."

Eliska turned to look and saw the waitress watching them, just casually.

"There are times," Ctibor said, his voice so muted she could hardly hear it, "when I think that she might be a police spy. Not all the time, you understand, just once in a while, not very often. What is it you want to talk about?"

"Look at your passport!" she said, not lowering her voice in the least. "Look at it!"

"Ssshhh, please!" But he took it from his pocket, held it deep in his lap like a purveyor of pornographic photographs, and opened it up and stared. He whispered, "Oh, Mother of all the Saints! What could have happened?"

It was back in his pocket in a flash, hidden in secrecy from the whole world, and he whispered, "Yes! We have to talk! We have to solve this problem. The same place, the same time, today."

"No!" Eliska said angrily, "not the same place, the same time! We talk here—and now!"

He was wailing, looking fearfully around him all the while, "No, not here. Never here! You must be mad!"

"Very well then, the same place. But not at twelve-thirty. We have to discuss this now! You hear me? Now!"

"I cannot leave this place! It is my office! I may have other customers coming!"

"But none," Eliska said, "as angry with you as I am! You know what is at stake now? Your reputation, you called it. It is in great danger now. How? I don't know. Don't force me to think about that. I may come up with some answers you won't like very much."

Ctibor whispered, "Very well, the same place and, yes, now. But we cannot be seen on the street together! You go, I give you five minutes, I follow. So go to the tower, go quickly and wait for me. I join you there, and we talk. Quickly!"

He was whispering still, and Eliska followed his nervous look towards the waitress. She was still watching them and—was that a faint smile on her face?

Eliska turned back to Ctibor and was very aware of his fear. He said, highly agitated, "We will talk; we must! There is never any problem that cannot be solved by mutual discussion! Believe me, please, I am as anxious as you are to set this matter right! I am your servant."

"Very well, then," Eliska said, and moved away. She walked off quite slowly and deliberately, and when she reached the famous square, she turned down the little street that was itself named for the tower and began that wearisome climb again. She reached the top and leaned on the railing there, getting her breath back and telling herself that this was going to be her last time ever on those damn steps. How could they put a museum up there? No wonder it was almost devoid of any visitors!

She looked at her watch; seven minutes already, and was that bad leg of his holding him up?

She wandered 'round to the south side of the tower and stared out at the picturesque and tiny little village of Trocnov, and thought immediately of Zdenek, for it was there that his famous ancestor John Zizka was born, only twelve kilometers from the apartment in which they now lived.

Ten minutes passed. Where was Ctibor?

The truth came to her in a rush, and she was almost ready to scream, not at Ctibor, but at her stupidity. She waited in bitter resentment for a few minutes more, just to make certain, and then she hurried down the steps to the square and walked quickly 'round to the Deminka. He was not there, but the waitress, smiling now, was waiting for her. "Madam Eliska Kucera, I think?" she asked.

Eliska nodded. "Yes, of course! Where is he?"

"Gone," the waitress said. "But he left a message for you. He asked me to say that he has suddenly been obliged to leave Ceske Bodejovice and will not return for quite a long while. Such a nice man, so very helpful always."

Eliska felt that she was trembling, and her cold fury was more than she could bear. She said tightly, "He told me that he thought you might be a police spy. Are you? Because if you are, I may have some information for you. Just give me a little time to think about it."

The waitress started laughing now, with very genuine amusement, "A police spy?" she asked, "Me? Spying on Ctibor? That's very funny!"

"You find it amusing? Eliska asked. "Don't you think it might be true, for God's sake?"

"That's not very likely, Madam Eliska, "the waitress said. "For God's sake, as you say, he's my husband. We've been married for twelve years. That must be a nice surprise for you. And he fooled you completely, you stupid bitch, didn't he?"

Eliska turned on her heel and stalked away. Now, she really was shaking with her fury as she hurried on to the department store's parking. There was the Skoda, and there was Zdenek, and she found it so very hard to hold back the tears. He took one look at her face, and said gently, "Whatever it was, sweetheart, there's not much the two of us can't overcome. You want to tell me?"

He listened attentively as she told him everything that had happened back there, adding to it another thought. "I can't forgive myself for letting him keep his hands on those passports. He just went on talking and talking and just not shutting up. I should have realized that he was plotting something or other, while giving me something else to occupy my mind. The bastard! And that waitresss! I could have killed her!"

"So let's go for a little drive, shall we, before we go home? Like down to the river? It's a beautiful day for a drive."

"Yes, it is," Eliska said, "but could we run over to Trocnov instead?

What a good idea. Let's do that. We can go the long way round, over the other river. What's it called, the Malso? Than on to Rimov, take a look at the lake for a while, then head back to Strakonice and we're practically there."

"Well, if we're going to the lake, we have to stop off and get some bread for the ducks. I can't remember when I last had the time to go feed ducks." She smiled. "Therapy".

He nodded. "It is indeed, and you're beginning to feel better already?"

"Yes, I am! We've a problem to face and we can face it when we get back home. And somehow, darling, I know we're going to find a solution."

"We sure as hell will." He started the car.

Eliska said, "Wait! Just one minute . . ." She jumped out and ran to the store, and when she came back a moment later, she was holding up a loaf of bread, "For our therapists," she said, "the ducks." She clambered aboard, and they drove off, keeping the speed well down as Kornel had said, and they soon came to lovely open country where the meadows were incredibly green and the trees were tall and stately and plentiful.

In twenty minutes they passed through Straskovice, and five minutes later came to the bridge over the little river. They stopped to lean on the railing and stared down at the water intently, looking for fish, like a couple of children enjoying the countryside.

"No fish," Eliska said in a moment.

And Zdenek nodded, "Must be their day off."

But at the lake, the story was quite different. There were ducks and drakes, some of them mallards, dipping deeply for their food, and a clutch of baby ducks came swimming to the shore as soon as they saw Eliska breaking bread, squawking angrily as they fought each other for it.

Eliska found the stump of a fallen tree close by the water, sat on it, and took off her shoes so that she could put her feet in it. She squealed, "It's cold!"

And Zdenek said, "Mountain water."

They stayed there for a very long time, occupied in some serious thinking, till Eliska said suddenly, "Enough, all right? I want to see that statue again."

"Me too," Zdenek said, "for maybe the thousandth time."

"And that's a sort of therapy, too, wouldn't you say?"

"Yes, I suppose it is."

"To be reminded of greatness when you're feeling so small. Yes, that's therapy all right. I love it."

A half hour later, just as the first signs of twilight were snails-pacing upon them, they stood below the Trocnov statue where the plaque said: Jan Zizka; 1376-1424. "Five and a half centuries ago," Eliska said.

Zdenek told her, "Actually, the date of his birth there is only approximate; nobody really knows for sure when he was born. The only thing that matters is that he was."

"That his son was born, and his son, until finally, a Zizka named Zdenek was found in the reeds of a river, wailing in a wicker basket."

"And a Princess named Eliska found him," Zdenek said. "Only that was a guy named Moses. So let's be on our way."

"Let's," Eliska said, "I did a whole lot of thinking with my feet in the water. That stimulates the brain, did you know that?"

"No, I didn't," Zdenek said politely, "but I'm very pleased to learn that."

"You do realize, don't you," Eliska asked as they got aboard and drove off, "that the important part of this family which is to say me, Martin, and Michal—we are in very good shape. We have a communal passport. So the misfortune is entirely yours, and yours alone. But I have found the solution."

"I can't wait to hear it."

"It means that I have to do a little of the driving."

"You? Heaven save us! The last time I tried to teach you how to drive, you managed, I'm sure you remember, to hit two other cars at the same time, about five minutes after you'd taken over the wheel."

"That is absolutely untrue," Eliska said. "They hit me, which is not the same thing. May I proceed?"

"Please do."

"You do most of the driving, getting us all as close to the border as possible. We drive along it for a while looking for the best place for you to smuggle yourself through, on foot. Probably more on your belly."

She was suddenly more serious, and she went on, "I just cannot believe, darling, that anyone with your amount of gumption, can't cross that fence! As I remember, it's all barbed coils, and a lot of the area is heavily forested. We wait to make sure you made it, we make a note of how many kilometers the nearest legal crossing is, get through on our passport, race back that same distance, and park there until you find us." She added, a little hopefully, "Isn't that at least possible? What do you think?"

"Actually," Zdenek said, and he was dead serious too, now, "that is very close to what I myself have been thinking. Yes, it can work, with one major change."

"Which is?"

"We can't afford, on the actual day of our escape, with all of us in the car, to hang around examining maybe a dozen possible places for me to cross. That is something we have to do well in advance, perhaps even several times, to make sure that the place we select is feasible. Just the two of us, cruising slowly along the border, looking for a promising place that turns out to be no good, we find another, and another, and if necessary, still another."

"That sounds to me," Eliska said, "like a great deal of the common sense I may be lacking in."

"No you don't," Zdenek said. "Don't belittle yourself! But reconnaissance, it's so terribly important! We find out first what we have to do, and then, we do it."

"Good," Eliska said. "When do you want to start?"

"Tomorrow. Instead of crying our eyes out, we start moving, we get the escape going. We'll leave at about six in the morning. Settle the kids for the day and drive to Bratislava first. There are no likely areas there—too near to Austria—so on to Komarno. That's three hundred and fifty kilometers. Then all the way for every inch of that border. Agreed?"

"Agreed," Eliska said, with a great deal of satisfaction. "The operation is now under way."

CHAPTER EIGHT

There was one little duty to be attended to in the morning before they could leave. At seven-thirty, the earliest reasonable time, Eliska thought—she took Michal 'round to the Stransky house, just up the street, and she arranged for him to stay there all day. "We might be very late," she told Mrs. Stransky apologetically, "is that all right?"

"I'll put him to bed with the rest of the mob," the good lady said, and that was that. Martin would be in school and was more than capable of fixing his own meals. Anything else, she wondered? No. But it was not until nearly nine o'clock that they actually left.

"I think," Zdenek said, once they were on their way, "we should take the normal route to Bratislava, but I don't want to get too close to the city itself, then head off instead for Komarno, not getting too close to the town there either. We both know how thick the border guards are in that whole area. But if we turn off east, on one of the subsidiary roads, we should be able to drive more or less along the border itself, but anything from five to ten kilometers north of it all the time."

"That's a long way if we have to walk," Eliska said, but Zdenek shook his head. "There aren't many main roads over there, but I'm sure we'll find a number of tracks going south into the forested areas, which is where we have to be very careful. The first block-house we see, the first tank, the first soldiers, we make a U-turn, get away from there and try again further on."

"Well," Eliska said, "that would seem to make sense."

They were driving, as Kornel had suggested, at not much more than forty kilometers an hour, and the traffic was heavy. There were cars whizzing past them at high speed, with a lot of raucous horn-blowing, and sometimes even sarcastic comments shouted at them from other drivers in more of a hurry, and Zdenek said casually, "Sometime during the day, I'll have you take over to get a little practice in while you can."

Eliska was horrified, "What? Not on this road, I hope!"

"We'll wait," Zdenek said, "until there are just two cars alongside us, so that you can have some fun."

"Beast . . ."

They came at last to a delightful little spa called Trebon, with small lakes all around it. Under normal circumstances, they would have stopped for a while, but it was only a ten-minute drive from the border, and Zdenek said, "I think we'll turn north here and take the road to Jindrichuv Hradec."

"We've never done that before," Eliska said.

"The border was never a worry for us before, but now . . . I feel a little guilty about it already. We can turn east there." He laughed. "Stupid, isn't it? But we know how heavily the border is guarded between Ceske Budejovice and Komarno, with no hope in hell of anyone sneaking over in this part of the world. We can turn south again a couple of hours further on."

"As long as we know where we are at least some of the time."

"Trust me".

"How much of the Hungarian border is there after Komarno, do we know?"

"I'd say about a hundred and twenty or thirty more kilometers before you hit the Ukraine."

"And we don't want to go there either."

"That's true enough, God knows."

But it was that stretch of territory that was the most promising for what they had in mind. It was mountainous and heavily forested too. The roads there were almost non-existent, many of them the "under construction roads" that first the Germans and then the Russians had worked on before abandoning them completely. In these beautiful, if often hazardous mountains, the roads twisted and turned every which way, so that you could never be sure if you were headed north, east, south or west. It was sometimes utterly confusing.

It was, after all, the Slovakian part of the Republic, peopled by what the Czechs liked to call their impoverished cousins.

They found themselves at long last hitting the D2 Motorway and filled up with gas there, but Zdenek wasn't too pleased about it. "Dammit," he said, "we're heading for Bratislava, that's the last place in the world I want to be." There was a minor road ahead of them on the right, and he swung the wheel around to bring the car onto it. It worried Eliska a little.

"We should go west," she said.

Zdenek grunted, "Yes, you're right, we should have gone left. Never mind. We'll swing around west as soon as we can."

But there was a tiny village ahead of them, and they drove into it and pulled to a stop. A stranger was passing them by, and Zdenek asked him, "The name of this village, friend?" and the man answered, "It's called Milovice, but if you're looking for Mikulov, it's just down the road a mite."

"Thank you," Zdenek said.

And Eliska whispered, "Oh, my God . . ."

She was looking behind them, and he swung around to follow her look. A military troop-carrier was pulling in a little way back, and a dozen or more soldiers were piling out of it, swinging their rifles.

Zdenek said tightly, "Mikulov, just down the road a mite, that's a border crossing. Great, isn't it? Just what we ought to be avoiding."

They saw now that a dozen or so troops were wandering around, not paying much attention to anything at all, and Zdenek said, "Back-up troops', they shouldn't worry us too much."

"They don't seem to wonder what we're doing here," Eliska said, "but we have to pull out of here the way we came in or else head for the crossing."

"We back out," Zdenek said. "We don't have anything to hide." He shrugged. "Just a couple of nice people on vacation."

"No," Eliska said emphatically, "in case they should start wondering . . . I see a bakery over there."

"Ah, yes, I'm hungry, too."

Eliska slipped away and was back in a few minutes with a sensibly sized package. "Four chlebickies," she said, "one for me, and three for you."

"Good, and I thank you."

He backed out, slowly turned the car around, and once more they were on their way.

Later in the afternoon, well up in the mountains, they came to a part of the road that was twisting around like a corkscrew with no help at all to the old-fashioned way of driving with the sun as the only indicator of direction. Zdenek stopped the car, looked around, and said, "A couple of minutes . . ."

He got out and scrambled up to a steep incline and stared around, and when he slid back down, he said happily, "We are absolutely not lost, whatever you might have been thinking." He pointed. "Down there below us, not too far off, there's a main road, a nice big river, and a good-sized town that just has to be Nitra. We've never been there, have we?"

"I don't think so."

"They say that the beautiful old castle there is well worth visiting, but we've more important things to do now. It's about one and half hours drive from the Komarno crossing, which is dead south of us, so . . ." He thought hard for a few moments, even scratching his head, and went on, "There is where the Hungarian border stops going roughly southeast from home and starts going northeast, right?"

"If you say so."

"So we'll take that road for about forty minutes, which should bring us as close to the border as we want to be. That's where we stop and assess the situation."

"Makes sense again."

"Then we turn left wherever possible, sneaking a little bit south if we can, we'll go all the way to the Ukrainian border if we have to, which is another several weary hours of these very crummy and exhausting roads."

"Wow."

"And we keep on stopping, getting out of the car and exploring." He checked his watch, "Nearly six hours since we left home. Of course, when we're ready to actually go, we'll know exactly where you have to drop me, where I have to start crawling, and it won't take so long. Thank God, the new engine's been run in by now, so I can start speeding up quite a bit, like twice as fast."

"Well, that's a blessing."

It was four o'clock before they made their first walk-about. They had actually come close enough on a forest track, to see in the distance great coils of barbed wire that marked the border, and there seemed to be nobody around, although they both knew that this was simply not possible. "I'm going to look around," Zdenek said quietly.

Eliska checked him, "Wait. Best to back up a bit, I'd say, quite a bit. And I'll come with you."

"No."

"Yes. Two of us together, like husband and wife, and I'm not dressed for anything dramatic. Much less suspicious than one man alone. In hiking boots yet."

"Ah, yes, you may be right."

"You better believe I'm right."

He backed up slowly for a while, until thick shrubbery almost concealed the car, and cut the engine. They got out to start moving quietly but casually around, not going far enough to lose sight of the vehicle. "Nothing, nobody," Eliska whispered, "and I don't believe it."

"A little closer," Zdenek said, "not too much. And look like you don't have a care in the world."

The silence was acute. There was not even the expected sounds of birds. Zdenek said, not quite whispering, "I smell trouble. What happened to the birds?"

"And there's the fence!" Eliska said, "My God, if you ran, you could make that in two minutes, maybe less."

"Much longer to get through it. Remind me that I'll need wire-cutters."

"And if it's electrified?"

"Rubber gloves, too."

And suddenly, there was a quite frightening crashing sound just behind them, and they swung around to see a soldier, a sergeant in the uniform of the Border Guards, landing lightly on the ground from the high branches of an oak tree.

Eliska reacted instantly, "Hey!" she said, and she was smiling broadly, 'you scared the wits out of me!"

The sergeant stared at them, "Suppose you tell me what you people are doing here?"

"That fox!" Eliska said.

"What are you talking about?"

"The fox!" Eliska said again. "You didn't see it? A beautiful red fox. We saw him back there, and he didn't seem a bit scared of us. We got out of the car, and he just sort of wandered off into those bushes there. I wanted so much to take another look at him. He's a real beauty!"

The sergeant put his fingers to his mouth and whistled shrilly twice. Immediately there was that crashing sound again as two more soldiers came clambering down from the trees. For a moment, they just stood there, their weapons leveled. The sergeant looked at Zdenek. "Did you see this fox, too?"

"Sure, he was a real beauty."

"Your papers." He looked to Eliska, "Yours too."

They handed over the requisite identification papers and the sergeant studied them carefully before he handed them back. "Get back to your car," he said.

Zdenek nodded. "Of course, and I'm sorry if we intruded." He too smiled. "I didn't realize we were so close to the border."

"You didn't?" the sergeant asked. "What did you think that fence is for? To keep the foxes out? Back to the car."

"Sure." They turned and walked back to it, not really surprised that the three soldiers were close behind them. Zdenek was looking up into the high branches of the trees, and thought he spotted three more of the hidden guards up there, or was it four? "Eyes ahead!" the sergeant said sharply.

"You bet," Zdenek said. When they reached the car, they were told to stand aside, and they watched the troopers methodically and meticulously search its contents, lifting out seats, opening the hood where any baggage would be stored and finding almost nothing there except a small toolbox. The sergeant located the sole remaining chleblicky, examined it, and asked, "This all the food you brought with you?"

"The remains of our lunch," Zdenek said.

"You won't mind if I feel obliged to confiscate it?"

"Be my guest."

"Now, be on your way."

The two of them got into the car, and Zdenek started the motor.

The sergeant held up his weapon for them to see. "You know what this is?"

"A gun," Zdenek said.

"You know what kind?"

"Assault rifle."

"Make?"

"It's Kalishnikov."

"How come you can recognize it?"

"There are a lot of Russian troops in Ceske Budejovice and they carry them. They haven't found out yet that our Skoda weapons are twice as good as theirs."

There was a little silence then, and it worried Eliska. But in a moment, the sergeant said, "First sensible thing I've heard you say. Now get going. Just remember—I see you again, you get a full magazine—that's thirty bullets—right through your guts. You got that?"

"Nice to have met you," Zdenek said politely, and they drove off to the safety of the highway.

Eliska was shaking her head. "I just don't know," she said, "how it is that you get away with being the way you are!"

"It's because I'm such a nice guy," Zdenek said. "And if that sounds like a joke, it's not. It's something a lot of people recognize at once, particularly the toughies, like our sergeant. The next stop is a couple of miles ahead, and we'll try again."

"Agreed." Eliska said. "Only next time, just don't make my blood-run cold like that, please! Any minute back there, my teeth were going to start chattering."

"There was nothing I said to that guy that could possibly have offended him."

"That's probably true. But it's a question of . . . of attitude, something I think you'll never understand."

"And that," Zdenek said, smiling in utter contentment, "is probably true, too. I love you, sweetheart."

"Then I wish," Eliska said sourly, "that you'd let it show a little more often."

Zdenek sighed, "Just try to be less of a pain in the ass."

The forest road was friendly to them now, saving them a great deal of wasted effort by letting them see, for more than an hour of driving, tanks and military transports almost everywhere in great abundance. They saw forts with the guns facing south as thought to ward off a Hungarian invasion, but all of them had embrasures on the north side as well, as though to shelter riflemen and machine-gunners.

"As bad as the Austrian frontier," Zdenek grumbled. "And why is it I never knew about this?"

"Because the only times we've ever been as far east as this," Eliska said, "we've been way to the north, nowhere near the border we're concerned about now. How could we even guess?"

They drove on and on and on, passing through Levice and then Lucenec, where Zdenek said, quite exasperated, "We're a good ten kilometers from the border here and in the last five minutes we've seen what? Three military posts? It's maddening! But this is a nice little town, well, not so little. I used to have relatives here."

"Used to?"

"In the good old days, there were two other Zizka families living here, and the Hussites fought a huge number of important battles around the town, some of them very prolonged. But they all got wiped out a couple of hundred years later, the Black Plague."

"Oh, God."

"No, not him. He wasn't around much then. Almost the whole population of the city got to be burned and buried in mass graves. So much for the Zizkas.

They drove on to Rimavska Sobota, which Zdenek said was not much of a place, simply because this town, too, was crawling with troops. Away to their right they could see two gigantic metal buildings, nicely painted sky-blue, with heavy cables leading out from them everywhere. "Generators," he said. "They must have this area lit up at night like you won't believe."

They drove at length through a very large city, past a huge and astonishingly beautiful cathedral. Eliska was in awe of it. "Did you ever see anything like it?" she asked.

"Still open to the public," Zdenek said, "by the gracious permission of the Party. The priests, of course, are not allowed to preach there anymore."

"And what is this town?"

"Kosice. And dammit, we're nearly twenty kilometers from the frontier. How the hell did we finish up here? Next road on our right, I'm taking it."

"Kosice?" Eliska asked. "I've heard of it, of course, but I've never been here before. Heard something about it quite recently," she said, "but I can't remember what it was."

They turned a corner to the right, down a very dilapidated road where the houses were all sadly in need of repair. "Falling apart," Zdenek said, "off the main streets, much of the town is just that, falling apart."

Eliska's memory struck home in sudden shock, "The towns," Vaclav Cubirca had said to her, "some of them are really falling apart, nothing is being maintained properly." And Kosice was one of the towns he was visiting on his lecture tour.

Zdenek was looking at her. "Something?" he asked. "Are you thinking of something special?"

She shook her head. "No," she said, not lying exactly, but just being discreet, "nothing of any importance."

The sun was going down by the time they reached Michalovce, at the edge of the mountains, where Zdenek cut the engine and said wearily, "Our last stop, you want to wander around here for a while? Stretch our legs?"

"I think so," Eliska said. "Where are we exactly?"

"A small town called Michalovce, of not much importance to anybody, especially not to us."

To the south of them, the sky was beginning to be brightly lit as the border flares started coming on in the distance. "How far is that?" Eliska asked, "about twenty kilometers?"

"A little more, perhaps."

To the north of them, the outline of the Carpathian Mountains was darkening, and Zdenek saw that she was staring at them. "That has to be Poland, no?" she asked.

"Forty minutes drive from here, yes. And if we go straight ahead for about half that, we'd find the Russians welcoming us with open arms."

"The Ukraine?"

"Uh-huh." He sighed, and threw out his arms and started rolling his shoulders to ease them. "Three frontiers in our sight," he said disgustedly, "and the only one we can't cross is the one we want. Hungary?"

"Yes, I could do with a bite to eat."

"In this part of the world, everything shuts down very soon after dark, so we'd better find somewhere right away. But the food should be good; there's a strong Hungarian influence here."

"Goulash and dumplings?"

"You said it. And we need gas. I hope to God they have a gas station here."

"And if they don't?"

"They surely must," Zdenek said, beginning to worry about it. In some parts of the country these days, gas stations were few and far between. But a passer-by he questioned told him, yes, there was one, gave him directions, and in ten minutes their tank was full again. "Won't get us more than half-way home again," Zdenek said, "but we'll be taking the main motor roads all the way now, so there shouldn't be any problem."

They found a small restaurant that was still open, though almost deserted, and as they waited for their goulash, Eliska said very quietly, "It looks as though we've been defeated, doesn't it?"

"On our first try, yes. But first attempts at anything often fail, don't they?" He smiled. "Like your first attempt at driving, and I never did give you the wheel today, did I? Too late now. I don't want you driving in the dark, my life's too valuable."

"You mean we have to try this again?"

"I was wondering if I should perhaps take another look tomorrow. The same thing, but alone."

Eliska was alarmed, "No! Zdenek, no, please! We already know how dangerous that can be. No, no, no!"

"Well, it was just an idea. What we need to know is more about the whole general line of the border. In my underground group, as you possibly suspect, we keep an eye out for possible new members for any of the cells, and send them . . ."

"I did suspect it was something like that," Eliska said, "odd little comments here and there, all adding up. I never wanted to ask you about it, of course."

"Of course, and I appreciate that. But what I was suggesting is that my group is no good to us here. The only one I truly know could help us is Lenka's, and we already decided that we mustn't use her."

"Was that a good decision, do you think?"

Zdenek nodded. "I'm sure of it. She's not untrustworthy—that's not the right word. She's too unreliable."

"Yes, I'm sure of it."

"And there's no one else, is there?" Zdenek asked.

Eliska was silent for a moment, and Zdenek asked again: "Is there, sweetheart?"

But then the cook brought their dinner, two huge bowls of steaming goulash and a very large plate of dumplings, and it gave Eliska a few more moments of worried thought. But the woman was gone after wishing them *dobrou chut'*, and they were left alone together again.

"There is someone else," Eliska said flatly, her mind made up. "Vaclav, Vaclav Cubirca."

"Ah, yes," Zdenek said, calmly enough to dispose any misgivings she might have. "Vaclav. I probably know more about his underground duties than you do. Because he travels so much, lecturing, he has a sort of rowing commission, picking up interesting information which he then gives to-guess whom?-for placing wherever it's needed."

"To Lenka," Eliska said.

"Exactly. So talk to him, sweetheart. Find out everything that might be useful to us about that whole area."

"Very well, I'll do that."

"Discreetly, of course."

Eliska sighed heavily. "The life we lead today," she said, "it's made up of so much lying and deceit, I've become hardened to it. But with one's friends? It's horrible."

134

"Yes, it is, and I don't like it much either, but it's necessary sometimes. In this case—vitally necessary. And when he finds out we've gone for good, he'll understand. That's the sort of man Vaclav is, a thinking man's man."

"Don't hold it against him," Eliska said tartly, "that he has to think to make a living."

Zdenek chose not to challenge it. "In retrospect," he said, "it will probably amuse him quite a bit."

"I truly hope so."

"I know it." He was attacking his food already, with some vigor. "Hey, this is a very good goulash! Very different from yours, and only half as good, but terrific!"

"A bit light on the garlic, maybe, but not bad at all. When should I see Vaclav?"

"As soon as possible."

"Tomorrow then, I'll call him first thing in the morning. Will you come with me?"

"No, I think not. I'm sure you'll handle it better on your own. We need every damn thing he knows—must know—about this area. Tell me when it is you hope to leave to start on your journey."

"I think," Eliska said, "that whatever adversities we have to find solutions to, ten or fifteen days should be a very generous time to overcome them. Starting early tomorrow morning with Vaclav."

"So do you figure we might leave, say, around late July?"

"Yes, I do, give or take a few days."

"Accepting the fact," Zdenek said, "that so far, just about nothing has happened the way we expected it to happen, and also that other, quite unexpected calamities may arise, are we being overly optimistic?"

Eliska nodded. "Probably. But isn't it a matter of setting our minds to it? I think it is."

"Good for you! It's wait and see again, isn't it? Great. And I'm with you all the way."

They finished their meal and paid for it, then got back into the car. Zdenek said, checking his watch, "Fourteen hours of driving! I can't even keep my eyes open."

"So get in the back," Eliska said, "and go to sleep. I'll drive."

He stared at her, "In the dark? Are you out of your mind?"

"We have great headlights. Go lie down, go sleep."

"You're crazy! Do you even remember the gear-shift?"

"I do, yes. And I'm insisting."

It made no sense to him, and yet . . . He suggested finding some hotel here and staying the night, but Vaclav, she told him, was the next item on the agenda. That was tomorrow morning, and nothing was going to prevent her from seeing him at the earliest possible moment.

She had already taken her place in the car, at the wheel, and Zdenek threw up his hands and clambered into the back. There was not a lot of room there, but he curled up on the seat, and the last thing he heard was her comment, "I forget where the light switch is. No! I found it!"

In a state of utter exhaustion and of the carelessness that goes with it, he was dead to the world in a matter of moments. And Eliska knew, with absolute certainty, that his fatigue had little to do with too many hours of driving, that it was more a matter of the bitterest disappointment he felt and simply would not admit.

It was the strong smell of gas that woke him up at last. He struggled to a sitting position and found they were in a service station and that Eliska was refueling the car. They were up in the mountains, and the moon was very bright. "Where are we?" he asked, a little groggily.

Eliska said happily, "Well, welcome back to the land of the living. We're in Třebíč."

"Třebíč?" Zdenek asked, startled. "What the hell are we doing in Třebíč?"

"Going home is what we're doing. Did you get a good sleep?"

"Yes, I certainly did. Do you feel all right?"

"A little tired," Eliska admitted.

"Třebíč! You came a long way around."

"Those narrow roads were scaring me a bit, but I found a motorway, which is much easier for a beginning driver."

Zdenek looked at his watch. "Two o'clock! Sweetheart, do you realize you've been driving for more than four hours? Bless you! No trouble?"

"Nope, But if you want to take over now . . ."

"You bet. We're nearly home! We'll be there in no time at all."

"And never a more welcome sight."

Now he drove very fast, right up to the little cars maximum, and by four o'clock they were both in bed and fast asleep. Until six-thirty, when Eliska was already heading for the shower. "Vaclav," she said, "he probably leaves the house soon after seven, and I want to be sure to catch him before he goes out." Yes, he was home when she called, answering his government phone immediately.

"What a welcome surprise!" he said. "Are you calling from home?"

"Yes, I am."

"And is Zdenek there?"

"Y-e-s, he's right beside me." She saw that he was standing there in his favorite dress for the early hours, a wrap-around towel, and that he was smiling at her, enjoying, she thought, some secret joke.

"So what can I do for you?" Vaclav asked, and he sounded amused, too.

"Nothing, really," Eliska said, "I just thought it would be nice if we could have an espresso together sometime. Like this morning."

"What a wonderful idea! How about the Korzo? They serve the best coffee in town, I'd say."

"One of my favorite cafés ever."

"Around eleven?"

"How about nine? Than you can buy me breakfast."

"Nine o'clock it is," Vaclav said.

"Good," Eliska said, and hung up.

Nearly two hours to wait, and she thought they were the longest hours she'd spent for quite a while. She could have set the meeting for eight, but a show of over-anxiety itself might have been a mistake. The story was to be about a pleasant ten days abroad, no more that that, a continuation of the deceit that had become more hateful to her every time she practiced it.

"Could I take the car over to the Korzo myself?" she asked. "A little more learning?"

"After last night," Zdenek said, "I have this feeling that you can take the car anytime you want it! But in the town's heavy traffic? It's not like one of those country roads, you know. I'm not too sure that it would be a good idea. In fact, I'm pretty sure it would be too dangerous by far.

Do me a favor and let me give you a few more lessons first."

"Maybe you're right. I'll take the bus." There was a little pause, and then, "No. Why don't you drive me over there, give me a lesson on the way, park somewhere out of sight and wait for me? Like we did with that bastard Ctibor, remember?"

"I'll never forget it! Very well, let's do that. When we find a way for me to cross, you'll have to do the cross-the-border bit in the car yourself anyway."

"So let's go now. It'll help pass the time."

"Now? Should I put on a pair of pants?"

"Not unless you really want to," Eliska said, glad that in such a trying time they could still make their little jokes together.

On their way to the café, he gave her a few of the simpler lessons, "That guy ahead, he's trying to cut in ahead of us. So you watch his front wheel, always the front wheel." And, "If you think you may have to slow down or stop, cover the brake with your foot, always cover, don't wait until the last moment. And if the driver behind you is too close, tap the brake a few times; the brake light will tell him to get off your tail."

They came to the little street behind the Korzo, found a parking place, and Zdenek said, "I'll be here when you're through."

"I might be quite a long time."

"I hope you will be, there's so much you have to find out."

And a long time she was indeed. It was vital, she thought, to show no distress whatsoever, just to ask Vaclav a few questions and try hard to justify them. She even found herself laughing a little. "Stupid," she said, looking around carefully to make sure no one was within hearing distance, satisfying herself that theirs was the only sidewalk table occupied. "Stupid!" she said again, "the only word for it! But I told you about our little vacation, I think. Well, Zdenek can't get a passport, so, believe it or not, he wants to sneak over the border on foot some place, while I drive Martin and Michal through Customs and Immigration. He's crazy! But he's convinced it can be done; said people do it all the time. Is he right? Me, I just can't believe him. I'm going to have to leave him behind, I'm sure of it."

She broke off at the look on Vaclav's face of absolute shock, and of something more as well. He too looked around, and lowered his voice even more. "You may or may not know what my duties in the underground are," he said, 'but in case you don't . . ."

He broke off, and was smiling suddenly as the waitress approached. "A good day to you," he said to her politely. "We'll just have coffee, please. Large espressos."

When she had gone, he said very quietly, continuing and looking deeply disturbed, "I'm breaking all our rules now; I must. I don't belong to any one cell, or lodge, and yet I'm part of every single one of them." He was whispering now, "As I am constantly on these lecture tours all over the country, I pick up a great deal of useful information, which I pass on to certain representatives all over the country. I won't tell you who my contact here is."

Eliska whispered something, and he said, quite shocked, "That is something you ought not to know, and I hope to God it wasn't Zdenek who told you."

"It wasn't. It was Lenka herself."

138

"Oh, my God . . . But darling Eliska, don't let him do it! Forget your plans altogether or leave him behind! Has that man no brains at all? You know how much I like him, and what I'm doing now is saving his damn life, it's as simple as that!"

"Well," Eliska said, not quite sure of herself and pushing for more information, "I'll talk with him, of course."

"God dammit!" Vaclav hissed furiously, and looked around again, knowing that he dared not raise his voice. "I will give you a figure, just one figure that will surely convince you—and Zdenek—of the danger." His voice was so low now she could hardly hear him. "In the last six weeks," he said, "four hundred and eighteen innocent Czechs have been shot trying to do what Zdenek wants to do, smuggle themselves over the border. Some of them were killed instantly, and those who were not were taken off to the prisons, where they were simply beaten to death. Not a single one of those four hundred and eighteen is still alive."

"Dear God . . ."

"And I have no figure for those who actually made it, because that figure is zero." He was patting at his pockets, and he said angrily, "I need a smoke, I really need one now, and I left my cigarettes in the pocket of my other suit. But there's a store, isn't there, just round that corner?"

"That's right," Eliska said.

"Full of apology, he asked, "Give me two minutes?"

"Of course. I can't wait to hear more."

"What more is there to hear?" Vaclav asked wearily. "Except to tell you that Zdenek is signing his own death warrant."

He left as the waitress came with the coffee. She looked at his disappearing form and asked, "Would you like me to keep it hot for him?"

"No, no," Eliska said, "he just went for a pack of Lípy. He'll be right back."

She sipped her coffee as she waited, and as Vaclav had said, it was great. She looked at her watch when six minutes had passed. She sipped some more, and when ten minutes came up, she began to worry. When her watch told her twenty minutes, she knew that something, but what?, had gone wrong.

She dropped some money on the table and went to find Zdenek, and he saw at once the absolute fury on her face. He asked, "No good news, huh?"

She told him, almost word by word, what Vaclav had told her, and he said, trying not to sound entirely devastated, "Rough, yes, it's not easy. But

139

the answer is quite simple. You go with the family just about any day now, and leave me here to my own devices. Sooner or later, I will find a way to join you."

"No," Eliska said clearly, and very sure of what she was talking about. "Ten minutes after Vaclav disappeared, and I hope to God we'll find out what happened to him, I knew exactly what has to be done."

"Which is?" Zdenek asked.

Eliska told him "I'm going to smuggle you over the border myself, in the back of the Škoda! Tomorrow, in a nice open space where we can't be seen, I want to tear that car apart with my two bare hands and find out just how to manage it!"

Zdenek slowly shook his head. "Do you think," he asked sourly, "that I'm not depressed enough already? Do you really have to throw a stupid idea like that at me?"

"Try a little confidence in me," Eliska said. "In a few days' time, we'll find a way to double you up and fit you in there, somewhere, somehow. Did you notice that when we got stopped yesterday by those border guards, they never looked in the rear at the engine compartment?"

"They never do," Zdenek said, "but for God's sake . . ." There was nothing he disliked so much as getting angry with her, but now he was furious, and his voice was rising. "You know how hot an engine gets? You expect me to sit on top of it? And you want to shrink me down to the size of a midget?"

"Listen to me . . ." Eliska began, but he interrupted her curtly, "No! I will not! I won't even discuss it!"

"And right now, if you're just going to yell at me, I don't want to discuss it either."

"So forget it then."

"No," she said, quite calmly, "neither of us is going to forget it. In bed tonight, if you dream, don't bother about me. Just dream about being wrapped around the engine of a four cylinder Škoda. Because that, lover, is your next port of call. You hear me?"

"Oh, shut up," Zdenek said bitterly. "Just forget it."

All the way home, neither of them spoke another word.

CHAPTER NINE

It was after three in the morning when the realization came to Zdenek that this night he would find no sleep at all, and he knew why. He leaned over and touched Eliska gently on the cheek. When she awoke and stared up at him, he asked her, "Did you know that a guilty conscience can rob a man of his sleep?"

She nodded. "Yes, I think so," she said sleepily, "So now you want to rob me of mine, too? Shame on you." But she kissed her own fingertips and then reached up to touch his lips with them. "You want to talk, is that it?

"Uh-huh. I'm afraid I was rather bad-tempered with you yesterday, not very nice, and I'm sorry. The absolute helplessness of our position finally caught up with me, something I've been denying for so long."

Well, it does seem to be a little desperate, that idea of mine, about the compartment, I mean. We have to call that sheer desperation."

"I've been thinking about that," he said, "and it does have a certain value. Not quite as you think, but . . . shall we go to the veranda? It's a gorgeous night, a full moon."

"Yes, let's do that. Blankets?'

"I'd say so."

She pulled them off the bed, and they wrapped themselves up and went outside. He held her tightly and kissed her. "The moonlight," he said, "it does something to your skin—it makes it luminous, lustrous, more lovely than ever."

"Nice," Eliska whispered, "but not what we came here for."

"True, true. So . . . there is indeed a lot of space in the Škoda engine compartment, but there's no way that even a much smaller man could get in there, unless the back seat were removed. And even then, the heat would be unbearable, and the poor devil would be roasted alive. But some rebuilding of that rear compartment . . . I don't know, it seems to have some possibilities. And your idea, sweetheart, of tearing it apart to see—that is exactly what we have to do."

"Some place where we can't be disturbed. Down by the river, maybe?"

"Once we get out of town, you drive, and we go over to the oak trees, where our friends the cows are. It means a little off-road driving, but that's no problem, we can get the car right up to the riverbank if we want to."

"We'll set up a picnic again," Eliska said. "If anyone should row or sail by, we have a reason for being there."

And so it was decided. In the very early and sunny July morning, Eliska was parking Škoda in the shade of the oaks and setting out the picnic stuff. Zdenek lifted up the cover of the engine compartment in the rear, and stared at it for a while. He said at last, "Room for a very much smaller man! Let's see what it looks like with the back seat removed."

He went to the front, lifted up the hood, took out the toolbox and wrestled with the bolts and the screws, some of them rusted in firmly, until at last, he was able to pull out the squab, exposing the engine, and then the seat itself.

Eliska asked him, "Is there room for you to lie down in there or not?"

"Plenty, he said. "But what then? No back seat; you throw a blanket over me and hope for the best?"

"Try it," Eliska said. He clambered in there and wriggled over onto his side, and she said, "Try moving further back."

"How can I?" he asked, "the vent's in the way."

"Could it be removed?"

"Yes, but that's what cools the engine. Without it, it would overheat and seize up in a matter of minutes. But I wonder if the floor could be lowered? Let's take a look."

He squirmed his way out and lay down on his back on the dew-damp grass, hauling himself under the car and studying the configuration carefully. In moments, he pulled himself out, and said, disgustedly, "No way! The damn floor's practically flush with the frame. And that rear seat simply must finish up in its original position, which means zero room back there. No, it was a clever idea, but there's no way it can be made to work."

But Eliska simply would not give up. She rolled the squab of the seat over onto its side, and said, "Just look at the thickness of that cushioning! Could we cut all that out?"

"Yes, there's a possibility there, I'd say." He examined it for a while, measuring it with his spread fingers. He said at last, with a great deal of enthusiasm, "I think you've got it! I really do! The whole seat has to be remade into a kind of skeleton. That vent has to be re-routed, a sheet of aluminum put there to hide what's between the front of the engine and the back of the seat, which will be me. And none of this are we capable of doing ourselves. We need professional help."

Eliska was silent, worrying about it.

Zdenek went on, "The seat alone, that's as difficult as the rest of the work! The springs and the cushioning have to go, leaving the original seat covering intact, and that means professional work. It's the only possible way."

"Kornel?" Eliska asked, "It's so terribly dangerous!"

"No." Zdenek said, "it's not."

"My instinct tells me that we can trust him, as you obviously do, but we both know how highly the Secret Police would pay for this kind of information."

"He will not go to the police, or to anyone else. He wouldn't ever want to, but even if he did, he can't do that."

"Why, because he's a Gypsy? We don't harass the Gypsies here."

"Because under another name, and even I don't know what that was," Zdenek said, "he is an escaped prisoner from Bratislava, wanted for the murder of an officer of the Secret Police."

"Oh, my God!"

"There are times," Zdenek said clearly, "when the killing of another human being can be justified."

"I'm not at all sure about that. I don't know; there could be circumstances, I suppose."

"As in this case," he went on. "I don't know if what I'm telling you was told to me by Kornel in confidence or not; he's never suggested that. But what happened to him is hardly a matter for everyday talk. I never wanted to tell you about it, but now . . . I feel that I should. It's about his wife."

"Oh, he's married?"

"Not anymore. In Romania, where he comes from, he married a famous beauty named Libuse." He hesitated for a moment, sighed deeply, and then went on. "You remember that when he came to the apartment, he stared at you and said something about a lovely lady, meaning you?"

"Yes, I remember, of course I do."

"He told me once that Libuse had the palest gray eyes he'd ever seen. Like yours. Apparently, it's very uncommon among the Gypsies. Anyway, it seems that all the other women in her tribe—just because of her great beauty, of course—disliked her intensely. He himself was not making a living because they treat the Gypsies very badly there. So they emigrated to Czechoslovakia, legally, and finished up in Bratislava. But there they were stopped because the license plate on their car was falling off—a trifling matter. He says the cops were very rude to Libuse, making physical jokes about her, so . . . he hit one of them. The back up came, they were both arrested, and he was thrown into the lock-up while Libuse was being questioned. I guess you can imagine what happened to her then?"

Eliska stared at him, "Dear God . . ."

"Yes," he said, "she was raped, by this same rogue cop, and under her tribe's law—and, I think, among a number of the Gypsy tribes—it's mandatory for a woman who has been violated to kill herself. She cut her wrists. He tells me that it took him nearly a week to break out of prison, find this guy, and kill him. And now, he's just lying low in Ceske Budejovice, hoping they'll never find him."

"And how long ago was this?"

"A little over nine years."

"I think I want to be sick," Eliska said. "It's enough to make you weep, isn't it? I agree, let him do the work, but . . . what about the hired help he has?"

"They're all Gypsies. They won't ask any questions, and he won't volunteer any information."

"You are sure of that?"

"Absolutely."

"Then the sooner we talk to him, the better," she said.

"How right you are." He was dumping the seat back into place. "No sense in trying to bolt it in," he said, "half the bolts are broken, but he'll want to remove it all anyway. There's very little town driving to get to his place, so you drive.

"Will do."

She took the wheel, started the car, and maneuvered it across the meadow and onto the road with fairly tolerable skill.

"Nice work," Zdenek said, and a half-hour later they were sitting together on a garage bench, ready to explain to Kornel exactly what had to be done. He was listening to them in silence.

"We have decided to leave the country," Zdenek said quietly. "For Eliska and me, life has become unbearable here, and our two sons . . . the eldest is seventeen, almost a man, and he has somehow learned to take for granted the oppression that has been forced on us. The other boy is a child, and to have him grow up under these conditions . . ."

Was he floundering a little? He looked to Eliska for help, and she said quickly, "But it is not only for them. It is for all of us. The decision was Zdenek's and mine only. I have a passport; the Secret Police have taken Zdenek's from him. I will therefore smuggle him over the border in the back of the car. It means some highly-skilled alterations to the car's body."

Kornel turned and looked directly into her eyes, and she tried to smile, but could not; she was thinking of the pain that was still buried deep inside this man's heart.

He said to her, very warmly, "Your reasons are not my business, dear lady. It is enough that you seem to want my help, which I will gladly give you, because you are my friends. Zdenek may have told you that I myself once felt the need to escape from my own country. I understand these things. I will miss him sorely; but, yes, I understand. But . . . to hide a man in the back of a Škoda? You think it is possible? Because I do not."

"It is," Eliska said firmly. "It means remaking the back seat. May I show you how?"

He stood up abruptly and said, "Yes. Show me what you have in mind."

They went to the car, and with a couple of hefty tugs, Kornel dragged out the two sections of the seat and the steel frame itself, dropping them onto the ground. For a long, long time he just stared at the emptied space they had occupied before, and at the now-exposed engine. "Interesting," he said. "I would never have believed it."

But he moved away, and paced up and down for a while, frowning. He picked up the naked steel frame, put it back where it belonged, and stared at it some more. He then began pacing again, picked up, in a few moments, the squab of the seat, and examined its cushioning carefully. At last he said, "Zdenek, my friend, be so good as to climb in there for me."

"Be glad to," Zdenek said, and crawled into position, curling himself up and twisting onto his side. "There's just this air vent in the way," he said, "if that could somehow be moved . . ."

Kornel nodded, "Yes, that can be done." He reached in and gave Zdenek a hand to help him out, and turned to Eliska with a smile of very genuine amusement. "What you suggested," he said, "seemed to me to be, forgive

145

me, madness! But now, I see that you were right and that I was wrong. Yes. This can be done, and I will do it." The smile broadened. "It would seem," he said, "that you know your Skoda better than I do."

"Not likely," Eliska said. "But can you say how long this would take?"

"Let me tell you that," he answered, "when I have done a little more thinking about this very unusual undertaking." He scowled at the seats, and thought about them; then he picked up the squab and examined it again. "I will remove the covers first," he said, "which must be done very carefully with a razor-blade so as to leave no sign of tampering. Even the stitching must be the same. We will discard all that padding and all those springs. Then I will shape plywood sheets to screw to the frame and glue thin foam and the covers onto them. And I hope that you will then have a new seat that should pass any inspection, though it may be a little hard on your passenger."

"Who will be kids," Zdenek said. "That won't matter."

"And then," Kornel went on, "I will re-route the air intake to give you still more room. If my thinking is correct, as I am sure it is, your needs will be satisfied. And this idea of a shield there, to hide you if someone should open the engine compartment, is very good." He shrugged broadly, "If anyone should see it and wonder what it is, you will tell them that it is your own idea, a wonderful invention to improve the engine's cooling system. This is good, because it will actually do just that. The Skoda factories should have thought of it themselves. But these days," he went on with more than a little scorn, "they are all far too busy building tanks for our dear Soviet friends. Do you have a fixed date for your departure?"

"Not really," Eliska said. "When the car is ready we will be ready."

Kornel nodded. "Then I will work day and night on it," he said. "The rest of today, tomorrow, and maybe the finishing touches the next morning."

"And we shall miss you sorely, my dear friend," Zdenek said.

Eliska echoed the thought. "Yes, Kornel, both of us. And just when I am beginning to know you better, to know what a wonderful friend you are."

Kornel took a key from his pocket and handed it to Zdenek. "The loaner," he said gruffly, pointing to it, "over there. So go now. Go! And let me work!"

In thirty minutes of heavy late-afternoon traffic, they were home again, on what was fast becoming their favorite spot in the apartment, the veranda, now furnished with two comfortable chairs and a small coffee table. "A bit early in the day," Zdenek said, "but this calls for a celebration. Do you realize that in a couple of days or so, after so many calamities we'll actually be on our way? What about a drink?"

"I think that under the circumstances," Eliska said, "that is a very good idea. I'll get them."

But just then, an incipient disaster arose, which, had it not been quickly ended, would have destroyed their undertaking altogether. As it was, it was enough to send them both into the depths of despair until quite unexpected relief came . . .

The phone rang at that moment, and Zdenek said, "Well, who can that be, I wonder?"

"It must be Lenka," Eliska said. "There aren't many people who have this number."

"You get it then," Zdenek said, "while I fix the drinks. That woman's a non-stop talker."

Eliska picked up the phone, "Hullo? Oh, Peter, what a pleasant surprise! How are you?"

"Fine," Peter Tuka said rather shortly. "Comrade Franek wishes to see you."

It made her quite angry, "He does? Well, that's just too bad! Doesn't he know that office hours are over for God's sake, and I'm on my time off anyway!"

"He's not only your boss, Eliska, but he's a Party Chairman, too."

"He's got some nerve."

"And if a Party Chairman tells you to jump off a very high cliff," Peter said coldly, "that's what you do, or face an Examination by the Chair, which might well be quite a lot more painful."

"That makes me sick."

"Tomorrow morning at ten" Peter said, "and bring your passport, he wants to examine it."

Eliska felt the blood draining from her face. "My passport? But . . . whatever for?"

"Tomorrow at ten," Peter repeated, and the phone went dead.

Zdenek had heard. He put down the empty glasses and the bottle, and he saw how white she was. "No!" he said. "Don't tell me he wants your passport."

"He does," Eliska said.

"Do you know what for?"

"No. I don't know how much more of this I can take."

She broke off, and was beginning to cry. He put his arms around her and held her tightly, "By God, there's nothing in the world that hurts me so much as to see you in tears! My darling, it may well be nothing at all! Like, perhaps he forgot to make a note of its number for his damn records! You know how important records are for these people!"

She tried, sniffing, to brush the tears away. "You really think it might be that?"

"Or something equally harmless, yes, I do!"

"Or perhaps he wanted to make sure he used the right stamps? Just maybe?"

"It could be something like that," he added, earnestly.

"We don't know for sure, that something is wrong, do we? We're just back to the good old wait and see. It's not the first time, and it probably won't be the last."

"I hope it is the last! I won't sleep a wink tonight."

"So let's have that drink and forget that you ever had that call until tomorrow morning."

"All right, if you say so."

They went back to the veranda, and Zdenek poured the rum for them both—just a little heavier than usual—and raised his glass to her. "Na zdraví" he said, "to your health."

She raised her glass to him and said, "To both of us."

They spent a little time in desultory conversation, trying, as Zdenek had said, to forget, but not with very much success. The boys came home, but Martin sensed an atmosphere that was uncomfortable, and as they went about their own business in their own sanctuary, the holy of holies that was their room. Dinner came and went, not much of a meal, and when bedtime came, both Eliska and Zdenek found that sleep was once again elusive.

Nonetheless, an angry and determined Eliska was up quite early. Showered, perfumed, and beautiful in her smart beige costume, she was back in her Telephone Department some five minutes before her ten o'clock ordeal. She was surprised to see that Peter Tuka was smiling broadly at her.

"How good to see you again!" he said, "I imagine you guessed why I had to be so off-hand last evening?" He jerked a thumb at Franek's office, "The boss of bosses was right beside me when I called. Did you bring your passport?"

"Yes," Eliska answered, "do you know what he wants with it?"

Peter shrugged. "To examine it, he said, whatever that might mean. Go on down. You'll find out."

She walked down the long, bare corridor to Franek's office, and the famous secretary looked up at her and checked her watch. "One minute to ten o'clock, Eliska," she said. "Good. You know how Comrade Franek likes punctuality. Go on in. I think you know the routine."

"Thank you," Eliska said, and in a few moments she was facing the man she knew to be her enemy. He was smiling at her, but the smile was only around his mouth; there was no place at all for it in his hard eyes. "Mrs. Kucera," he said, "how good it is to see you again! Did you bring your passport?"

"I did, Comrade Franek."

"May I see it, please?"

"Of course." She handed it to him and he spent an interminable time turning all its pages, and studying every one of them. He placed it on his desk at last, and said, choosing his words very carefully, "You must know, I am sure, that I have nothing against you personally. As a matter of fact, I like you very much, though I am truly disturbed by the amount of time you have been taking off from your work."

"With Comrade Tuka's permission, of course," Eliska said. "And my holiday in Yugoslavia seems to require a lot of time consuming documentation. However, Comrade, I will be working full time again very soon now."

Was he looking into her eyes, those eyes that always told the world at large that she was lying? He leaned back in his expensive leather chair, and said, frowning now, "Ah, yes, your vacation. We have a certain difficulty there."

It was very hard for her to keep her emotions in check. She asked quietly, "A difficulty, Comrade Chairman? What kind of difficulty would that be, if I may ask?"

"You may certainly ask," Franek said. "Well, let me see how I can best explain this. As you know, I already gave my approval a while ago."

"For which I am very grateful."

"Kindly do not interrupt me. But three of our Telephone Company employees, to whom I gave similar approval a month or so ago, have not returned from Yugoslavia, having chosen to defect and put out their abominable ideas on what they call freedom in thousands of leaflets now flooding the streets of Belgrade." He took a little moment for effect, and repeated, "Belgrade. The capital of Yugoslavia, a hot bed of anti-communist

149

propaganda. As a direct result of this treachery, I have been ordered by the Party to re-check all future requests for vacations in foreign countries that do not palpably follow the desirable philosophies of our own Leninism. This means, dear Mrs. Kucera, that you can spend your vacation in Russia, or Poland, or East Germany—or even in Bulgaria. But not in Yugoslavia. So why don't you reapply for Yugoslavia next year?"

Eliska felt that her whole world was tumbling down around her. Trying to control her trembling, she asked, "May I at least have my passport back?"

Franek shrugged. "This is a passport for Yugoslavia only, it is useless to you now. No, you may not have it. And you are dismissed now. Good Day".

She turned abruptly and left him, and walked down that hateful corridor back to what she knew as her own usual workplace. She leaned against the wall there, emotionally distraught to the point of physical pain, and Peter was staring at her, quite bewildered by the suffering he saw on her face.

"But, what happened?" He asked, stammering.

Eliska took a long, deep breath, "He has confiscated my passport. There will be no vacation now. Go to Bulgaria instead, he says. Next year perhaps, he says. And I don't even believe that."

"If there's . . . if there's anything I can do . . . ?"

"Like what?" she asked bitterly.

"Yes," he said, apologetically, "that was a rather stupid remark, I suppose."

"See you, Peter," she said, and left the office.

When she arrived home, Zdenek saw her deep distress at once, and he listened attentively as she told him what had happened. He held her tightly in his arms, a time for commiseration and nothing else. He said at last, "There's no one we can appeal to, is there? No higher authority that can help us?"

"None," Eliska said. "In all these years we've never made any friends in high places. How could we?"

"And Franek's a very rich man, the only kind of bribe he would want is way beyond our means."

"He has dollars in the hundreds of thousands and even if we had it . . . he hates me so much! If only you could have seen his face! Hard, hard eyes, just gloating."

"Then it's the end."

"Yes," she said, "it's the end."

"So what do we do now?"

Eliska shook her head, "There's nothing we can do."

"No," Zdenek said, "I mean for the rest of the day? For tonight? For all the days and nights to come?"

"I think that for now," Eliska said, "I will go and lie down. And you?"

"I don't know, I'll just sort of hang around, I guess, and try to avoid going around the place shoving my fist through every pane of glass, every window we have. That's how I feel."

They were both in the depths of the worst kind of despair, a feeling of utter helplessness sweeping over them. Shortly after five o'clock, the relief came at last. There was a knock on the front door, and Zdenek went to open it. To his acute astonishment, it was Peter Tuka. "Well," Zdenek said, "good evening. This is quite a surprise, what can I do for you?"

Peter was smiling broadly. "Is Eliska home?" he asked.

"I think she's sleeping, but if it's important . . ."

"Just tell her," Peter said, "that I find myself in the happy position of bringing her back her passport, all stamped, and ready for use whenever it's needed."

Zdenek could only stare at him, "You mean . . ."

"Yes I do."

"Well, I'll be damned! Come on in, for God's sake, and I'll go get her."

He almost ran into the bedroom. Eliska was stirring there, half awake. "Did I hear voices?" She asked sleepily, and Zdenek took her wrist to drag her body out of the bed.

"You did," he said. "It's Peter Tuka, and he's brought you your passport, so come!"

He was pulling at her, and she almost shrieked, "Wait! My hair! It's a mess! What? He's got my passport?"

"Yes, he has, and don't worry about your hair, you never looked more lovely."

He pulled her into the living room, and Peter was holding up the passport for her to see. "Good evening, Eliska," he said very gravely, though his eyes were alight with his pleasure. "Your passport, dear lady, in perfect order, all permits stamped in there for ten days in Yugoslavia."

Her hands went to her cheeks, "My God . . . Is it true?"

"True," he said, and slapped it down on the table. "All ready to go."

"My God," she said again, "I can't believe it!" She picked it up, flipped through its pages, and shook her head. "It's a dream, a dream after a nightmare. What happened?"

Peter was obviously only too anxious to bask in his temporary glory. "It's a long story," he said deprecatingly. "I'm afraid it might bore you."

"No way!" Eliska exclaimed. "Tell it, Peter! We both want to hear!"

"We do indeed," Zdenek said. "Would you perhaps care for a glass of something?"

"Well, would you happen to have any vodka?"

"Of course," Zdenek said. "Hold everything," as he went searching. When the vodka and the rum and the glasses were all ready, he said briefly, "So tell . . ." And Peter began his story.

"First," he said, "do you happen to know about my family?"

"Well," Eliska said, "Tuka is a well-known name I would say, highly respected everywhere."

"Did you ever hear of Bohuslav Tuka?"

"No, I don't think so."

"He's my uncle, Peter said, "a Party Chairman and also a member of the nomenclature of the very highest of the ranking, and one of Franek's most powerful bosses. Like most of his group, he is a very wealthy man. And do you know just how these people get to be so rich?"

Yes, Zdenek knew, and so did Eliska. But she chose to be a little cautious. "It is rumored," she said, "that on occasion, some of them do help themselves to other people's monies. I'm sure that no Tuka would ever do a thing like that."

"Oh, but they do!" Peter said, and he was laughing now. "My good uncle Bohuslav up in Prague, once 'confiscated' a huge sum of money, a fortune in American dollars, in one single, quite daring robbery. They dragged him into court. He would have been disgraced and thrown into prison, had I not gone to his rescue."

"Interesting . . ." Eliska murmured.

He had raised his glass. "To your health," he said, and tossed the vodka, Russian style, down his throat. He went on, "It so happened that I was in Prague at the time, and I gave him an alibi. I swore that he was with me, out of town, at the time of the robbery. Knowing that I am essentially a very honest man, the judge believed me, and Uncle Bo was released. They even apologized to him! And on the way home, he said to me, 'I'm in your debt, young fellow. I owe you. Never forget it.' And I never did."

He turned to Zdenek. "You must know," he said, "how very fond I am of Eliska. I made just one call to Prague. One single call. And Uncle Bo made one single call to Franek. End of story. So now . . . Enjoy your holiday."

"How can I ever thank you?" Eliska asked.

Zdenek added, "It would seem Peter, that we are greatly in your debt, no?"

But Peter was slowly shaking his head. "No," he said, understanding, and the look on his face could only have been called benevolent. "Eliska will tell you," he said, smiling, "that I am almost a professional nice guy. No—though I thank you."

He shot out a hand to Zdenek and shook his, very firmly. "I am only sorry," he said, "that you will not be going, too. Well, perhaps next time. And I must go now. I thank you for your hospitality."

"One for the road?" Zdenek asked, indicating the empty glass, but Peter shook his head again. "A heavy date this evening," he said, "two guys, two gals. We'll be doing a lot of drinking. See you both again soon." And he was gone.

"Can you believe all that?" Eliska asked.

Zdenek said cheerfully, "We have to! It happened! And now, all we have to wait for is the car. What day is it today?"

"Saturday, of course," Eliska said.

"We just might get it tomorrow."

"And be on our way! It's a very good feeling."

"Yes," Zdenek said, "it really is."

A little later, Martin came home and there was a very serious question to be faced now—just how much could he be told about the plans they had. This was not something that had come upon Eliska suddenly or unexpectedly; there had been quite a few inconclusive discussions with Zdenek on the matter, but she had always known that the final decision would be in her hands. It was not easy for her to balance the pros and the cons and make any sense out of them.

She knew how skillful the schoolteachers were with their children, constantly encouraging them to spy on their parents, to listen in on their conversations and report them. She knew how prone Martin was—like all other teenagers, she was sure of what was always known as "the loose talk that costs lives," to recall the Nazi and Russian military occupation of her city. It meant that the need for tight security was very apparent. The less the boys knew, the better it would be for them all.

On the other hand, how could she be expected to lie to her own children? Did the end, in this case, truly justify the means?" It was a question she found very difficult indeed to answer. Zdenek was watching closely, in silence.

And then, Martin was telling them about the three chess games he had just won, playing against three of his friends simultaneously. He was pleased with himself. The moment Eliska dreaded so much had come.

She made up her mind at once to test the waters at least.

Luck, she was thinking, *with any luck at all I might get away with it.* And now began one of the most heart-wrenching talks she had ever experienced.

"We have some problems," she told Martin as calmly as she could manage. "As you know, you and Michal are both on my passport for this trip, but Zdenek just doesn't have a passport at all. So, we are trying to find a way to get him to Yugoslavia without one. It's not going to be easy, but I think it can be done, one way or another, if we apply our minds to it."

"What?" he asked, startled. "Smuggle him? You can't do that! Do I have to tell you again? You cannot break the law!"

"But we really want that holiday, and there doesn't seem to be an easy way to get it."

"What you are suggesting," Martin said, interrupting her, "is that if you want something that's forbidden by sensible laws, it's all right to ignore those laws if you want it badly enough. Like, you want to break into your neighbor's house to steal his favorite painting, fine, go ahead, because you really want it."

"Oh, shut up!" Eliska said angrily. "That's not the same thing at all, and you know it!"

"So tell me the difference," Martin said.

"Morality is the difference! I do not find it moral to help Zdenek, without a passport, to get over that damned border!"

"For a short holiday . . ."

"For whatever," Eliska said firmly.

"Baloney!"

"Martin!" Zdenek said sharply, "it's your mother you're talking to!"

"Sorry, I should have said she's not talking sense."

"And that is just as rude!" Eliska said, "so what, in your expert opinion, are we expected to do?"

Martin shrugged. "I don't know, maybe try again to get him a passport."

"A waste of time."

"Then he has to stay behind. You and I and Michal go, and when we come back, we tell him in great detail what a fine time we had. Vicarious, perhaps, but it will have to do."

Zdenek said nothing, but Eliska was shocked, and it showed. "You . . . you wretch!" she said, quite unable to control her anger.

But he shrugged again, "Then you and Michal and Zdenek go, by whatever illegal means you can contrive. I won't have any part of it. I will stay behind."

"No, Martin, no," Eliska said. "I won't go without you, I won't even think of it."

"Then that would seem to be the end of the vacation idea. A shame, it was good while it lasted."

"Will you shut up?" she asked again, "and listen to me? This time—you must."

"If I have to," Martin said, puzzled.

She looked at Zdenek and saw the slightest of nods. She took a long deep breath; it was time for the plunge. "It's not just a vacation," she said clearly. "Far from it. We're going to America."

He could not have been more startled. "What? What on the earth are you saying?"

"To Austria first, "Eliska said, "and from there, we take a plane to America."

"No! No! No! I don't want to listen to this."

"You will, boy," Zdenek said.

Eliska added. "It's what Zdenek and I both want to do, and we want you to come with us."

"To America?" He was shouting now. "No! What's in America that we don't have here?"

"Freedom," Eliska said, "freedom to think, even to say, what we like to think and say. And do what we wish to do."

"Which means chaos!"

"Freedom is not chaos, Martin. That's an idea that's been constantly drummed into you here. We call it brainwashing. Even by your teachers, among others, who are employed by the government you like so much. Don't they tell you in school to spy on your parents?"

"No! They do not!"

"Don't lie to your mother, Martin," Zdenek said severely. "We know very well that they expect you to listen to your parent's conversation and report on what is being discussed."

"They want to know how they can improve our way of life," Martin said angrily. "You find something wrong with that?"

"And pass on those reports to the Secret Police? Yes, I find something very wrong with that."

"They do?" Martin asked. "Where's your proof?"

"I would rather you didn't talk to me like that," Zdenek said, holding back his anger.

"It's common knowledge," said Eliska, interrupting them, and taking control of the argument again.

"Common knowledge among the anti-communists," Martin said, "people you seem to agree with. And if you and Zdenek are going to America, lots of luck. But count me out. I'm staying here, where all my friends are. But Zdenek can't go, can he? With no passport? So it'll finish up with just you and Michal. Great, just great."

No one spoke for a while, and then Eliska broke the silence. "Martin, dear, I will not go without you. There can be no question of that at all."

"Family sticks together?" he asked sourly.

She nodded. "Yes, something like that. The family is very important to me."

There was another very long silence, and then Martin said, "Jeez . . . . leaving all my friends here? Can I think about it for a while?"

"Not for long," Zdenek said. "We leave very soon."

"And you are somehow being smuggled over the border. I hate it! How can I be part of it?"

"There may possibly be no smuggling involved," Eliska said. "There may be a legal way."

Martin stared at her. "Suppose you tell me how."

"No," Eliska said, "I will tell you when I'm ready to. And meanwhile, should you talk about this to anyone . . . you know what will happen to us?"

"I know," Martin said harshly. "I know! I will go to my room now. I have some thinking to do."

The passage of time seemed to be endless, but the next day Martin announced, with a great deal of reluctance, that he would, after all, come with them. On the Sunday evening, Kornel brought the car and showed Zdenek what he had done. "Tip up the back seat," he said. "There's your hiding place."

Zdenek did so and was astounded by it all. After much discussion, Kornel simply refused to be paid for his work. "Just have a good journey," he said. Zdenek went back into the apartment and told Eliska the good news.

When Martin came in she told him, refusing any argument, "We leave tomorrow morning. Zdenek will drive to within a few kilometers of the border and he leaves us there. There is a legal tour going to Yugoslavia, government sponsored, and they will take him across, we will pick him up later on. This is the legal method I think I mentioned to you."

Martin frowned, "Well, I suppose that's all right."

"It is," Eliska said, "so quit worrying about it."

But now she turned to Zdenek, and he was shocked by the awful hardness in those pale gray eyes. She said coldly, "Vaclav. Before we leave, I must know what happened to Vaclav."

"Oh." He stared at her for a moment, and there was a little silence, but then he said briefly, "I'm going out for a while. I'll be back. Start packing." And then—he was gone.

Martin asked, dismayed, "What on earth was all that about?"

But Eliska shook her head. "God alone knows," she said heavily.

They went about their work disconsolately, and it was nearly three hours later that Zdenek returned. "Well?" Eliska asked.

He told her, "My Lodge, My Cell, was having a meeting this evening. I had decided to skip it. A wine cellar, with a dozen or so people all sick to death. Vaclav . . . I think we knew part of what must have happened to him, but now I have confirmation—and the details. He was picked up by the Special Police and thrown into prison. There, they beat him—to death. He didn't . . . he didn't break. He told them nothing."

Eliska's hands were at her face, and the tears were beginning to come. "Dear God," she whispered, and Zdenek went to her and embraced her.

"What can I say?" he asked.

She shook her head, "There is nothing anyone can say."

Then she heard Martin's voice, a whisper seeming to come from very far away, "Vaclav? Vaclav? He was the nicest guy who ever lived, a friend, and . . . they beat . . . they beat him . . ." He broke off, and turned away, not wanting them to see how very close to tears he was, too.

It was a miserable evening and night for all of them, but the morning came at last, and Eliska, unusually pale, said with a certain determination, "It has never been possible to change the past, has it? So now, let's do what has to be done."

Soon after midday, with Zdenek driving, the family was heading out of Ceske Budejovice, on their important and eventful journey.

It was Monday the first of August, in the year 1983.

CHAPTER TEN

It could not have been a more felicitous day for them. The midday sun was high over their heads, but there was cloud enough to stifle its heat, and the traffic, once they had left the city, was not too bad at all. They had first contemplated driving to the Bratislava crossing, but there was always the old argument that since this was the most important of the Hungarian border posts, it would probably also be the most efficiently staffed. Since immigration and customs officials were their enemies of the moment, they decided on the extra two hours or so of driving on to Komarno, a town that was only about the tenth the size of Bratislava, situated where Europe's most historic river, the great Danube, was met by the river Váh. It was famous for nothing more remarkable than the fact that the famous composer, Franz Lehar, was born in its nearby sister town, just over the river.

"Fewer people around to bother us," Eliska said decisively, "and I have this awful feeling that since we've been so lucky all the way along, we're maybe counting on luck a little too much."

Zdenek agreed with her. "You're right. Let's not take any chances that we don't really have to."

There was another argument greatly in Komarno's favor, as Eliska pointed out to him. The population here was mainly Hungarian. Its sister town in Hungary itself, Komarno Mezö, just across the bridge over the Danube, was within easy walking distance.

"Great," Zdenek said, "it means that at least, some of the official staff there will be Czech Hungarians, far less likely to worry about us."

They had also made the decision long ago that wherever they chose to cross it would be very late at night, when it was at least probable, they both thought, that the official personnel would be more tired than during the daylight hours. (In actual fact, this turned out to be a gross miscalculation.)

Zdenek, as was his habit, was driving at a fairly high speed, enjoying the recently rebuilt engine.

Eliska murmured, "We have about what, four hours of driving to the frontier?"

"Closer to five," Zdenek said.

"So what's the hurry?"

"Oh . . ." He slowed down a little and turned around to the boys in the back. "You kids all right back there? How does the new seat feel?"

"Hard," Martin said. "What happened to it?"

"Kornel had to work on it," Eliska said quickly, "two of the springs were broken, a couple of sharp ends poking up into the upholstery, and they could have hurt somebody's rear end. So he rebuilt it, made it as firm as it was when we first bought the car."

"He overdid it, of course," Martin said sourly. "He made it too hard. But it figures, I guess."

"It's great, Michal said, "I like it."

Martin said, "Well, at least it's bearable."

"Bearable?" Michal echoed. "What's that supposed to mean?"

"Bearable," Martin said pedantically, "means able to bear bears. Bears can sit on it without suffering. Like I am."

Michal looked up at him disgustedly. "I hate teenagers," he said, "you know that? I just hope I never get to be one."

"Our permanent child," Martin said, and Michal slugged him in the stomach and fell silent.

"So we have plenty of time to waste," Zdenek said, "We'll hang around for a while when we hit the more forested areas. Stop for some sandwiches in the evening. And soon after that, you have to drop me on the highway for those tour people to pick me up."

"Tour people?" Martin asked, scowling. "Yeah, I think you mentioned something about that."

"I did not just mention it," Eliska said, "I told you! There's a government sponsored tour going to Yugoslavia, and we've arranged with them to take him over the border, so that we can pick him up there later on."

"Bribery?" Martin asked. "And how much did it cost you?"

"That's none of your damn business!" Eliska said.

159

Zdenek added, "No bribery, boy, that's quite the wrong word. We just made a charitable contribution to the organization; it's all perfectly aboveboard."

"Sort of . . ." Martin said. "So where are these famous tour people now? Like, somewhere behind us? Or up front?"

"Oh, for God's sake," Eliska began.

But Zdenek said at once, "They're behind us, way behind us. All I have to do is wait by the roadside at the rendezvous and watch for a big yellow bus."

"Satisfied?" Eliska asked. But Martin said no more on the subject.

It was a plan that she and Zdenek had discussed at great length, and they were convinced that it would work—or at least that it was better than any other alternative they could find. Worrying about it, Eliska had said disgustedly, "That Martin!" I truly love him but sometimes he can be so . . . so pig-headed."

They were still in the agricultural areas at the lower elevation, with the mountains quite a long way off to their left. They came at last to a town called Trnava, on the river Trnavka, which had come here all the way from the distant Carpathian mountains. They stopped here for some espresso coffee, then wandered around the town for a while, just passing the time. When they came to the beautiful old cathedral, they stopped. Eliska asked Martin, curiously, "Did you ever wonder why it was that all of these places of worship got to be closed down or at least stopped functioning?"

"No, why should I?" Martin said, shrugging. "We know very well that religion always takes people's minds off far more important matters."

"Like what?" Zdenek asked.

Martin gestured, a little angrily, "Like well-organized government!"

"I suppose there is an argument there," Eliska said, "but there's an awful lot of people, I've been told, who disagree with it."

"A minority," Martin said. "We surely can't be expected to give every minority in the country its own foolish way. Can we talk, if we have to, about something else?"

Eliska sighed. "I guess so," she said.

Zdenek too was a little impatient. "Preferably," he said, "about something less argumentative. Now, shall we be on our way?"

All around them were fields of wheat, flourishing marvelously well in the rich dark soil, and there were deep ditches on both sides of the road, sometimes running with water from the area's multitudinous lakes, some of which were very large, some no bigger than tiny ponds.

"The wheat fields," Zdenek said. "Later on, we'll wrap Michal up in a blanket and put him to sleep in one of them." He looked to Eliska, "You, too, perhaps?" But Eliska shook her head. "I won't sleep a wink until we're well over that damn frontier." But there was another problem on her mind.

The governmental control of children here was even more severe than it was for adults. She knew well what would happen if Michal, at seven years old and still very much a child, were to be found by the border authorities wide awake in the car in the middle of the night; they would simply take him away, put him to sleep in some home under their control, and heavily penalize the parents by probably arresting them, or most certainly making them wait until well after daylight before releasing him.

She explained this carefully to Zdenek, who was not quite as well informed in such matters as she herself was. She made sure that both Martin and Michal heard his, too.

She asked Michal, "You know what this means, baby?"

"Baby?" he asked, quite shocked. "Did you say baby?"

"What I meant was darling," she said. "Sorry, I'm a little nervous just now."

"What for?" He asked. "If you want me to be asleep, you just tell me when. You want me to snore, too?"

"No, darling, let's not overdo it."

"I snore all the time at home to annoy Martin, I'm very good at it."

"Correct on both points," Martin said.

Eliska went on, very gently, "Just a convincingly sound sleep, even if someone should shake you by the shoulders to make sure that you really are asleep."

"Someone does that," Michal said darkly, "I'll bite his hands. Both of them."

They drove on until well after darkness had set in, passing through the small town of Nové Zámky, where Zdenek said, with a great deal of pleasure, "My ancestors built this little town, too, as a fortress to hold off the Turks, of all people."

"The great John Zizka himself?" Martin asked, always glad to know more of the family history.

But Zdenek shook his head. "No," he said sadly, "John, or Jan, was long since gone. His grandsons. But when the old man died, the Hussites were losing more battles than they won. Today, they're just memories."

161

"Which is where," Martin said, "the best people always live. In other people's memories."

They left the town and came to open country again, and Zdenek said to Eliska, "We're as close as we dare got to the frontier now, less than a half-hour's drive. So now—the wheat fields for those who want to sleep."

He parked the car a little off the road, a few trees and bushes there, and they all jumped over the running-water ditch and went into the field. Martin was carrying blankets, and Zdenek had both hands full of the bread and cheese and sausages that they had brought with them. Michal, it seemed, was already fast asleep on that hard back seat. Eliska picked him up and carried him heavily, set him down, and wrapped the blanket around him against the cold night breeze. When he was well tucked in, he said clearly, "I'm sleeping, Mommy. You want me to snore now?"

"You're an absolute wretch, aren't you?" she said, "and I can't think why I love you so much. Sleep tight, darling."

"G'night," he murmured, and was asleep almost immediately.

"Me, too," Martin said. "I'm going to stretch myself out and doze for a while."

"I think we can all do that," Zdenek said. He looked to Eliska, "Are you alright?"

"Of course I am. You too?"

"Sure." He squinted at his watch in the moonlight. "Nearly ten o'clock. I'll keep watch and wake up at midnight. I have this idea that you're not getting nearly enough sleep. Is two hours going to be enough for you?"

"For God's sake," Eliska said, "quit worrying about me. You can be very boring sometimes, can't you?"

"The only reason I worry," Zdenek said, "is that I believe it's lack of sleep that's keeping you in such a lousy mood. A real wet blanket. Try cracking a joke once in a while." He was scratching at his beard, wishing he could trim it.

"The only joke we have on this operation, as you call it, is yourself," Eliska said. "It would help us a great deal if you'd think about that."

She lay down on her back on the soft straws of the crop, stretched herself out wearily, and looked up at him. "It's going to be one o'clock in the morning before we drop you off. Martin is going to wonder how come the tour bus is driving all through the night. We didn't think about that, did we?"

"As a matter of fact, I did."

162

"Of course," Eliska said, scoffing, "I should have known that. So what solution did you come up with?"

"The obvious one," Zdenek said, "the one that says the hell with it. So why don't you just curl yourself up now and go to sleep? G'night."

The waiting time passed slowly, but midnight inevitably came at last, and with it, the border preparations began. Zdenek woke them all up and said, "About thirty minutes to the frontier from here, by my reckoning." And for Martin's benefit he added, speaking to Eliska, "Where was it they said they'd pick me up? Soon as I can see the lights? Something like that?"

"What they said," Eliska answered, "was keep to the edge of the forest until you can see the reflection in the sky of the border lights. Step out of the trees and onto the road as soon as the headlights of the bus flicker; that's their signal. Once the bus with you in it is over the border, they are going to drop you off at an old abandoned gas station there, about two kilometers down the road, just a wreck now, but a very good point of reference, very easy to find. That's where we pick you up again."

"Got it."

They drove on, with Zdenek still at the wheel, until there they were, the bright border-post lights putting all the stars into obscurity and offense against nature in itself. Zdenek said, "Well, this is where we part company for a while."

"Right," Eliska said, "but there's one thing to be taken care of first." It was a little matter they had decided would be the best thing to do.

She turned to the half-asleep Michal, "Darling, we might be a very long time crossing over this border, if you have to go, you won't be able to go there. Best you go now."

"Mama," he said sleepily, "I don't want to."

Smiling at him, Eliska said, "And I have to go, too . . ."

"Oh, all right then."

She turned to Martin, "Take your flashlight and go with him, I don't want him falling over in there. Take his hand, he's only half awake."

"I am not," Michal said, but he took Martin's hand anyway.

"I'll start walking then," Zdenek said. "See you all in Hungary. Won't that be nice?" He sounded still very much on edge, a man who liked his sleep and missed the comfort of a decent bed. He hated, too, the necessity of forcing himself to wake up at a given time for this damned midnight crossing, which he had never really thought was much of a good idea; would they all not be better prepared to handle any emergency if they tackled the bureaucrats when they themselves were wide awake instead of being half asleep? Sure, he'd agreed when Eliska had suggested it, but he was beginning to wonder why it was that he was always so damned acquiescent with her.

The toilet visit took only a few minutes, and when they returned to the car, Zdenek was no longer to be seen, and it was Eliska who took the wheel and drove on for little more than a half kilometer or so, with Martin beside her, and Michal asleep again on the back seat.

When they reached the frontier, the lights were blinding in their intensity, but as they had always hoped, there was very little action going on. There was only a single car ahead of them, a late model Mercedes with East German license plates. Three officers were going over it as the driver and a woman who may have been his wife were standing there and not trying to conceal the bad temper they felt. They both had that indefinable look of tourists, the kind that always demand unjustified respect.

The officers had opened up the Mercedes' huge trunk, had removed and opened three suitcases, and were tossing the contents, item by item, carelessly onto the ground. One of them said to the woman pointing to her feet, "Your shoes, I wish to examine your shoes."

It made her furious. "Warum?" she shouted. "For why?"

He shouted back at her, as angry as she was, "Sofort! At once!" For a moment their eyes met. It seemed to Eliska, watching, that he was about to seize her and throw her to the ground. But in a moment she gave way and muttering something, she bent down and took off her shoes. The officer snatched them from her and studied them meticulously, paying particular attention to the heels, even putting them to his ear and shaking them violently. Apparently satisfied, he tossed them to the ground and gestured to her, "Hände hoch," and when she raised her hands there was murder in her eyes.

He patted her all over her body, beginning at the armpits and continuing all the way down to her thighs, the sides, the back, the front, not even sparing her breasts.

Watching, Eliska wondered why the women's husband—if that's what he was—was accepting all this so readily. A wimp? Or was he, too, perhaps enjoying her humiliation?

But there was a far more important worry on her mind now. This was obviously a search for smuggled money. What if they were to treat her the same way . . . ?

It seemed that Martin was reading her mind, "They're looking for money," he said.

She nodded. "Yes. I think that's probably what they're doing."

"I hope you're not carrying your money on your body?"

"The legal allocation from the bank is in my purse," she said patiently. "The good stuff is hidden away, and yes, it's on my body."

"Oh mother! Whereabouts, for God's sake?"

Eliska dropped her eyes for a moment. "Never you mind," she said quietly.

Martin said nothing, but he was plainly discomforted. They waited, and waited, and waited some more. Finally the Mercedes ahead of them was almost finished. The two German tourists were trying to repack their belongings, but two of the officers were 'helping' them by gathering clothing up in bundles from the ground and just tossing them into the car all higgledy-piggledy over the floors, until they were through. The arm of the barrier swung up, and the first officer said to them gruffly, "Aus, aus, aus, get out of here." Eliska thought it sounded a little like a dog barking. The big car drove off, and the steel barrier, painted in red and white stripes, dropped down again to prevent any hurried escape if someone wanted to risk the assault-rifle shots that would surely follow any such foolish attempt.

The officer looked back at the Skoda and signaled it forward, and as Eliska started up again, Martin whispered, "Smile, Mother, smile everywhere. We're nice people on a ten-day vacation."

"Of course, I know that. I'm not a fool."

"Just trying to be helpful," Martin said, sighing.

Eliska drove on slowly, then stopped correctly at the hand signal and said politely, "Good evening, officer."

"Your passports, please?" he said coldly.

She told him, handing it to him, "There's just the one. My children are included on my own."

"The child in the back there? Is he sleeping?"

"Of course! At eight o'clock every night, wherever we may be, we put him to bed. And he sleeps like an angel."

"An angel?"

"The angels of legend."

"Your husband is not with you?"

She knew that they would check it out, a lie was not permissible now. "I have no husband at this time," she said. "I have a companion, with the permission of the Party."

"His name?"

"His name is Zdenek Zizka."

"Ha!" the officer said. One of the Zizka trouble-makers?"

"No," Eliska said, "the Zizkas are no longer antigovernment. Quite to the contrary, they are known as strong supporters of the Party."

"And very good people." Martin said.

The officer turned his cold eyes on him, "You will talk to me, boy," he said, "when I tell you. Not before."

"My apologies, Comrade," Martin said. He hated being spoken to as though he was a child, but one thing he was sure of was that it was never safe to argue with a cop.

The officer held his look for a moment, but then gave Eliska his attention again. "And why is it that your Zizka is not traveling with you?" he asked.

"He cannot leave his work," Eliska answered.

"Which is?"

"He is a leading agriculturalist. At this time of the year, he's very busy."

"How much money are you carrying?"

"A little spare change," she said, "plus six hundred Yugoslav dinars which the bank kindly allowed us for a ten-day vacation in Yugoslavia." She reached into her purse, took out an envelope, and handed it to him. "Twelve fifty-dinar bills," she said, "together with the authorization."

He thumbed his way through the money, checked the permit, and handed it all back to her. He studied the passport now, scowling as he flipped the pages, and at last he said, "I will study this. You will wait here." He turned sharply away and went into his office with it.

For a long, long time they waited, and holding on to her patience was a very severe problem for Eliska. She looked at her watch, twenty minutes had passed already. She said angrily to Martin, "What the devil is he doing, can you answer me that?"

Martin shook his head. "I have absolutely no idea. I never was much of a mind reader."

He got out of the car and moved a pace or two around, stretching his arms out wide and bending his knees up and down as though to get the stiffness out of his bones. One of the officers by the barrier called out to him, jerking his thumb out in a gesture, "Get back in the car, boy! You hear me? Back in the car! Now!"

He clambered back in, and said quietly to Eliska, "That window there, I couldn't see much, but he was on the phone. It may well be that he was calling Ceske Budejovice—just a guess, of course—to check up on Zdenek. Or he could have been calling his superiors for instructions. Who knows? Patience, Mother. If anything's wrong we'll find out in time."

166

They still had to wait, and Eliska was fast becoming more and more devastated, both mentally and physically. Another twenty minutes went by, and then the hour was up and she was deep into the worst kind of acute despondency. She was conscious that her hands were shaking, that she was even perspiring, though the night was cool. She said to Martin, quite savagely, "This is absolutely intolerable! There can be no reason for them to behave like this!"

Martin said shortly, "It may just be possible that they're doing what they believe they have to do, no? If you'll only compose yourself for a couple of minutes, you'll know that everything's all right. They just have to check us out, so stop worrying, calm down and we'll find out as soon as . . ."

He broke off and then, "Here he is now. Calm, keep calm, take a good deep breath."

The officer was approaching them, the passport in his hand. He held it out to her, and she took it from him with a movement that was almost subconscious. "You may go now," he said. "You're free to go."

She could only stare at him. She said, stammering, "I beg . . . beg you pardon . . . What did you . . . did you say?"

He answered her rudely, "What's the matter, are you deaf? I said go! So you go, you understand? Or should I talk German now?"

Eliska pushed the gearshift into first, and it grated horribly.

"The clutch, Mother," Martin said urgently, "your foot on the clutch!"

She came to her senses partly, and threw the clutch in while the accelerator pedal was still floored. The car leaped forward like a savage animal pouncing on its prey, and in moments they were on the famous bridge over the Danube and slowing down to a more reasonable speed.

Martin sighed with relief, and Eliska sighed too. She asked him, quite exasperated, "How can you expect me to concentrate on my driving? He let me through without any kind of a check? And there I was worrying my head off in fear of a body search! He didn't even want to look at our baggage! He didn't want to know what other kind of money I was carrying. I can't believe it! And what was he doing all that time with my passport? For well over and hour, if you please. And you expect me to drive this wretched car intelligently? You've got some nerve, I must say!"

"But, Mother—"

"And don't 'but, mother' me, either. We're getting close to the Hungarian customs now, so calm down."

Martin did not answer her. It seemed hardly the time to pick a new confrontation.

They came to the second half of the frontier, where the Hungarians gave her hardly any problems at all. They examined the passport briefly, handed it back, and then just wanted to ask a whole lot of questions, most of which seemed to be quite unimportant.

"Are you carrying, between you," the officer asked, "more than five hundred cigarettes or more than one hundred cigars?" He added, "The young man is over sixteen, I think, is he not?" And therefore old enough to smoke?"

"Going on eighteen," Martin said, a little sourly, and Eliska said, impatiently, "Neither of us smokes, Officer."

"Or more than five hundred grams of tobacco?"

"No tobacco, either."

"Any small gifts exceeding a cost of one thousand forints each?"

"None whatsoever."

"Your Tourist Board will have told you, I am sure, that you may bring in any amount of foreign currency, but that you may carry with you only one hundred forints in Hungarian currency and it must all be in coins, not bills. I am also sure that you must be respecting this regulation?"

"Of course, Officer," Eliska said. Martin added, "You bet."

It still went on: "Are you carrying with you any works of art valued at more that one thousand forints?"

"We have nothing with us worth so much," Eliska said, trying to hide her anger now. "In fact, we are carrying with us no works of art at all."

"But should you buy any while you are here, please remember that you need an export permit for them."

"Of course. Are we free to go now?" She indicated Michal, asleep back there, to the officer. "I really must get the child into a proper bed. Can we go, please?"

"You may," the officer said, unsmiling. "Just remember that our traffic laws are very strict here. You are no longer in your Czechoslovakia."

But Eliska was already moving off fast. "These Hungarians," she said furiously, "they can drive you nuts without even trying."

Komarom Mezö, a town of very little size or importance, save for the crossing, seemed to go on forever, but at last the buildings began to thin out and in another ten minutes or so they were once again in open country. The moon was bright, and Martin asked, a little casually, "Is this where we start looking for that old abandoned gas station to pick up Zdenek?"

168

"A little further on, I think," Eliska said, and she was right, Only a few minutes later, there it was ahead of them, more of a ruin than anything else, just a few old sheets of corrugated iron and some bits of lumber hardly worth carrying off. It was mostly just the sign there, in rusting reds and blues, indicating what its original purpose had once been. She pulled up, stopped, yawned hugely, and said, "Well, he obviously hasn't arrived here yet. Why don't we all go into the forest and sleep for a while?"

"Why don't you and Michal do that?" Martin asked. "I'd rather sleep in the car." He paused very slightly for effect, and then added, "On that excessively hard seat."

The sudden realization hit her hard. Was there room for denial? She knew that there was not. How then, to handle such a worrisome eventuality? How even to gain some time to find a response. She looked Martin straight in the face and said coldly, "If you have something to say, Martin, why don't you just say it?"

"I'm not really too fond of beating around the bush," Martin said, "but there are, now I come to think of it, a couple of things that intrigue me."

What was that emotion trying to force its way into her consciousness? Was it truly only anger, or was there some hatred there, too? "Such as?" she asked, almost trembling with an unwanted emotion. He answered her at once, "Oh, I was wondering how come we never saw or even heard that tour bus of yours. Wondering if it ever really existed. Wondering, too, how that rear seat in the car came to be so hard, as though someone removed all that nice, soft cushioning and built, what, a sort of baggage compartment underneath it? For purposes of smuggling something over the border. Or maybe somebody? Like Zdenek?"

How was she ever going to face this calamity? She knew there was a fight coming up and hated it; knew also that the only thing she could do now was to hit it hard. She held his look for a moment, trying to gauge the depth of his emotion, and then, forcing upon herself a calm that did not come naturally, she turned away and helped Michal, only half awake, into the front. Then she knocked tree times on the side of the seat, the sign to open the bolts in there. She heard them thrown back, and she took hold of the seat with both hands and threw it forward almost savagely, as though it were an enemy itself.

"Come out, darling," she said to Zdenek, very quietly. He stepped out and stood for a moment staring at Martin, not understanding. Martin held his look, and then turned to Eliska and said, with barely-contained fury, "All I want now is to get the hell out of here!"

"Martin!" Zdenek said angrily, "you will not use such language on your mother!"

"I want to get back to Ceske Budejovice, where I belong." Martin went on, quite out of control now, "but I can't do that, can I? I'm on the wrong passport, so why the hell couldn't you have told me?"

"Martin!" Zdenek said.

But Martin went on, bitterly. "You couldn't trust me, is that it? You can't trust me to keep my mouth shut? Your own grown son? It makes me sick to death."

"Will you listen to me?" Eliska asked.

But he shouted, "Just tell me one reason why I should!"

"Because," Eliska said, holding onto her composure, "Zdenek and I decided that the less you knew about it, the better for all of us, even though you made such a stinking fuss about it! And keep your voice down. Michal's trying to get back to sleep."

"And that's your biggest worry."

"No! My biggest worry is that my own grown son, as you choose to call yourself, won't do me the courtesy of listening to what I have to say."

"I'm listening," he said coldly.

She went on, "It was not an easy decision, Martin. We both decided that if we should be caught, you ought to be in a position of being able to say to the police, in all honesty, that you knew nothing about it."

"And you think they would believe me?" Martin said, not hiding the sarcasm.

"We hoped they would," Eliska said. "I did tell you, it was not easy for us."

"So now?"

"Now," Zdenek said deliberately, "we drive on for a while to leave the frontier further behind us. We sleep in the fields till daylight, and it's my hope that when we wake up this foolish quarrel will be behind us, not to be spoken of again. You hear me, Martin? You understand what I am saying?"

"Yes, sir," Martin said again.

With Zdenek at the wheel once more, they drove on, and within the hour they found a very promising area of vast barley fields on one side of the country road, and a huge orchard of peach trees on the other. They parked the car, went deep into the field, spread out a couple of blankets, and dropped off to a welcome sleep, with the air sweet with the rich scent of the ripening peaches.

It was the sun that awoke Eliska at last, coming up over the distant skyline. They were in the lowlands here, with no mountains to slow the spread of gold and red to the east. She looked at her watch, just after six in the morning, which meant about three hours of good sleep behind them. She saw that Michal was still sleeping, that Zdenek and Martin were both slowly opening their eyes in that early morning, lazy half-awakeness that is sometimes so pleasing.

She stood up and stretched her arms out, and looked over to the road and stared in sudden shock.

"Zdenek," she said quietly, urgently, "don't move, darling, don't move an inch. Martin, wake Michal and pass him to me, then follow me back to the car. We have visitors. The police, two of them. One in the police car, the other examining the Skoda."

"Oh my God," Zdenek said. Martin was shaking Michal awake, pulling him up and pushing the sleepy body to Eliska. She held him tightly by the arm, "Come with me, Michal dear."

They moved towards the road, no more than fifty or sixty paces, and she was smiling at the officers when she came to them.

"Good morning, Comrades," she said, "and what a glorious day it is."

Martin added his, "G'morning."

"Is this your car, Comrade?" the officer asked.

She nodded. "Yes. I'd been driving for too long. I was afraid of falling asleep at the wheel. I hope we're not breaking any rules by stopping here? I just had to sleep for a while."

He looked at the license plate, "You are tourists, I see."

"Yes, we're on our way to Yugoslavia, for a short holiday by the sea. Ten days."

"Do you know that you left your car unlocked while you were sleeping over there?"

"Er, yes, the lock doesn't work very well. Sometimes I lock it and can't unlock it again. It's a very old car."

"I see. We do not have a high crime rate here, but still—always lock the car when you leave it unattended."

"Yes," Eliska said apologetically, "I will be more prudent in the future."

"May I see your driver's license, please?"

"Of course." She handed it to him, and he merely glanced at it and handed it back to her.

"But," he said, "I would like to be assured that all the contents of your car are still there, just as you left them."

"Yes, I understand."

"I'll take care of it right away," Martin said. He went to the front of the car, flipped the lever, and raised the hood. "Three suitcases, "he said, "a picnic basket of food, a tool box, a jack, a can of oil, a foot-pump for the tires. Yes, looks like everything's there that should be there, officer."

He looked across the road to the peach trees, "Could I pick, say, half a dozen of those peaches to take with us?"

The officer stared at him for a moment, scowling, "As you ought to know," he said, "those orchards are government owned, and what you are suggesting is the theft of government property, for which the penalty is not less than sixty days in jail, plus a fine of one thousand forints.

Take one single peach, young man and I will feel obliged to arrest you."

"Oh," Martin said. "Got it."

The officer turned back to Eliska. "Be advised," he said severely, "always lock your car when it is unattended."

"In the future," she answered, "I always will. I thank you for your advice." Without another word, the officer went to his car, and they drove off.

"Five minutes," Eliska said, relieved but still cautious, "just to make sure they're out of our hair. Then go get Zdenek."

She made Michal, still sleepy, comfortable on the hard back seat while they waited. When at last Martin shepherded Zdenek back, and she told him what had happened. "So close, now," he said, musing. "Haven't we learned that it's so often at the very last minute that calamity hits us?"

"I think you're right," Eliska said, "and I'm always worried that we're maybe getting a little too over-confident sometimes."

It was true, of course. The amount of actual and careful planning that had been put into this escape was disastrously small for so demanding an enterprise; two people beaten down by oppression and determined to elude it—but with very little experience of the kind that would assure them of success. Zdenek knew that it was so.

He nodded, and sighed heavily. "No way can we get careless now," he said. "We'll do what has to be done, of course we will, and we must."

"I hate it, darling, as much as you do." Eliska said, "But, yes, it's back to your prison, I'm afraid, until we get off this road. That police car is ahead of us. If we should overtake him and find him parked somewhere and he sees you aboard—even driving—no, we can't allow that to happen."

Zdenek agreed and hid himself, and Eliska drove off again. Ten minutes later they saw that same police car parked, exactly as she had prophesied, on the roadside, turned around now and facing the way they had come. She waved to them cheerily as she passed by, but they paid no attention to her at all.

After a sensible twenty more minutes had passed, they came to a right-hand intersection. Martin said, "Take it, Mother, we're too far south anyway."

Eliska did so. After ten more minutes, Zdenek was out of his cage and once more in control of their destinies as they headed for the border of Yugoslavia.

CHAPTER ELEVEN

It was frustrating for them to realize that once they had crossed the Czechoslovakia/Hungary border, they were only a twenty-minute or so drive from the border with Austria, which was to be their next step along their momentous migration. It meant an almost subconscious need to drive directly west, as though the little Skoda had a mind of its own and wanted to take them to their destination.

But the frontier there, so tantalizingly close, would be as heavily and dangerously guarded as that directly from Czechoslovakia itself. Martin, pleased with his new job as Navigator-in-Chief, was constantly telling whoever was driving, "South, we have to move more to the south." It was he who carried the maps they had brought with them, long out-of-date as they were. Zdenek himself knew most of the route from their previous visit, but this time it was the northernmost part of Yugoslavia they needed, not the southerly area of the pre-paid beach house where they might have gone.

"Slovenia," Martin said, "Slovenia is the part of Yugoslavia we need, which is now due west of us. Too far south will take us into Croatia, which is something we can do without."

He was right; the Croatians had always been alarmingly difficult people, especially in their treatment of foreigners, a rough-and-ready race who just naturally disliked outsiders. The Slovenians to their north were the elite of the country, for the most part gentle, intellectually inclined, and correctly thinking of themselves as sophisticated Europeans rather than as artless Balkans. Though their own language was Slovene, a form of Serbo-Croatian, their main lingua franca was German, except in the extreme west, where it was Italian, and English was also spoken by the better-educated classes.

174

(This linguistic richness was brought about by the fact that the Serb and Croatian family of languages were all quite unintelligible to anyone not born into them, employing between them two separate alphabets, both the Latin and the Cyrilic.)

Now Zdenek was once more easing to the south, leaving behind them the rich and fertile bank of the Raba river, which they had been following for more than an hour. The highway they were on was marked 18, but it suddenly changed to 6, and Martin said, "Hey, hold it everybody, we've come too far."

Zdenek pulled to a stop, and turned to him. "Too far for what, exactly?"

"Too far for safety." Martin replied, "There's a small town ahead of us." He was straining his eyes to study the tiny print, the map colors faded. "Looks like it's called Bayânsenye. It looks too like it's a border crossing, just a couple of minutes down the road. The nice guy driving our car doesn't even have any papers." He sounded very bad tempered.

Zdenek was already making a U-turn and heading back at speed, and when the road sign changed back to 18, he asked Eliska, "Are we still thinking of crossing at midnight? It hasn't helped us a great deal so far."

"Third time lucky, they say," Eliska replied. "Yes, we cross at midnight."

"So that gives us plenty of time for a good solid meal someplace, and a nap in the barley fields for a couple of hours, too."

"You're hungry again?"

"What do you mean, 'again'?" Zdenek asked. "I'm always hungry, you know that."

"Yes, me too," Martin echoed. And Michal put in his two cents' worth, "How about some apple pie?"

"Take the next turn to the left," Martin said, "a minor road, there's a village along there—I can't decipher the name. Hang a left, and then a right at the fork."

"Goulash," Zdenek said, relishing the idea, "real Hungarian goulash, and the hungry man's personal gift from God." And fifteen minutes later, they were there.

It was a tiny vine-growing village, the forest all around it, with two small state wineries set a little apart from one another. All the houses, not more than a dozen or so of them, were built from the local red sandstone, a few of them had a Turkish aspect in their turreted chimneys, a reflection of the long gone days when this was Turkish territory. There was a small but

175

very strong stream running nearby, with an old watermill straddling it, no longer functioning. There was a two-pump gas station there, one for gas and one for diesel, a general-purpose store, and restaurant and bar. "Praise the Lord," Zdenek said.

And Martin echoed the thought, "Great, I love it."

The restaurant was quite an experience for them. The only other diners there were two men, quite well dressed, who had about them that indefinable air of government employees. The men stared at them as they entered, then whispered quietly to each other. "At a guess," Zdenek murmured, "state wine inspectors?"

"I think you might be right," Eliska said, "take a good look at their table." Their plates were piled high, and there were four bottles of wine there, too.

It seemed that this tiny restaurant was run by one person, and one person alone, an elderly lady who seemed to be the cook, the waitress, the cashier, and the general factotum. She came to their table and began to tell them, in Hungarian, what was on the dinner menu. Eliska said, amiably, "Deutsch, bitte? German, please?"

It seemed that the good lady chose to speak only Hungarian when she told them what the menu for the meal would be, not one word of which they understood. They nodded their heads politely from time to time, and for good measure Eliska added a ja, ja, jawohl, or a gut, gut, once a while, but when the meal came at last they could not believe their good fortune.

First, there was an excellent soup with goose-liver dumplings, followed by pancakes stuffed with chopped lamb, braised in tomatoes and sour cream, and finally a sweet strudel filled with cherries and cheese curd. And just automatically, there was a bottle of the famous wine, known almost worldwide a Bulls' Blood.

Zdenek could not have been more satisfied, and he wanted to put forward an idea that he was half sure Eliska would reject. "A long and very tiring journey," he said to her, "and how long ago was it that you had a good sleep in a good bed, even for just a few hours?"

Eliska catching on at once, was already shaking her head, but he went on, nonetheless. "This place is almost certainly an inn as well as a restaurant."

"No darling," Eliska said.

He wanted to be heard. "I can't get a room here, I have no passport, but you and the boys? I can walk out, you pre-pay for a couple of rooms, get a good sleep for a few hours, move out at around two in the morning, and we'll meet some place and hit the border. Don't you think that's a good idea?"

"I think it's a great idea," Eliska said, "and I thank you for it. There's only one thing wrong with it."

"Which is?"

"It won't work." She sounded terribly frustrated.

"How come?" Zdenek asked.

"Two reasons. First of all, if you were to walk out of here and leave us alone, don't you think it might look a little suspicious? Especially since our two government friends over in the corner table there are still throwing very doubtful looks at us every so often—no, don't look at them now."

"Oh."

"Even more importantly, my passport, as you must know, would have to be handed in here for the night. My passport! The only valid document we have between us! No way is it ever going to leave my possession for even a couple of minutes."

"Ah, yes, you have a point there. So it's bed in the barely fields again. Well, so be it."

"There's not the scent of ripening peaches to lull us to sleep here," Eliska said, "and grapevines honestly don't smell very nice. But did you notice the old water mill there, right at the edge of the forest?"

"Sure."

"There's all the heavy shrubbery in the world there," she went on. "Right next to the sound of falling water? What do you think?"

"I think that's a wonderful idea," Zdenek said. "and since this is our farewell to Hungary . . . what's the name of that apricot brandy they make here?"

"Barrack," Eliska said, "Yes, I think that's a wonderful idea, too. Perhaps we can regard it as celebrating the end of our difficulties."

The elderly lady brought them the two drinks they ordered, and she looked at Martin, pointed to him, and asked, "Sö r? Bier?"

"Beer?" Martin asked, "No, thank you, not this time around." He looked at the very large brandies they had been served, and shyly said to Eliska, "I may have to take over the driving sometime."

"What, you drive?" she asked, "Since when, might I ask, have you been able to drive?"

"Oh, about six or seven months, I think," Martin said shortly, and when she and Zdenek just stared at him, he went on. "Some of the guys at school, they drive their parents' cars all the time. Once in a while, I kind of help them out. I'm very good at it, as a matter of fact."

"I can't believe it!" Eliska exclaimed.

He answered her very seriously. "Try me, Mother," he said. "Why don't you do that? Just try me."

Zdenek was shaking his head slowly from side to side, "Learn a little something every day," he murmured. "They do say it's character building."

And Michal chimed in with his small contribution. "It's true," he said. "He's taken me for a drive. He's even let me sound the horn."

"Well, I'll be damned," Zdenek said. "We'll have to think about that, won't we?"

He raised his glass to Eliska. "Na zdravi," he said.

She raised hers to him and to Martin, too, "Na zdravi, good health, to all of us. Every day now seems to be better than the one we just left behind us. I think . . ."

The elderly lady came soon and started clearing the dishes away, which Zdenek thought might be a sign that closing time was approaching. He paid the bill, infinitely small for such a splendid meal, and they returned to the car in very good spirits.

All right, Zdenek said to Martin, "you drive."

"You mean I can?" Martin asked.

Zdenek nodded, "That's what you told us."

"Great!" he said, and got behind the wheel.

"You'd better sit in front with him," Eliska told Zdenek, quite unsure about all this. "You might have to grab the wheel, or hit the brakes, whatever. I'll sit in the back with Michal; he's going to be fast asleep soon now."

"No, I won't," Michal said. "I'm gonna wait for the waterfall, so there."

"Manners, child," Eliska said, sighing.

As Zdenek climbed in beside him, Martin said hesitantly, "I think we should drive a little to the east when we leave here, sir, not to give the impression that we're heading for the frontier."

"Oh? And why would that be?"

"If those two nicely-dressed gentlemen should be watching us," Martin suggested, "it might be better if they think we're just ordinary tourists, heading back to Gyor, or maybe Budapest. It's just a feeling I have, no real reason." He sounded quite unsure of his argument and was surprised how quickly Zdenek agreed with him.

"Our feelings," Zdenek said, "are often far more valid than reason is. Let's do that."

"We turn off the road as soon as we hear the waterfall again? Into the forest?"

"You've got it."

They followed the road till they were out of sight of the restaurant, with the forest on their left getting more heavily wooded the further they went, and then Martin slowed down and finally stopped, listening. "That's it, I think," he said.

Eliska nodded, "The sound of falling water," she said absently. "I like it."

She could not quite understand, at first, why the crecent euphoria seemed to be drifting slowly away from her, but the more she thought about it, the more clear the reason seemed to be, and she hated it. "I'm so tired," she muttered to no one in particular, but Zdenek swung around and reached a hand out to take hers.

"It's natural enough, sweetheart," he said. "How much real sleep have you had since we left home? A few restless hours wrapped up in a blanket on the ground? And the anxiety."

"Yes. It's mostly the worry, I think," Eliska said wearily. "There are moments, just moments, when I feel that my nerves are shot to hell and gone. It's not a very pleasant feeling. At other times, I'm even ashamed of it."

"Don't be," Zdenek said, "we're close to the end of it all now. The Hungarian border is coming up soon after midnight. These people have all been good to us so far; there shouldn't be any problem. And when we hit the Yugoslav side of the frontier . . . well, we've done that before. I don't expect any difficulties."

"Last time," Eliska said, worrying sorely about it, "you were driving and doing all the talking. This time, if there's any trouble, I'll have to handle it myself, because you'll be cooped up in your wretched cage." Her voice sounded forced, and Martin looked at her, and then looked quickly away.

Zdenek squeezed her hand tightly. "For the last time," he said. "and first of all, my hiding place is uncomfortable, yes, I must admit to that, but it's certainly not wretched. And as far as your worrying about the stupid questioning that we always have to suffer is concerned, I have the utmost confidence in you. I'm quite sure you can handle it with no difficulty whatsoever, just as you've done before. Damn sure."

"Yes, of course," Eliska mumbled.

179

Martin had turned off the road now and was easing the Skoda over the meadow, the headlight dimmed as he searched for an opening among the trees. He found one that seemed suitable and drove into it slowly.

Zdenek said, "Good, nice driving, and we're very close to the stream now. Can you hear it?"

"I hear it," Martin said, "and there it is."

He swung the wheel over and drove on a little further till they were on the bank of the stream itself. The fall was a little downstream from them now, the sound of it very satisfying to them all. The old water wheel in the distance was faintly visible in the bright moonlight.

They found some soft grasses to lie on, and Zdenek spread out the two blankets for Eliska and Michal. He saw that they both fell asleep very quickly indeed. He moved away with Martin and said in a whisper, "Good night, young fella." And soon, they, too, were both fast asleep, with the comforting sound of running water.

It was Zdenek who was the first awake, as always, very soon after midnight. He woke Eliska first, with a gentle hug and kiss and a quiet, "Sleepy-time over, sweetheart, but we'll have some more very soon now, plenty more. How do you feel?"

She stretched out her arms and yawned. "Fine," she said.

"Truly?" he asked.

And she nodded, "Truly. I was a little depressed before, perhaps, but now . . . yes, truly fine."

"So let's be on our way, shall we?" Zdenek asked. He went on, "We're quite close to the frontier now. Once we're in Yugoslavia there'll be no more of this night-time crossing business, which has been a burden for all of us. To cross into Austria, we'll cross that bridge when we come to it, and by all reports, a whole lot of refugees seem to have done that. So it can't really be very difficult."

Not difficult? There was simply no way that any of them could have known how very far from the truth this assertion would turn out to be, eventually.

It took them no more than fifteen minutes to reach the border, and theirs was the only car there. But the nighttime officer on duty was not in the least as tired and weary as Eliska had hoped, and indeed expected. Instead, he looked full of the kind of energy that so often suggests satisfaction in an important job being well done. But he was polite and courteous, and even a trifle jovial.

"Good evening," he said. "What a wonderful night it is! May I see your passports, please?"

"Just the one," Eliska said, as usual. "My children are on my own."

"Ah, yes, of course." He took it from her and handed it back after the most cursory glance imaginable. Then the obligatory questioning began: "Exportiren zie," he began in German, the tourists' lingua franca, "are you exporting any Hungarian works of art, and if so, do you have the necessary permits?"

"No works of art," Eliska said, "and therefore no permits."

"Have you any Hungarian currency in excess of one hundred forints in bills, not coins?"

Martin saw the impatient look on Eliska's face, and he answered quickly, "We have no Hungarian currency at all, officer. We're just on our way to a ten-day vacation in Yugoslavia."

The officer turned back to Eliska, "Regulations demand," he said, "that I inspect the baggage you are carrying. If you would be kind enough to open the hood for me?"

"Of course," Eliska said. Martin saw that she was fuming. She got out of the car, went to the hood, fumbled there uselessly, and in a moment she just gave up. She said, in a very loud voice, "Where on earth or in hell is the lever to open this damned hood? Martin, where is it?"

Martin was out of the car in a flash, and he said, forcing a broad grin, "Mother! Don't you remember? I fixed that hood last night. I know it's hard to get your hand under it now. Let me do it for you."

He threw the lever, opened the hood, and said to the officer, "Last night it was rattling horribly. I had to tighten up that lock. Looks like I might have overdone it. I'll fix it in the morning."

The officer said to Eliska, teasing her, "You're driving in a foreign country without knowing how to open up the hood of your car? Lady, it's hard to believe!"

"My fault," Martin said, still grinning foolishly, "I'll take care of it."

The officer pulled out a single suitcase, opened it, just fumbled around inside it for a moment, closed it, put it back where it belonged, and slammed down the hood. "That will be all," he said.

"Thank you," Eliska said, forcing it. "Are we free to go now?"

"Yes, ma'am," the officer said, smiling. "I'll not hold you up any longer."

Eliska got back into the car and slowly drove on to the Yugoslav side of the frontier. There it was even less of a hassle for them. The Slovenian officer merely checked the passport, wished them a happy vacation, and waved them on.

"Hallelujah!" Martin said. "We're in Yugoslavia at last! The next item on the agenda, Mother, is to free Zdenek, once we're clear of the town. Would you like me to take over the wheel, give you a rest? I'm sure you must need it."

Eliska shook her head. "No," she said flatly, "I don't like your driving too much." But she smiled, put a hand on his knee, and gently said, "No offense, Martin dear. It's just that I'm more comfortable about my own driving. Yours takes a little getting used to." She patted the knee and said again, "No offense, all right?"

"Sure," he said, "no problem."

She drove on for a while as the buildings around them gave way to farming country, large meadows with animal manure in great piles by the roadside waiting to be picked up and smelling strongly of just that, the rich and not unpleasant odor of good farmland. They passed a huge cigarette factory with large billboards everywhere illustrating its function. They came at last to a great field of tall-growing plants on strong stems that turned out, on investigation, to be sunflowers, their huge heads bent down with the weight of their seeds, awaiting the harvesting.

There was no traffic at all now in this quiet and pleasant rural area. Zdenek was quickly released from his prison under the seat. He stretched his arms and his legs and looked over the fields. He said, "Ah, yes, sunflower seeds. It's a big industry here." He looked at his watch, and said, "Nearly one o'clock," he said, annoyed about the lateness of the hour. "That gives us four or five hours of sleep. The farmers here will be up and about as soon as it's light." He turned back to Eliska, "You think that will be enough for you?"

"Enough," she said briefly. "You'll take over the driving in the morning and I can doze very nicely in the car if I get sleepy, though I don't think I will. There's too much to worry about, for instance, how to get into Austria, now that we're nearly there."

"Don't worry so much," Zdenek said. "Sleep first. We'll worry afterwards, if we must. We've always solved our problems somehow or other, and that's what we'll do again."

They slept well among the sunflowers, trying hard not to destroy any of them, for a very good reason. They were no longer in a country where every worthwhile enterprise was state-owned for the profit of the state alone. This was all private property now and, as such, respected.

182

It was Zdenek's reliable instincts that woke him, just as the sky to the east of them was beginning to brighten with long streaks of a beautiful red-gold, the rising sun not far behind them. He checked his watch again, five-twenty, and woke the others, as they went to the car. He opened the front passenger door for Eliska.

She said, "No, I want to drive today."

He looked at her in surprise. "But don't you want to doze for a while? You only had about four hours sleep."

She said, "No, I'm not tired. We're nearly there. I just want to get my hands on that wheel."

He nodded, understanding, and smiled, "Of course, whatever you say." As they set off again, they saw that the first of the farmers was coming out of his cottage. Some more of them were carrying rakes or hayforks to start their day's work.

Eliska took her eyes off the road to swing around and ask Martin, "How far is it to the frontier?" A truck was coming at them, sounding his horn, and Zdenek grabbed the wheel, but Eliska was holding it firmly. "Relax," she said, "I saw it." But then, she slowed down from her high speed and was even laughing softly. "Sorry about that," she said lightly, "I plead guilty to a moment of carelessness. But I assure you, it won't happen again. And does anyone know how far we are from the border?"

Martin took a moment or two to recover from incipient panic and studied his map. "Depending on where we want to cross," he said, "seventy or eighty kilometers, call it an hour to an hour and a half of driving. There seems to be quite a number of border crossings in this area."

"Look for a village called Kaltic," Zdenek said. "It's a border point, apparently not very far from Maribor, which is a major city."

"Kaltic, Kaltic, Kaltic," Martin mumbled as he searched, and Eliska asked, "What's so special bout Kaltic?"

"Underground stuff," Zdenek replied. "You're not even supposed to know about it, but since we need it now," he sighed and went on, "you may or may not know that in my Cell, my Lodge, we try to keep tabs on refugees fleeing the country. It's not always easy. But in the last six months, from Ceske Budejovice and its environs alone, nineteen refugees have crossed over into Austria, or tried to cross over. We know for sure that fourteen of them made it, as we've heard from them. The other five? We know that two of them were caught and imprisoned. The other three? No news at all. Perhaps they made it and didn't bother to let us know. It can happen. We believe that a few of them may have just lost themselves in the forests

183

and died. But the chosen crossing place has always been Kaltic, where it seems, there is a very flourishing smuggling industry. Not only in cigarettes, which cost in Austria nearly three times what they cost in Yugoslavia, but electronics as well, and also people. Refugees. They guide them over the mountains, in exchange for cash, their cars, whatever they have to barter with. And so . . . look for Kaltic, Martin. That's where, one way or another, we cross over."

"Kaltic, Kaltic," Martin muttered, "there's no such place." But then, "Hey! Wait a minute!" he said. "I found it! Take the next side-road on the right, Mother, in forty minutes we're there."

And they were. Eliska drove around for a while and found at last the crossing point, where more than a dozen cars were lined up, being allowed through one by one. The Austrian post was quite close to that of the Yugoslavian, and just as busy. She parked there and just sat in the car watching. And in a little while Zdenek asked, "What is it you're looking for?"

"Just wondering what we have to do next," she answered. "I'm finding it out." She asked Martin, "This is Kaltic, is it not?"

"Yes, Mother," Martin said, "this is Kaltic."

She looked at Zdenek, "The smuggler's paradise?"

He nodded, "I guess you might call it that."

She drove around some more, away from the crossing, and found a small street in which almost every building seemed to be a bar. She indicated one at random. "In there," she said, very much in control of herself, "find me a smuggler I can talk to. I'm going to get us over that damn frontier, come what may."

"If you're sure of what you're doing," Zdenek said, "I'll see what I can do."

"I know exactly what I'm doing," Eliska said, "and that's something of which you can be absolutely sure."

"Very well."

He went into the bar at once and ordered a beer. Even at this early hour, it was quite busy. He sipped the drink and said to the barman, casually, "Looks like a nice little town, Kaltic."

"Not too bad," the barman said, polishing glasses.

"Got one hell of a reputation."

"It has?"

"Smugglers everywhere, they tell me."

"Not true," the barman said. "Sure they hang out at one or two of the bars, looking for stuff to smuggle over the border; that's what they tell me."

"But not this place . . ."

"No way." He grinned. "The owner's son is a cop. We have to behave ourselves. And so do our customers."

"Suse." Zdenek finished off his beer in one long gulp, and asked, "What do I owe you, friend?"

"Six dinars."

Zdenek laid a twenty on the bar and slid it across, "Why don't you keep the change?"

The barman looked at him, and Zdenek asked very quietly, "Any other good bars around here, maybe?"

The barman slid the note into his drawer, found another glass and started polishing it. He looked around, this way and that, and mumbled just as quietly while studying the glass, "The Florida, two streets up, turn left." He raised his voice and said affably, "See you again sometime, right? Been nice talking with you."

"You too," Zdenek said, and left. He went to the car and said to Eliska, "Two streets up on the left-hand side, a place called the Florida."

"Nice work," Eliska said. "So jump in."

They found the Florida with no difficulty. There was a garish sign under its brightly painted name that said, in English: 'American drinks served. Hi-balls. Jack-on-the-rocks.'

"A tourist trap," Zdenek said. "So be it." He started to get out of the car, but Eliska stopped him. "My turn," She said. "Just wait for me."

"Well, I don't know" Zdenek began.

She interrupted him, "There are a whole lot of things women do better than men," she said, "and negotiating is one of them, right?"

"Right," he said, and grinned at her. "So go to it."

She seemed to be in the best of spirits imaginable as she stepped out and went to the bar, and there, inside, a stranger was sizing her up almost at once.

She was sitting at the near end of the long counter, and he was a little further down, alone. There were perhaps a dozen or so people in the room, but she was the only woman there. She caught his eye, half-smiled, and turned away again, toying with the ginger ale she had ordered.

He was tall and broad-chested, a physically powerful man, and quite good-looking, with carefully combed hair and a neat mustache, with dark, deep-sunken eyes. He wore a well-cut gray suit with a white shirt and a conservative tie that made him look like a prosperous businessman.

He moved along the bar towards her, smiling. He said in German, "Good morning." And that he asked the almost mandatory question in this part of the tourist-busy world, for him in its simplest form. "Deutsch? Srbska? Italiano? Maqyar?" Meaning: what's your language, and where do you come from? Then he added, surprisingly, "Czech?"

It surprised her indeed, but she answered in her mother tongue. "Yes, I'm Czech, and you?"

"Born in Prague," he said, laughing. "My family came here nearly ten years ago and decided not to return. I soon found work, soon found out too, that private enterprise is far more profitable than working for the profit of a detested state. So now I make a very handsome living taking cigarettes into Austria, Yugoslav cigarettes, the Austrians go crazy for them." He looked at her ginger ale, "Buy you a slug of vodka to put in that?"

Eliska shook her head. "No, thank you, too early in the day for me."

"What about this evening? Are you doing anything for dinner?"

"I hope that somehow, with your help, perhaps, I'll be better occupied."

"Oh, really? Well, that sounds exciting. Tell me how."

"How often do you make that trip over the border?"

It seemed to puzzle him and bring on a slight frown. "Oh, three or four times a week on the average. Why do you ask?"

She smiled. "I find it fascinating."

The frown did not go away, and he asked her, "What is it exactly you are doing here alone, in this rather disreputable bar?"

"Looking for someone like you," Eliska said. "And I can't tell you how pleased I am to have found you."

Now the frown went, and there was a large smile there instead. "Well", he said, "how nice! So again, what about dinner tonight? They do have a few very good restaurants in this little town. We can go to my very comfortable house afterwards."

"Wait!" Eliska said, interrupting him, "No! We have business to discuss! Very important business for both of us!"

He stared at her. "What . . . what kind of business?" he asked her, and he was obviously getting angry.

She stared back at him. "Am I getting some sort of a runaround?" she asked. "You smuggle cigarettes over the border. I take it that you can smuggle people, too. There are four of us, two adults, and my two sons. We

186

have a very good Skoda car which we are prepared to hand over in full or at least part payment for showing us one of those hidden tracks through the mountains we've heard about so much. So, can we talk shop?" For quite a long time, he held her look. He said at last, in quite a friendly manner, "Will you believe me when I tell you how pleased I am to learn that you are not, as I thought, a prostitute?"

She was in sudden shock. "What?"

"We are both mistaken, Madam. I came here looking for smugglers, as I believe you are so doing also. But my reasons are legitimate. I am the area manager here for Alpha cigarettes, and we have a huge delivery to make this evening. We go through the customs, paying all the necessary fees and part of my job consists of making sure that there are none, or very few of our mortal enemies, the smugglers, in the immediate vicinity." He sighed. "They sometimes hold us up, even on the highway, and loot our trucks. They carry guns; we cannot. I have not found any that I know by sight, which is most of them, here today. Perhaps I am luckier than you are, dear Lady. Now, will you accept my offer of a drink? I feel you might need it."

"No," Eliska said, her voice coming straight from an iceberg, "I will not. I do not. Good day." She turned on her heel and stalked out, a picture of wounded dignity. But there was a furious anger there too, and when she reached the car, Zdenek saw it at once.

"No luck?" he asked.

"None," she said flatly. "But there's not far to go now. I will try something else."

"Such as?"

"That's what I have to find out."

She backed the car up and made a U-turn, quite capably, and drove back to within sight of the frontier, then she stopped and just watched. The Yugoslavia side was open, the barrier arm in the raised position, and the guards there were just signaling the cars through one by one. The Austrian barrier, however, was down, being lifted for each individual car to pass through after inspection. "Wait for me here," Eliska said, and left the car to move in closer on foot and wander around there.

Zdenek, puzzled, looked to Martin. "Have you any idea," he asked, "what she's doing now? Because I'll be damned if I do."

Martin gestured helplessly. "A mystery to me, too," he said. "All I know for sure is that when Mother makes up her mind to do something, there's just no power on the face of the earth that is going to stop her."

"That," Zdenek said contentedly, "is absolutely true. What she's up to now, I guess we'll find out soon enough." He smiled, and added quietly, "The famous philosophy at work again, I guess. Wait and see."

So, they just waited.

Eliska was in the fullest possible control of her senses as she watched the action around her very carefully, until she saw that a Yugoslav officer was, in turn watching her, too. He was quite young, good-looking, with no official air of severity about him. He beckoned her over with a raised finger, and she went to him, smiling.

"What are you looking for, lady?" he asked casually.

"Oh, just looking," Eliska answered. "It's not that much of a big deal, is it?"

"A big deal? I'm not sure what that means!"

"No one being checked this side, just a few minutes for each car on the Austrian side."

"Well, that's the way things are around here, most of the time. Are you going through to Austria?"

"Thinking about it," Eliska said, holding the smile.

"You have a passport?"

"No."

"Oh." He scratched at his chin for a moment, and said at last, "Tell you what. You go, start walking. When you get close to my comrade over there, start running, fast, real fast. You just might make it."

"That's great," Eliska said, "the only thing is, there are four of us, and we have a car."

His expression changed at once, and he shook his head slowly. "A car?" he echoed. "No, lady, that's a different matter altogether, and maybe you'd better just forget all about it."

"No!" Eliska said sharply. "I don't want to forget it! So what's the best thing for me to do? Will you tell me that, give me some advice?"

"Lady," he asked sternly, "all right with you if I pretend I didn't hear you?" He moved away, turning his attention to an approaching car, and Eliska called out to him, "So if you didn't hear me, maybe you can't even see me either, right?"

The officer looked back at her and said nothing.

She went back to the car and drove over to take her place in the line. When Zdenek asked her what she had in mind, she just shook her head and murmured, "That officer there, he may not know it, but he gave me a very good idea. You'll see. In a very few minutes now."

188

The line moved slowly forward, and she was passed through the Yugoslav side, like all the others, without stopping, with five or six cars ahead of her, a half-car's length apart. One of them, she saw, was very close up to the vehicle ahead of it. And in this case, the arm of the barrier stayed up.

She turned to Zdenek and said quietly, "Soon, now, very soon."

"Soon what?" he asked, but she made no reply at all.

In a moment there was only one car ahead of them, a fine Mercedes limousine. She eased forward slowly, fumbling in her purse as though she might have been looking for the necessary paper, until she was almost bumper to bumper with the Mercedes.

"Oh, my God." Zdenek said, understanding now, his face lighting up into what was almost a wide grin. Martin too was staring at her, astonished, excited, and speechless.

The barrier stayed up for the limo, and Eliska floored her pedal at once. They shot forward and she wrenched the wheel over fast to hit the grass verge of the road and wrenched it back again as she shot past the Mercedes, missing its highly-polished body by less that the thickness of her little finger.

Zdenek yelled, "By God, you made it!"

Martin was yelling excitedly too, "Mother! I don't believe it, we're in Austria!"

Eliska steadily held her course, forcing every iota of speed out of the Skoda, and she held it even as a siren far behind her blared out its angry, urgent note.

Now, its siren adding to the din, a police car came racing after her, with a second one close behind it. In moments, the lead car was passing her, swerving rapidly in front of her, and Eliska virtually stood on the brake pedal to avoid the inevitable crash. The second car braked to a sudden halt close behind her.

In moments, the police were pouncing on the Skoda, guns in hand, throwing the doors open and pulling them out. Someone was shouting, "Out, out, out, the kid stays there! Everyone else out! Up against the vehicle!"

Zdenek, Martin and Eliska were thrown against the car, and the shouts now were, "Hands on the roof! Come on! Spread those legs, spread'em!" Zdenek was shouting, "Take it easy, for Christ's sake! You beat up on women here?"

Even Michal, crying his heart out, was shouting too. "Please . . . please . . . don't hurt her!" And not one of the officers was paying them the slightest attention. A sergeant said angrily, "Weapons check. Come on, get with it," and there were hands all over the three of them, with a voice at last, "Nothing. No weapons, Sarge."

The sergeant turned to Zdenek, "Where are you from?"

"Ceske Budejovice," Zdenek said, "that's in Czechoslovakia."

"I know where Ceske Budejovice is," the sergeant said, "so what are you doing down here?"

"We're refugees," Zdenek answered, "looking for asylum in Austria."

"Asylum? Join the crowd. Crashing through the border post? That's a hell of a way to start looking." He addressed one of his men and indicated Zdenek and Martin, "These two, back of your vehicle, I'll take the woman and the kid in mine. I'll need a driver for the Skoda, too."

"My child!" Eliska cried.

The sergeant tried to comfort her, "No one is going to harm him, lady! Come to that, no-one's going to harm you folks either. Unless, maybe, we have to."

"So what happens now?" Zdenek asked, sensibly trying to control the fear that was still in him.

The sergeant told him, "Now is when the interrogation begins." He said coldly, "A place called Triskirchen, at the Border Patrol main offices. That's where we're going now, just a few miles up the road from here. Maybe long enough for you people to realize the severity of what you've tried to do." In the momentary silence, he added, "Last time someone tried that trick, his car was faster than ours and we had to open fire. You want to think about that, maybe?"

In a very short while the little convoy was on its way, a somewhat shopworn Skoda and two bright and shiny police cars. When they arrived, Eliska got out of the car and Michal jumped out and ran to her. He was in tears. "Mama!" He said, "What's happening to us? Are you all right?"

"Of course, darling," she said, "I'm fine."

Martin moved to them and laid a hand on Michal's shoulder. "It's going to be all right, kid," he said, "just hang in there as best you can. Will you do that for me?"

"Don't see why I should have to," Michal said sullenly. He was already brushing the tears away.

The sergeant elbowed his way past them and took Eliska's arm. "You'll come with me," he said roughly. He turned to one of his subordinates, "The

190

older boy and the kid can wait in the office till someone comes for them. Put the big guy in one of the cells. I'll start off with the woman."

"For Christ's sake!" Zdenek began furiously.

But the Sergeant shouted at him, "Shut up! You hear me?" With no more ado, they got hustled off into the building.

CHAPTER TWELVE

Eliska fought hard to contain her anxiety at what was happening, knowing full well the difficulties that were surely awaiting them all now. She knew, too, that she would find a way out of them. She quickly came to the decision that an extremely polite and courteous attitude would be advisable now.

The sergeant had taken her to his office, sat her down opposite him at his desk, produced a notebook for his use, and was sharpening a pencil with his pocket-knife. On the wall behind the desk there was a large photograph of President Rudolf Kirchschläger, and a much smaller one of Chancellor Sinowatz, a large board of police photographs marked "Wanted," a bookshelf crowded with legal manuals, a few wooden chairs, three large filing cabinets, a smaller desk with a typewriter on it, and little else.

The sergeant sat down at last and looked at Eliska in silence for a while, as though trying to figure her out. "Your passport, please," he said, and she handed it to him. "Madame Eliska Kucera, Yugoslavia only," he said, flipping the papers.

She nodded. "Yes, in my country these days, that's the only place you can visit outside the Warsaw Pact countries."

"Yes, we know that. What made you want to emigrate? Was it economic difficulties?"

"Well, no," Eliska said. "As a matter of fact, I was very well paid as assistant to one of the senior staff at the Telephone and Electricity Company."

"Then were the police after you, perhaps, for some kind of criminal activity?"

"No!" Eliska said, "Nothing like that at all!"

"Were you a member of the famous underground?"

192

"Not that either."

"So was your decision to leave the country prompted by purely political reasons?"

Eliska hesitated. It sounded to her rather like a trick question, but what could she do? She said, sure that the truth was the best answer, "I suppose you could call them that, yes."

"Are you, or have you ever been, a member of the Communist Party?"

"No, absolutely not. In order to get my passport, I had to sign up for a projected series of lectures on Marxist-Leninist philosophy, but we escaped before I actually got to attend any."

"Which presumably you did not want to do."

"That is correct. I would have hated them."

"Is it also correct," the Sergeant asked, "to describe you as anticommunist?"

She knew that the Austrians were quite fervently Catholic, which meant, she was sure, that she was on safe ground here. "Yes," she said, "I am, emphatically so."

"But you never joined the underground. Why not?"

"I felt that it might put my two sons, or perhaps, I should say, the whole family, in danger."

The sergeant worried about it for a moment. Then, "That sounds a little obscure to me. How so?"

"In our schools, they teach the children to spy on their parents. Had they believed, or even suspected, that I was actively involved in the antigovernment movement, it could easily have severely damaged our family relationships. As it was, there were subtle efforts being made to turn my eldest son, who is seventeen, into a communist."

"Successful efforts?"

"It's very hard to read the mind of a teenager, but I do know that ever since he was old enough to think for himself, he was being thoroughly brainwashed, as all the school children were."

The sergeant grunted. "The man with you is your husband?"

"He's my companion."

"Meaning what, exactly?"

"Meaning," Eliska said easily, "that we are not married. We have been living together for about four years now."

"With no thought of regularizing the relationship?"

"There's always been plenty of thought about it. He wants to marry me. I have always refused."

The sergeant was very uncomfortable. "I could ask you why," he said, "but I suppose that's none of my business. Is he a communist?"

"Far from it," Eliska said, "very far from it! He was always a very active member of the underground."

"But you chose not to be."

"If his activities were discovered, he would have been put in prison and probably killed. Who then, would take care of my children?"

"You had no objections to his underground activities?"

"No! I was always very proud of him! He will confirm everything I have told you."

"Give me a few moments," the sergeant said, and began writing in his pad. He looked up in a while and said slowly, quite genuinely puzzled, perhaps even a little sympathetic, "You were reckless enough, I might even say mad enough, to try and force your way past our Immigration and Customs post. I must ask you then, is there any insanity in your family?"

"No," Eliska said. "There never has been, none at all. I know what I did, and I knew what I was doing when I did it."

She hesitated for a moment, and then asked, "May I speak quite frankly, sergeant?"

"It is my hope," he said, still puzzled, "that you will continue to do so."

"In that case," she continued, "perhaps I should tell you how very desperate I was. I was not thinking only of myself and of my companion. Yes, we hated the life we were forced to live! But of much more importance was my conviction that both of my two sons were being indoctrinated into communism. I must also tell you that this is no imaginary fear. Quite to the contrary, it is very, very real."

Her hands went to her face as the memories came surging painfully back. She went on, "I have personal knowledge of this danger. Many years ago I fell in love with and married a man who later became the most dangerous kind of communist. He was the father of my son, and the husband I subsequently divorced. He too knew how easily children can be brainwashed. When I crossed through that barrier, my only thought was that I would do anything to prevent this from happening again. Yes, it was desperation! On the Yugoslav side, a Border Patrol officer suggested that I might make a run for on foot. I tried to do it in a car. It was a mistake, and I readily admit it."

The sergeant rose to his feet and began pacing around, his thumbs stuck into his belt, a look of intense concentration on his face. Shortly, he turned back to Eliska and said, "You have of course, committed an offence against our immigration laws, and you will surely admit that your defense is a very unusual one to say the least."

"Yes, I suppose I must agree with you. And this is the time to tell you something else. We are hoping for asylum in Austria, but only for long enough to arrange further transit to our eventual destination, which is the United States of America. We have been told that there's an organization here in Vienna, that will help us do that."

Was the sergeant beginning to sympathize with her? At the very least, being less antagonistic? She thought that perhaps he was. He said, nodding his head, "It's called The Political Refugee Assistance Organization. But they need clearance from us, to weed out the criminals for them."

"For heaven's sake," Eliska said, "do we look like criminals?"

He permitted himself something like a smile. "Lady, most criminals do not wear a big red 'C' on their foreheads! We have had a few cases here where we have cleared honest looking refugees for asylum, only to find out that a few months later they were arrested for burglary, bank robbery, fraud, assault, even murder. It is a risk we dare not take."

Then the questioning began all over again, mostly nothing more than a repetition of the questions she had already answered. It was driving her to distraction. She chose to put up with it as best she could, not letting her impatience show. And when, at last, it came to an end, the sergeant said, "You will remain here for a few days, except the two children will be kept in a home we have here for this purpose."

"What?" Eliska exclaimed.

He raised a placatory hand. "Please, have no fear, they will be very well looked after by an expert in child care until you and your companion are freed from our cells here."

The word horrified her, "Cells, you say?"

"Yes, but they are not severely uncomfortable, as cells go. There will be more questioning. We must be absolutely sure that you are telling the truth, and only the truth."

"Cells? Dear God! Are we going to be separated?"

He was back to his accustomed severity now. "Yes, that is mandatory. I must, Ma'am, forbid blasphemy in my office."

"Of course," Eliska said. "Forgive me, it will not happen again."

He rang a little bell on his desk, and when an officer appeared at the door, he said to him, "Take Mrs. Kucera to cell number three. Make sure the sheets are clean and the floor well swept. Then send in her husband, that is to say her companion. I'll see him next."

The officer escorted her down the long hall. When they passed a door marked with the sign "W.C." she stopped and asked him, "Do your cell have toilets in them?"

He shook his head. "No, Ma'am," he answered. "When you are in need, you bang on the door. Someone will come and escort you."

The cell was not as uncomfortable as she had expected. The bed had a straw mattress on it, a fresh sheet, and a single, fairly good blanket. The door was made of heavy wood, and the solitary window was batted, with nothing much to look at beyond it. She had heard it said that a prison cell without a window was purgatory, denying the prisoner the satisfaction of knowing that there was a world out there somewhere.

She lay down on the bed and wished she could sleep, knowing that this would not be easy. Wondering what the immediate future would bring, she doze off for a while at last.

It was midnight by her watch when she was awoken. It was a different officer, come to escort her back to the office for yet another interrogation. It turned out to be almost identical with the last. She wondered why the questions were always much the same and figured that it must be an attempt to trip her up, to find out if she had been lying previously.

These midnight examinations went on, incredibly, for a full week before her captors appeared to be satisfied, and she was back with the sergeant again. His attitude now had changed completely, all the severity seemingly gone, and replace by a mood that was almost benevolent. Most important of all, Zdenek was there, too, embracing her fervently as the sergeant waited politely for their greetings to end.

"Are you all right, sweetheart?"

"Yes, darling, and you?"

"Sure, and I think we're free to go as soon as the boys arrive. Someone told me they're on their way here now."

"True," the sergeant said. "A car has been sent for them. I have learned that they are both in very good spirits."

"Just to see them again," Eliska whispered.

"Very soon," the sergeant reiterated. "And you will be pleased to learn that your stories have both checked out. It means that you will now be free to go about your own business in Austria for as long as it takes to acquire permission to emigrate to the United States of America. That will be in a few months."

He went on to tell them that since authorities had to know where they would be, rooms had been booked for them in the Maribor Hotel in a small town called Neuhaus, some thirty kilometers from Triskirschen, where they were now. It was also thirty kilometers from Vienna itself, where the offices of the Political Refugee Assistance Organization were located. These people would find a sponsor for them to help in the emigration process. He also told them there was an American Ambassador whom they would have to approach for the necessary American entry visa. He gave them these two addresses.

It was all very exciting for Eliska, and she could hardly wait to see her sons again, to be with them after all this time. They hung around the office for a while, and the sergeant even sent for coffee to offer them. He told them that Neuhaus was a very pleasant little town, with good shops and restaurants. They would be free to find work there if they so wished, not necessarily for the extra money. The hotel bills and many other necessities being paid by the refugee organization as a loan. It would be expected to be repaid within a year of arrival in America. It is "the honor system," the sergeant said, "and we are told that it is very rare indeed that these debts are not honored."

At long last the boys arrived. They were indeed in the best of spirits. After the embraces were over, Martin told them delightedly that he had spent most of the time there teaching his lady guardian how to play chess. "I don't think she's ever going to be expert," he said, "but who knows? All she wants to do is play every hour of every day. It's considered a good sign."

Michal could only boast of the amount of ice cream that had been lavished on him. "It's good thing," he said seriously. "We should do more of that at home."

There were still a few details to be settled. The sergeant told them that they could keep the Skoda. It was technically being held as evidence if they were to be prosecuted for the attempt to crash the immigration barrier. "However," he said, "the court has decided that in view of several mitigating circumstances, which have not been explained to me, such prosecution is being held in abeyance against the various reports of your behavior while you are in Neuhaus."

"Oh God . . ." Eliska murmured, and then remembering, "I mean yes, of course, I understand."

"However," the sergeant continued, "before attempting to license that wreck of a car to Austria, you really will have to do something about the dreadful pollution of its emissions."

"It's a very good little car," Eliska protested.

"But there again," he said, "The refugee people will be only too pleased to help. They will show you where all the junk yards are when you choose to abandon it, as you surely will."

The time was passing, but at last an officer came in and said, "Ready, Sarge. The Skoda's been gassed up with one of our own cars on standby. The driver is Officer Haydn. He's all set to go. He's got friends up in Neuhaus."

"Oh, he has, has he?" the sergeant asked. "Well, I still want him back no later than eight o'clock tomorrow morning."

The office nodded, "I'll see to it."

The drive to Neuhaus was uneventful, and they found the Maribor to be a very good little hotel. The prospect of having to wait here for several months was a little depressing. On the third day of merely reorganizing themselves, they decided to drive over to Vienna to make contact with the group that was going to be so important an adjunct to their efforts. They also wanted to try and make an appointment with the American ambassador.

This was their first ever visit to what was perhaps the only city in Europe that could rival Prague itself in splendor, though of a vastly different kind. They were soon to find out that the people of Prague prided themselves not only in the splendor of their city, but also in a certain preference for efficiency in their activities. The context here was one of no worry, no rush. They had an attitude of laissé-faire on a remarkable scale. The culture here was a Kaffeehaus culture, which Eliska found quite delightful. Zdenek seemed to regard it with somewhat less favor. For him its first manifestation surfaced at the offices of the Political Refugee Organization.

They found the office on Leharg Street easily enough and were greeted by a young receptionist. She seemed to have heard of them. "Eliska Kucera," she said, stubbing out her cigarette, "and Zdenek Zizka. Yes, the immigration people in Neuhaus have told us about you." She flipped some pages in a file. "Your case has been assigned to Frau Ender."

"Then could we see her, please?" Eliska asked.

"Yes, of course," said the young lady, taking up her pen. "When would you like an appointment?"

"Well," Zdenek said, "right now would be great."

The secretary looked at her watch, and she was smiling broadly, "Not a good time of the day to find her," she said, "Frau Ender will be in one of the coffee houses. I don't know which one. Tomorrow, perhaps, around three o'clock?"

"Fine," Eliska said. So it was arranged.

The next call was at the American Embassy, where a very efficient young man introduced himself as Herr Raab. American of Austrian heritage. He was an assistant to the Case Disposal Executive. How could he help them? He asked. He listened carefully as Eliska explained their needs, interrupting her once to say, frowning, "Kucera, Kucera, yes, I think we have a record of that name." He found a file and opened it, and said, "Ah yes, the Political Refugee Organization gave us your names, Zizka and Kucera, yes." He spent a few moments skimming over one of the pages, and said, smiling. "You will be pleased to hear that you come to us with their highest recommendation. It seems that we are thinking in terms of political asylum rather than a visit, am I correct?" When Eliska nodded, he asked, "You are husband and wife, I take it? Or is it, forgive me, father and daughter?"

"Neither," Zdenek said. "You have a problem there?"

Under the desk, Eliska kicked his ankle, but the young man said easily, "No, of course not! It merely means that I have to give you two separate forms to fill out instead of just one." He handed them the two documents, four pages each. Indicating the far corner he said, "That table, you'll find ball-points in the holder there."

The questionnaires took them almost forty minutes of study, and halfway through Zdenek said sourly, "They want to know if I ever had syphilis. Can I tell them it's none of their damn business?"

"From me," Eliska said, "they want to know if I am a prostitute, or ever expect to become one. The answer to both questions is a polite no."

"They also want to know," Zdenek went on, "if I have ever been arrested. If so, for what offenses, and how much time did I serve? I think I should tell them that I prefer to keep my criminal record secret, and see what they make of that."

Eliska laid down her pen and looked at him. "What's come over you lately?" she asked. "Ever since we crossed that last border to safety, you've been as bad tempered as an ox that's lost his favorite sow. So what's the matter with you?"

"Nothing's the matter with me," Zdenek said shortly. There, as far as he was concerned, the matter ended.

They handed in their papers, and the young man told them that their immigration staff handled all requests for asylum. He told them that this department was grossly over-worked these days, so they should expect it to take a little time. He looked at the forms, "You are both staying at the Maribor Hotel in Neuhaus, I see. Expect to hear from us in about two months. You have a good day."

Out on the street, Zdenek said angrily, "Two months! Looks like nothing ever gets done the same day in Vienna. How can they live like that?"

"Let's go have a coffee," Eliska said. "Across the square, there, that looks like a nice place."

A nice place it was indeed. The mocha coffee was out of this world, and Michal was enthralled by the pastry they ordered for him. It was smothered with schlagsahne, the local heavy whipped cream. When the check came, Eliska was in shock, "Roughly four times the prices of the Deminka cafe back home," she said dispiritedly. "We're not only paying for what we ordered, but there's a 'Value Added Tax' as well, whatever that might be, and—can you believe it?—a 'Liquor Tax' as well? Did we have any drinks? I think not."

Imperatively, she summoned the waiter, who didn't really know what the obligatory VAT was either. The Liquor Tax, he

Explained, included the coffee and cream because sometimes the customers wanted a slug of brandy in their morning coffee and that the schlagsahne often contained a modicum of kümmel, a liqueur of formidable propensity.

"What?" Eliska asked, dismayed. "You mean that you serve alcohol here to children?"

"No, ma'am," said the waiter, "only if you ask for it."

She gave up, paid the bill, and turned to Zdenek. "You know what this means if we have to stay in Austria much longer?"

"We'll be running out of money?"

"We'll very quickly be broke unless we both find work. So let's head back to Neuhaus and start looking."

The next day they were back again in Vienna, to meet with Frau Ender, an elderly lady of great dignity who assured them, first of all, that her organization would be behind them every inch of the way. "We are dedicated" she said, smiling, "to the kind of assistance that only we can provide, through long experience with troubled refugees. You realize, of course, that when the time comes, you will be traveling separately?"

"But . . . but no," Eliska said. "Separately?"

"Oh, yes," she said, and explained that there were two categories to deal with in the organization, one being families, the other being singles. The one was always sent to one area in America; the other could easily be split up into different destinations, and at different times as well.

To Eliska, this was most alarming. "But we are a family!" she said. "We can't be separated like that!"

Frau Ender shook her head. "No," she said gently, "in our books, since the child is under sixteen, he must stay with his mother, but the elder boy, over sixteen, is classed as an adult and will be sent separately, as your, ah, companion will be." She sighed. "It would be so much simpler if you were married, but we have to classify you as an unmarried mother." She hesitated for a moment, and then went on. "It is none of my business, of course, but I really do want to help you. Is there any reason why you should not be married? Is one of you still married to someone else perhaps?"

"Nothing like that," Zdenek said. "She just won't have me."

"How very gallant of you," Eliska said tartly. She sighed, and told the good lady that they had contemplated it from time to time. They were in fact, thinking of getting married in America.

"Then do it here," Frau Ender urged. "Do that, bring me the certificate, and I will happily see that you remain together."

Zdenek turned to Eliska. "Looks like you're going to be stuck with me after all," he said. "Don't worry about it. I do have all the qualities that make for a good husband, you know."

"You do?" Eliska asked. "I just wish you wouldn't hide them so expertly."

Frau Ender, feeling that she was doing her good deed for the day, made the necessary arrangements for them. Three weeks later, once again back in Vienna for a civil ceremony, Eliska Kucera and Zdenek Zizka became man and wife. They had a certificate to prove it.

She told him that she wanted to keep her maiden name, still to be known as Eliska Kucera. He stared at her for a moment and then merely grunted in acceptance, and the question was never again raised by either of them.

Reflecting on this, Eliska wondered if it would have any effect at all on their personal relationship and, somehow, as the weeks went by, it seemed that almost nothing had changed, except for many more of those long silences that she had come to expect, over all those unmarried years, from her now-husband Zdenek. She was acutely aware of the fact that the bloom was falling off their relationship. They had gone through so much together seeming to leave only the thorns. It worried her, and far worse it also puzzled her.

But the urgent matter now was to find work to bolster the incoming monies. They needed sensibly paid work for all of them, and they held what might have been called a family conference to look at the options.

For Martin, the plethora of phones was astonishing.

"I guess I'll be working, too," he said, "but do you realize that just about everyone in this country seems to have a telephone? Don't they have any communication control at all here?"

"Chaos," Eliska said, and he accepted the jibe with a broad grin.

"Yep, that's what it has to be, and I'm beginning to like it. I wonder what the wages are like here?"

They were soon to find that out. In a matter of days, Eliska had accepted the first job she was offered, joining the staff of a very high-class restaurant. She discovered that much of the work seemed to be washing dishes, which she undertook with her customary vigor, with no complaint whatsoever.

Martin, meanwhile, had gone to work shifting books around in the Neuhaus public library. Just a few more days later, Zdenek was driving a truck on the milk-run. Most of the time Michal was in the hotel alone, realizing the necessity finding things to do with the few other kids there, not complaining at all.

After a few weeks of this, Eliska arose one early morning and saw that Zdenek was still fast asleep, long after his usual starting time. She shook him awake and asked him what was going on. "They fired me," he said causally, "for being late a couple of times, didn't I tell you?"

"No, you did not!" she answered.

He went on, "So who cares? You try getting up at three o'clock every morning for a goddamn milk run . . ."

"I care!" Eliska said, flaring. "You're earning more than Martin and me together. We need that money!"

He shrugged. "Don't fret about it, I'll find something else."

"When?" she asked tightly.

"Soon," he said. "When I'm ready." It was not until ten days later that he was working once again with another milk company. He, too, was beginning to miss the extra money, which was considerable. The work entailed not only driving a huge diesel truck, but also lugging around the very heavy galvanized iron milk containers and setting them just so in just the right places, then picking them up empty on the return journey, well into the overtime hours. It was the kind of utterly exhausting work that only a large and powerfully muscular man like him could cope.

There was only one item on their program left now, which would keep them in Austria, the all important interview at the American Embassy. For this they had to wait and wait, and then wait some more, the time seemed to drag dreadfully. The phone call came at last, and they were told that an interview had been scheduled for them on the Wednesday of the following week.

"Next week, next month, next year," Zdenek grumbled. "This crummy country is getting me down."

"Well, at least," Eliska said, "our major expense, the hotel, is paid in full."

"It's a loan," Zdenek said, interrupting her. "We have to pay it back within the year. If you ask me, we'll probably still be here, waiting for some damned interview or other."

"Oh, do shut up!" Eliska said. "Kindly remember that we are all getting very good wages here! You want to see my little account book? For your information, we are spending much less than half of what we earn; we're actually making money now." She tossed the little notebook across the table to him. "There, take a look."

He pushed it back to her. "It is not necessary. I'll take your word for it. But I wonder what a bottle of good rum costs here?"

Was she being too hard on him, she wondered? She weakened, and said grudgingly, "One bottle then, and it has to last until we leave here, however long that might be. Agreed?"

He weakened too, and grinned at her. "Agreed. And you know? You can be a very nice lady when you put your mind to it."

Eliska chose not to answer him. Since this was late Friday evening, with a weekend coming up, she decided that a trip in the countryside would do them both a lot of good. The following midday, a short workday for all of them with Sunday quiet free, she asked Zdenek, "Baden, have you ever heard of it?"

"Baden" he replied, "isn't that some sort of a spa?"

"Sulphur thermal baths," she said, "and it's only a half-hour run from here. One of the ladies downstairs was telling me about it. She says it's fabulous, so why don't we go take a look at it?"

"It's going to be full of tourists."

"Don't knock them. Isn't that what we are?"

"Yes, I suppose so. Well, anything to get the hell out of this dreary hotel for a while."

"It's nice to know that you're so enthusiastic about it."

"All right, then. All right, we'll go."

Martin and Michal were both truly enthusiastic about the idea. A little while later they drove on the old Weinstrasse. It was the Wine Road that ran through the grape growing countryside, to one of Austria's most

203

famous spas. Somewhat to her surprise, it improved Zdenek's state of mind enormously. They both spent hours luxuriating in the warm waters of the fifteen springs, while the boys spent their time on one of the thermal water swimming pools, where Martin was particularly pleased to continue with Michal's lessons, sure that they would eventually find, in America, other contests to take the place of the one they had left behind them in Ceske Budejovice.

Back in Neuhaus, Eliska was quite sure that Zdenek's demeanor had improved to a very noticeable extent. She was equally certain that it would not last for long. Sure enough, within a few days he was back to his grumpy, bad-tempered self again. She was beginning to wonder if she had ever really understood this man.

The time for the American Embassy appointment came at last, and it was back to Vienna for what they both sincerely hoped would be their last visit.

The same pleasant young Zherr Raab was still there to greet them. They were kept waiting for only an hour and quarter before they were ushered into a spacious and nicely furnished office. On the door was written the legend: 2nd Deputy. There they met with an elderly and very distinguished gentleman of the old school. He was tall, slim, and ramrod-straight when he stood up to introduce himself.

"My name," he said in quite unaccented German, "is Claude Wilcox. If you would be good enough to tell me which language you prefer? I deeply regret that my Czech is so limited as to be quite useless."

"German is fine," Eliska said.

He went on, "Good. Well, I am the deputy responsible for our Department Seven, which deals with questions of asylum. I understand is what you are both requesting, correct?"

"Yes, indeed, sir," Zdenek said. Deputy Wilcox resumed his seat and picked up the documents that they both recognized at once as the questionnaires they had filled out. In a few moments he was frowning as though he had seen something there he did not like very much. He put down the papers, thought for a while, and then asked, "Would you be so good as to tell me the reason, or reasons, which prompted you to apply for asylum in the United States?"

He was looking at Zdenek, but it was Eliska who answered him, "I will be most happy to tell you."

He switched his look to her and said, smiling and genuinely happy, "Ah, yes, the memories . . ." It was an old man reminiscing when he went on. "Many, many years ago, when I first joined our State Department, they sent me to Prague as a Fourth Deputy, merely because it so happens that I always had a flair for languages. I have five or six, but Czech, unhappily, never was one of them. I tried so hard to learn it, but it doesn't belong to either the Gothic or the Romance groups, does it? So after a year of, please, believe me, much deep study, I had to give up trying. I asked for a transfer to a French, Italian, Spanish or German-speaking country. But while I was there, I did discover that in Czechoslovakia, it is always the woman, not the man, who handles the negotiations. Most Americans, I am sure, must find this very strange. Even though a woman's position in the States today is much more formidable than it was when I was in my formative years. Please, go on. I will try not to interrupt you again."

"It's very simple, sir," Eliska said, developing a great liking for this kindly old gentlemen, "Czechoslovakia these days is not what is used to be in your time there."

"Ah, yes, I know that, to my great sorrow. It used to be such a wonderful country. Prague, I well remember the opera there. I saw a reprise of Don Giovanni there in the Stavovske divadlo. Am I pronouncing that correctly?"

"Perfectly so," Eliska said. "A wonderful performance . . . and if I may continue?"

"Of course."

"The Party in Ceske Budejovice was trying to turn my sons into communists and in part, perhaps, succeeding. Quite apart from that, my husband and I, both anti-communists, were afraid that sooner or later my dislike of the Party and his activities against it would surface. Than we would be, quite simply, thrown into prison, where the death rate of anti Party activists is frighteningly high. What then, would happen to my two sons? They would become wards of the Party. Need I say more?"

"This is true, Mr. Wilcox," Zdenek said. "My own work in the underground movement, if it were discovered, would have meant the end of our family. One way or another."

The deputy nodded in agreement, but was frowning again. He said carefully, I find your reasons for asylum to be perfectly acceptable, but unhappily there is a major difficulty here. It is a matter of policy."

"Policy, sir?" Eliska asked, worrying about it.

He nodded. "Yes. Our State Department policy has always favored the immigration of families over individuals, realizing that a cohesive family is less of a risk in a new country than the individuals themselves.

Here we have the case of an unmarried mother, I believe, which is unhappily very much to your detriment, meaning that . . ."

He saw Eliska' smile and broke off, saw her digging into her purse and producing a document to hand to him. "Our marriage certificate," she said. "Of course, you had only our previous questionnaire. I should have realized that, my apologies. Now we are husband and wife, with two wonderful children. A family.

He studied the paper and then positively beamed at Eliska. "Splendid," he said. "That is really splendid news! Well!"

"Does that mean what I think it means?" she asked.

He nodded. "It does indeed," he said, "and all that is required now is my recommendation to His Excellency the Ambassador, which is purely a formality, and automatically accepted. You will be notified within a very few days, three or four at the most, at which time we will have the necessary documentation ready for you to pick up."

He stood up, shook hands with them both, and said, mostly to Eliska. "This has been a very pleasant interview for me, and I'm happy that it turned out so well for you."

"It is wonderful news," Eliska said, "and we simply cannot thank you enough."

The old gentleman raised a didactic finger and said, smiling, "When you come for your papers, I will have Herr Raab out there send you in to me so that I may give them to you myself, personally. He well knows how busy I am, but . . . well, I'll have him squeeze you in, so to speak. I wish you now a very good day."

"To you, too, sir, with our gratitude," Zdenek said, unaccustomedly polite.

Outside, as they went to the car, Eliska said, "That's about the nicest old man I've ever met! I wonder if they're all like that in America.

"That kind of spotty, old-school gentility," Zdenek said, pontificating, "comes with old age. It doesn't come with nationality. I wonder why they haven't retired him, put the old sod out to pasture."

"High time, maybe, that I did that to you," Eliska said.

Three days later, all was well with them once again, because with the necessary documents in Eliska's purse, they were almost ready to leave. There was just the question of the Skoda.

"We abandon it," Eliska said. "Let's hope that whoever picks it up will be someone who really needs it for a while. We've had our money's worth out of it."

They were waiting on the sidewalk, their bags packed, waitng for the organization's bus. It came at last, not much more than three hours late, and they joined the crowd of fellow refugees aboard. There were refugees from Czechoslovakia, from Bulgaria, from East Germany, and from Poland. There was a sign over the driver's seat that said, in six or seven languages: "No drinking aboard," but the Poles were happily passing around their bottles of Vodka and, by and large, it was an experience for them that they rather enjoyed.

They were driven southeast on Highway 225 for half an hour at high speed to Vienna's Schwechat Airport, where they were scheduled to board an Austrian Air's DC9 aircraft for the eight hour trip to New York, and then on to Glendive, Montana, to meet with the Refugee Organization.

As they climbed up the steps to board that plane, Eliska said somberly, "This is it, isn't it?"

And she was right. This was, at least, the beginning of the end of Eliska and her family's escape to freedom.

EPILOGUE

The arrival in the United States of America was not without its disasters. It was April 30th, in the year 1984, and the flight from Vienna, Austria, to Billings in Montana, U.S.A., had been smooth and comfortable. Montana itself was so vastly different from the places they had lived in all their lives that this lent the place enormous interest. They were taken to a small town called Glendive, where their sponsor was located. They found these vast open spaces very impressive indeed.

The sponsor, Patty, a lady of impressive bearing whose mandate was the assistance of Czech refugees, helped the family learn the English language and to assimilate.

Personal relationships were much in danger here. Zdenek wanted to go at once to California, where they had Czech friends. Back than, Zdenek and Eliska helped them to escape. But they decided that for the time being, at least, they were to remain in Glendive. "Until," Patty told them, "we can find suitable employment for you, and you will no longer be in our care."

Just a few days later, Eliska entered their room to hear him on the phone saying, "Right, yes, see you guys then on Friday." then he put the phone down the moment he saw her.

"Who was that?" she asked, mystified.

He answered her rudely, "None of your business."

She bit her tongue to hold back the angry comment that came to her, and said nothing. On that Friday morning, he said to her casually as he packed a small bag, "I'm going to California for a while. See you when I get back."

"You can't do that." Eliska began.

But he cut her off, and said, "I can, and I will." He brushed past her and was gone.

She had a wretched time trying to explain to Patty what had happened, and the good lady told her, quite embarrassed herself, "Under the circumstances, Eliska, I feel you would be better off without him. He seems to be sometimes quite unreliable."

"Unreliable? Yes, on occasion I suppose that might be."

"Might be? Are you then suggesting that you are unaware of your own husband's character? I find that very strange."

For several moments, Eliska was silent. She said at last, slowly, "I am beginning to think . . . to think that . . . that quite possibly . . . I never really knew this man. It is a thought that horrifies me."

Zdenek returned to Glendive two weeks later and chose to assume that nothing untoward had happened. In spite of her justifiable antagonism, Patty found him a job as a janitor in one of the better local schools. Very soon Eliska was working too, as an accounting clerk in one of the social services companies, and Martin and Michal were both studying hard in English language classes. For the rest of the year, life just jogged along for them all, but for Eliska, very unhappily.

One day she came upon Zdenek lying barefoot on the sofa in their room reading a magazine when she thought he should be working. She asked, expecting the worst, "So why aren't you still at the school?"

"I don't like toilets," he said. "I quit."

She stared at him, "Say again?"

He tossed the magazine aside, stood up and started pacing back and forth. "They want me to clean out their damn toilets," he said, gesticulating wildly. "Don't they know who I am, for God's sake? I'm a Zizka! So I quit! I'm leaving town. I'm going to stay with our friends in California. Come with me, please. I hope to God you want to, Eliska sweetheart, because I'm tired of me not being as supportive of you as I should be. It all will change in California. We will start all over. So, are you coming with me?"

"No," Eliska said briefly, and that was that.

In a few days, Zdenek was gone. He came back once trying to persuade Eliska to leave with him, but she declined. As the months rolled by, she realized that the time had come for her own pride to take its natural place in her life. She began proceedings for divorce. She quickly learned it was remarkably easy to do in this still strange new country.

A single woman again, she moved with the boys to Arizona, where the local elementary school accepted Michal. Martin went back to Montana where he liked it best.

In the course of time, she met and fell in love with a distinguished American of French-Canadian origin, a highly successful and worthy man who loved her as sincerely as she did him. It was quite a short time before this sensible affair came to its logical conclusion, and they were married.

For the first time ever in her life, Eliska now felt free to experience those of life's wonderful gifts that had for so long been denied her: trust, honesty, openness and, most of all, freedom and true love.